# The Factory

# The Factory

## Ihor Mysiak

translated by
### Yevheniia Dubrova · Hanna Leliv

Atthis Arts

УКРАЇНСЬКИЙ ІНСТИТУТ КНИГИ

This book has been published with the support of the Translate Ukraine Translation Program

# The Factory

by Ihor Mysiak



Cover art and design by Ihor Dunets
Used with permission from our friends at Tempora Publishing

English edition design and editorial review by E.D.E. Bell
*To Ihor, a believer, a fighter, a poet, a kin—it's a shame I could not know you.*
*Yet the work continues. The joy is worth it. Tridents forever.*

Published by Atthis Arts, LLC
Detroit, Michigan, United States
atthisarts.com

ISBN 978-1-961654-24-2

Library of Congress Control Number: 2024947496

*The Factory* was published at the time of the full-scale Russian invasion of Ukraine. Back then many Ukrainians left their homes in search of a safe place, their shelter from the war. And Ihor's novel also wandered around the world, together with Ukrainians. My husband's friends sent him photos of his book from different parts of the world, and Ihor was happy that *The Factory* saw the light of day and visited countries where we had not yet been. Today, this novel was published in English, which means that more people will read it and it will also travel, as my husband Ihor and I loved to do.

Ihor would be very happy with this news. It was his little dream that came true. Memory lives longer on paper. Ihor lives in his texts and in our hearts. Thank you for reading this novel about life.

**Maryna Mysiak**

Discovering a unique talent and displaying it to the world brings enormous joy to every literary agent. I was blessed to meet Ihor Mysiak who was not only a gifted writer, but an extraordinary person too—kind, joyful, devoted, persistent, hard-working, very passionate, and modest.

His novel *The Factory* got proposals from several publishers as soon as our Literary Agency OVO submitted it. A rare chance for a debut writer and a good sign for a literary agent that you have found a gem.

Ihor was a believer. He really believed. Most of all he believed in Ukraine and was ready to defend it again as he did in 2014. He believed in love and his beloved wife Maryna, to whom he dedicated a lot of poems. He believed in his brothers and sisters in arms, in his family. And he believed in me and in the success of his novel.

*The Factory* was published in Spring 2022. One of the books, if not the first, published after the full-scale invasion and it was as a sign of hope that we will stand. It spoke to the sense of happiness; where to find it or how to make it are the questions to which the answers are always fleeing us.

We last met with Ihor in November 2022. A short fleeting moment. He was happy. His book was well accepted by the audience and he was sharing with me his dreams of seeing his book in bookstores around the world. For all people to read what happiness is made of . . .

Ihor disappeared on April 1st. We kept hope for almost a month and a half before the territory where he was last known to rescue people was deoccupied and his body was found.

Now you have his dream in your hands. Thank you for reading and please share the word about *The Factory*. It will make Ihor Mysiak's memory last long.

**Viktoriya Ma, Ihor's literary agent, Literary Agency OVO**

# Foreword

Military literature, namely that which emerges from the experiences of those who have served in war, is increasingly resonant in Ukraine today. My brothers and sisters in arms are fighting, creating, and laying down their lives while I am writing these lines. I would say that if one wants to read texts from Ukraine during this period, it must first be something by a military author. Many have joined the fight since February 2022, driven by an urgent need to engage with these critical moments of our modern history. It is also my story. Ihor Mysiak, however, had been serving since 2014, when this chapter of the Russian-Ukrainian war, in fact, began. Since then, his joyful spirit and deeply romantic view of life have been extensively coated by sweat, resilience, and sorrow. Like many of us, he has faced a lot, yet I never once witnessed him succumb to despair. I wonder if readers will discern in Ihor's writing the unmistakable mood of military life that permeates his novel. For example, those short character appearances as the chance encounters with strangers at the remote outposts, brief remarks just like reporting to the commanding officer, or surrounding nature descriptions which reminded me of my own observations during succinct breaks in the shadowy woods. This narrative serves as a mirror of how our society is feeling like, reflecting the relentless nature of war—there are no pauses, only an unceasing march forward. I find myself pondering the essence of happiness, a concept I struggle to define. While I have little idea of what it means to others, I am intrigued to read, sometimes between the lines, what Ihor means when he thinks about happiness. Could we trace his ideas back to monumental works of literature, perhaps like *One Hundred Years of Solitude*?

In the end, we all become memories—mere memories. Well, I don't know . . . Ihor has crafted a novel that made me recognize, reflect, and dream. More than that, he reminded me about the powerful beauty of embracing life, even amid the darkness of war. It is so important to live. As much as to be happy despite all the efforts of evil.

**Pavlo Matyusha, writer, veteran**

*To Dage.*
*He was the first to read this book.*
*It's a shame you did not know him.*
*There will never be anyone like him—*
*he died at a different factory . . .*

[By "different factory" Ihor means Azovstal, a steel plant in Mariupol that served as a shelter for as many as 1,000 civilians and final holdout for thousands of Ukrainian fighters, including many from the Azov Brigade. In 2022, it was under siege by Russian troops for almost three months.]

*" . . . and where you once lived, now there's only sand."*

*Mykola Vorobiov*

# The Factory

# 001

Nothing will happen if you do nothing. At this very moment, other people are doing what you do not dare to do. They master the art of living, drinking their cup, letting it spill down their chins.

What did the people I want to tell you about do? They simply lived. I knew them; I broke bread with them. Before you jump to conclusions, listen. Maybe after this story is over, you and I can talk about time—if any of it is still left by then.

Things started a long time ago, when old Schneider bought this factory. Back in the day, it was just an old, useless building—without history, without a past, without a future. The villagers always remembered the factory as miserable as it looks now. "No one cares about it," they said, "let it just sit there." It was home to mice, rats, and wild pigeons. Weasels, too, and that was it.

Schneider himself did not know the history of the factory but always wanted to buy it. He already owned a garment factory that allowed him to live comfortably. No one noticed when he first arrived here. Schneider did some construction work—fixing, building, remodeling. Sometimes, he hired locals, paying them well. Some said he planned to open another garment factory, while others claimed he would grow mushrooms. More intricate theories circulated too, but I cannot remember them all.

He ended up buying the factory though calling it a 'factory' was quite a stretch. A few buildings stood on the lakeshore, pushed right up to the forest edge. You would not even notice those gray structures if you drove by. You would probably just spot the chimney of the half-ruined boiler-house. The factory was hiding behind the trees.

Trucks began to frequent it. Local mushroom foragers said that windows were installed in some of the production facilities, front doors were replaced, and the fence was fixed. Others claimed they did not see anyone there and that everything was locked up.

Fishermen said they saw a bunch of strangers lugging large crates. Later, someone claimed to have spotted armed men, and people began to steer clear. Rumors spread that bandits were hiding on the forest edge, holding hostages. An old woman who lived in the last house on the street claimed to have seen a car driving in that direction at night and have heard an inhuman scream. She was hard of hearing but still insisted that eerie sounds later came from the factory too.

Halia, a local woman who picks berries to sell at the market, said someone shot at her near the old factory as she was returning from the forest. The bullet swooshed over her head and hit a dry pine tree. Halia swore she could show the mark on its trunk. People went to look but did not find anything.

The village lost sleep, having no idea what was happening. A local drunkard tried to sneak behind the curtain, but nothing came of it. When he slipped into the building to search for anything to sell, he was brutally snatched and given a solid thrashing with a stick. Later, a sign reading "PRIVATE TERRITORY" appeared on the large metal gate.

Nothing was clear; the village was still losing sleep.

Trespassing attempts stopped only when Schneider fired the guard who collected the fee for fishing in the lake and allowed everyone to fish freely.

Only the unusually hot September drew people's attention back to the gray walls of the factory. As they finished harvesting and birds gathered to migrate south, work at the factory was in full swing. Schneider's car—locals had already figured out it was his—shuttled between the factory and town.

People's minds boiled with confusion and curiosity. They desperately wanted to know what was happening but got no answers. Schneider, who seemingly appeared from nowhere, stole their peace of mind. They had heard about him before. Some of the women had worked at his factory, but this was not enough to truly understand what kind of person he was.

He gave the impression of always wanting the best for people. It was this drive that brought him to that place and pushed him to invent a device on which his people now worked day and night. This device was supposed to turn the world upside down, leading people to find happiness.

It was said later that he had entertained this idea for a long time, and the technical solution dawned on him just before these turbulent events. By the time he and his tiny team arrived here, his dream had almost been turned into reality. The place was bustling with activity. Later, a member of the inventor's crew revealed some details that went beyond the scope of rumors and gossip. This whole story is tightly connected to that man, but more on that later.

What did Schneider want? He wanted to help. Imagine having a small box in your apartment assisting you with all kinds of things. It improves your well-being, saves electricity, and reminds you to turn off the water and lights. It has a positive impact on your house plants and protects them from dying when you forget to water them. Thanks to this device, your wife does not suffer from headaches, and you feel strong and capable. Your children do their homework on time, and you do not even need to check on them. No one can afford the luxury of lying. Your cooking feats never burn your pots, and you never forget things or lose focus. Decisiveness and courage fill your soul, so despicable just a few minutes ago. Everything changes;

everything gets back to normal. All you have to do is bring a small box home and turn it on.

The device does not create any distortions—it simply unlocks your potential. With its mechanical heartlessness, it prompts you to do what you could do yourself but often do not.

How much would you be willing to pay for such a device? Would you buy it? Maybe as a gift? Even if you believe you do not need a nudge, you surely know someone who does. I do not know what stage the work reached by the time some people affiliated with a local MP, or a businessman, or a businessman MP, turned up at the factory. Their visit was clearly not a courtesy call. They arrived in the dead of night and disappeared about an hour later. The work ground to a halt. No one shuttled to town to pick up supplies anymore. Schneider's car vanished. The building became deserted.

A month later, people learned of a possible reason. A local MP known as Snout (his mother's maiden name, not a made-up moniker) set his sights on the factory and the lake. It was not its gray walls but the smooth surface of the lake that interested him—it seemed only fitting to build a resort in a location like that.

Snout's arguments were made of metal and had wooden stocks. Schneider, no longer young, stepped back. He did not even remove anything from the factory; he simply vanished. Schneider sold off all of his businesses, including the garment factory, which now produces warm uniforms for Scandinavian workers.

People gossiped that Schneider had sold his house and car, too, and moved to the United States where his older son lived. And it was true. Schneider never returned here.

Snout rubbed his hands in anticipation of launching his big construction project. But as he struggled to push through the bureaucratic maze, someone even more powerful expressed interest in the lake. Snout buried his head in the sand, but before long, his entire body was buried in the ground.

The factory with its equipment and all sorts of junk that had been hauled there kept people awake at night. They rushed on a looting spree, as if it were the end of the world. But the feast did not last long.

On a cloudy day, an explosion rocked the factory site, killing a local villager and his son. The scene was horrific, but that's another story. After that incident, people decided the factory was mined and they had better stay away. Someone claimed to have seen Schneider and his team planting mines all over the site to prevent Snout from pilfering his stuff.

In reality, the village and his son stumbled upon an old shell while digging up scrap metal. They tried to take it apart. The outcome is well-known.

The rumors about Schneider and his factory subsided, but the explosion was remembered for a long time. Since then, people fished in the lake for free.

The former guard did not dare to return.

# 002

Christmas passed, followed by Epiphany. January entered its last week. The sky was tall and gray. The weather spared no one; the wind blew off your hat as soon as you ventured outside. The clouds it chased westward herded together. The temperature was above freezing for several days now, though not at night. The snow in the fields blackened, and the ground turned into dark slush that froze at night and stuck to the boots during the day. The air was humid. The sun had not reappeared since Epiphany. The days were lengthening, but no one noticed that. The villagers were still recovering from the holidays.

The surface of the lake, covered with a fine layer of ice, was dotted with the prints of birds and small animals. The place looked deserted.

A car was coming from the village. It headed toward the factory, brown mud scattering from under its wheels. It almost reached the dilapidated gate when another car appeared on the road. It also turned onto the dirt path and followed the first one.

The cars stopped by the factory, and people got out. There were three of them—two men in the first car, and another in the second one, a half-dead Volkswagen Golf. The car looked tattered, as if giant children played with it as a toy. If someone peered inside, they might have thought that a grenade had exploded there and the music was turned on afterward.

One of the men said to the Volkswagen Golf driver:

"I offered to give you a lift, but you said no. Where did you get that beater? Is that a new model?"

"You know what, boss? It's a decent car. A work in progress," the driver replied and slammed the door.

He was slim and on the short side, no longer a youth but not a solid man either. He had a thin, drawn-out face. His eyes, always looking away, gave a nomadic vibe. People called him Boss because he always slipped that word into his speech. He spent his days and nights under cars; his hands were always smeared in soot, but cars were his only source of peace. He entered the building last.

The scene they witnessed was worth remembering to compare later how much things had changed.

Destroyed furniture, crates, old china, and fragments of glass, brick, and plaster were scattered all over the floor. Some metal fittings remained intact. However, all the cables had been ripped out, and there was not a single trace of engines. The visitors walked further down the hall, where a large production facility transitioned into a two-story maze of utility rooms. They went upstairs and entered a spacious room with three big windows. Two of them were intact, but where the third one used to be, there was now only a boarded-up old wooden frame. On a surviving windowsill lay a handful of screws, a few empty cigarette packs, an old newspaper, and a painting—a copy of Chagall's "White Crucifixion." The painting was in a plain frame, obscured by a layer of grime on the glass. Yuriy picked it up to have a closer look.

Back in the day, he worked with Schneider. You could guess why he returned here, to this same room, to this same window. Schneider's device robbed him of his peace of mind. He wanted to return a long time ago but due to certain circumstances, could only do so now.

The two other men just stood there, embarrassed, staring at Yuriy. The silence grew, filling the entire void, the entire chaos, the entire room, in the middle of which the man was sitting on a chair. He took off his gloves and put them into the pocket of his old dark blue jacket. Hryhoriy approached him. Boss remained standing in front of the window, his body turned toward the woods, as if he had heard a sound coming from there.

Hryhoriy removed his glasses and rubbed his eyes. He was of average height, with a round face decorated with a small but deep scar concealed by the thick rim of his glasses. His eyes looked calm. He scratched the scar with his long, thin fingers and put his glasses back on.

"We have to check the basement and then leave. It's getting dark."

The sound of several pairs of feet stomping drowned out all noises still audible inside. The men strode through the large production facility, disappearing into the darkness. The flashlight blazed up and then dimmed somewhere in the distance. Down below, keys jangled, and a metal door screeched unbearably loudly.

"Everything's here. I knew it." Yuriy's voice echoed, tinged with excitement.

It had gotten dark outside, and the wind did not relent.

"We'll be back in two days. I'll stop by."

The door of the black car slammed shut.

Yuriy was not an ordinary guy. He used to work at the factory with Schneider. They had known each other since childhood. Schneider helped him get into the radio engineering department. Yuriy became a fairly successful businessman; an owner of several repair shops fixing cell phones and computer equipment. His brother was a high-ranking public official, but people said he had not been in touch with Yuriy for a long time.

Two days later, early in the morning, they all returned to the factory. The snow merged with the lake, and the landscape around them sparkled so hard their eyes hurt. Their two cars pulled into the yard. The men hauled an old makeshift stove out of the trunk, then a chainsaw and a few bulky packages.

Judging by all these preparations, they did not plan on going back anytime soon. Boss rummaged in his car for a while and apparently found what he was looking for—a small object which he shoved into an inside pocket of his jacket. He threw the backpack over his shoulder and joined the others.

"Welcome to our new home," Yuriy said, smiling.

His face was flushed, radiating joy.

"Right. But your 'new home' looks more like a shithouse. You two might as well clean it up," Boss teased him.

"What do you mean 'you two'? Aren't you going to help us?" Yuriy asked.

The guys lugged the stove to the familiar room on the second floor. It was probably the only livable space in the whole building. The smell of a place long abandoned struck their nostrils.

They started to clean things up. Yuriy brought some bin liners, and the men began to stuff them with junk. Then Yuriy and Hryhoriy went down to the basement, while two others—Boss and a new guy who was not with them the last time—stayed upstairs to finish the cleaning.

"Water." That's how Yuriy introduced him. He was a sullen man of average height, with eyes as clear as two drops of water. He looked no more than thirty. He took off his green puffer jacket and hung it on a nail. Then, without saying a word, he picked up a liner and started gathering trash.

"Get a smoke first. Can't start work without a cig," Boss said, holding out a pack.

"I could use one," the newcomer said, pulling out a cigarette.

They walked over to the window and lit up. They stared at the woods, the smoke slipping outside through the broken window pane. Boss went on.

"How did you end up here?"

"Yuriy and I went to the same school. We've known each other forever. And it's tough to land a job now, so I took him up on it. He promised some kind of interesting work, but it's all quite vague now. But Yuriy won't mess with me, I know him."

"We're going to make this device. Cool stuff. You'll like it. It's not just something you've never seen—I bet you haven't even *heard* about anything like this. Yuriy will fill you in. Oh, and why do people call you Water?"

"It started back at summer camp. I was afraid of water."

This nickname had stuck so long ago and so firmly that no one, maybe not even he himself, remembered his real name. He was still a little kid at the time and could not swim, and there was not anyone to teach him. One day, he went to the river and asked older kids to teach him. A boy just pushed him into the water, saying it was the best method. He came to lying on the ground. Someone had pulled him back onto the riverbank. He had been terrified of water ever since. A few years later, at a summer camp, the children heard him scream in his sleep, horrified: "Water! Water! Water!" So, that's what they started calling him. Over time, the nickname lost its scornful tone and transformed into its present-day, familiar version of 'Water,' its origin hidden deep down.

"Let's just get on with cleaning."

They continued to stuff the liners with all sorts of junk.

Hryhoriy and Yuriy sorted through whatever was left of Schneider's old supplies. They wanted to sift through it all to see if they could still use something. Nearly all the spare parts were damaged, just like the packaging materials. Only a few things survived.

"We'll have to order it all," Hryhoriy said. "These supplies aren't reliable. I hope we get down to work soon. I know I'm working for you and all but I don't do anything much, and people don't get paid for that."

"Hryhoriy, we've already talked about the money. You'll get what you were promised, don't worry."

"Okay, okay. We have to do something about the electricity, too."

"That's exactly what I'm doing. Why don't you think about what we need to buy? Let's have a coffee later and write up a list. This will be your first task. It's serious work, right?"

Yuriy smiled, and Hryhoriy's eyes flashed. He went back to rummaging through old boxes of circuit boards with even more energy.

The guys upstairs continued to clean up. Water knew he would be staying here, so he picked up the trash thoroughly to prepare a room for himself. This was his decision, even though it was not particularly necessary, especially during such a cold spell. But they had hired him, had they not, so he might as well work as a guard or a janitor at least. Uncertainty was bringing him down, knocking him off his feet. Yet, Yuriy had promised him good money. He had asked him bluntly how much he wanted to be paid—and agreed to it. This burdened Water with responsibility, and he tried to keep himself busy.

"Spare a cigarette?" Water walked up to Boss, who had just tied another bin liner full of trash and propped it against the wall.

Hryhoriy and Yuriy returned from the basement.

"Hryhoriy and I are going to the grocery store. Do you need anything?"

"Can you get me some water? I've got the rest. I'm staying here overnight," Water said.

"Here? But this place will be empty for two days." Yuriy was clearly puzzled by his decision.

"It's alright; you know me well," Water said with a childish grin. "Just get me some water."

"Okay."

Having caught up with Yuriy, Boss whispered into his ear, "Hey, get him some cigarettes, too."

Outside, rays of sunlight playfully skipped across the glossy surface of the ice.

Boss, just out of the factory building, shouted to Water: "We'll rest for a bit. I'm going to take a short walk and will be back soon."

No one answered.

"You can go down, too, if you want."

"It's okay. I'll be here," Water yelled back.

When they removed all the junk, the room seemed to shrink. Water stared at it in disbelief that so much could fit in here. It immediately became clear that old floorboards were enough to cover only half of the room, and the other half was bare concrete. This, along with the shabby walls and ripped-out wiring, did not promise a comfortable existence, but Water resolved to settle here.

He decided to check out the stuff in other rooms on the second floor, counting the total number of rooms as he went. There were quite a few of them—six at the very least. Water started his exploration with a small room next to his. He quickly stumbled upon a table and lugged it to his would-be den. Other rooms revealed hopeless, apocalyptic-like scenes, strewn with pieces of brick, plaster, and broken glass. In one of the rooms, a window had been knocked out along with the frame, and a small patch of snow lurked in the corner.

The farthest room, cluttered with old desks, metal army beds, broken china, and dirty kitchen utensils, intrigued Water the most. He was stunned by its metal walls and ceiling. Sheets of metal covered the entire room; it was kind of a metal box overflowing with junk. Perhaps they had been developing military projects here. Water quickly felt uncomfortable in this bunker, eerie even. The smells, any and all, tore his nose to pieces. Water walked out. He felt sick; a headache set in, and everything went black. A breeze blowing through a knocked-out window in the hallway returned him to life. He trudged toward the staircase and then downstairs. Seeing nothing of interest on the first floor, he walked outside to finally take a deep breath. Boss was nowhere to be seen. He was inspecting other buildings.

Boss particularly liked one of them, an old garage cluttered with construction debris and boards. It was divided into a few sections where cars were parked back in the day. He thought he might well find a repair pit beneath all those heaps of trash.

Yuriy brought some food, and they had lunch together on the lakeshore. The sun hung above them. Boss and Water puffed the smoke into the clear skies.

"Relaxing this much is bad for you. Let's go. We should make some space for Water to sleep if he insists on staying here," Yuriy said, scooping the trash into the liner.

They installed the makeshift stove, routing the pipe out through the window and using a piece of plywood to cover the gap. They set up a guard post for Water, even though it was not clear what he was even supposed to guard.

Water went into the woods and came back with a bunch of twigs. The wind had knocked down a young fir tree, so he was able to cut some excellent bedding for himself. Water loved sleeping on fir twigs.

When he returned upstairs to his room, the guys were almost done boarding up the window with old plywood.

"Oh, what's that?" Boss asked, laughing.

"This will be my mattress."

"Are you sure you want to stay here? We won't be back for another two days," Yuriy asked. He sounded nervous for some reason.

"It's fine."

"Alright then."

Water began arranging his sleeping spot near the stove. The room filled with the scent of a winter forest and rosin as he scattered the twigs on the floor.

Water pulled up his backpack while Boss and Hryhoriy watched curiously, wondering what he would take out of it. But he only unfastened his sleeping bag and pushed the backpack back into the corner.

Yuriy brought two large plastic bottles of water.

"Just as you asked. There's also a chainsaw here, so you can cut some firewood. And we have a surprise for you." He chuckled. "Come on, Boss. Give me a hand with it."

Boss reluctantly went downstairs.

"Aren't you scared to stay here all alone?" Hryhoriy asked Water, watching his new, oddball friend roll out his sleeping bag. "I wouldn't stay here even if you paid me."

"It's not as scary as you think."

"What about rats?"

"Rats aren't scarier than wolves."

They heard heavy stomping.

Yuriy and Boss hauled a small diesel power generator upstairs, setting it down in the hallway. Yuriy also brought a duffel bag and placed it by the window.

The sun no longer felt warm as they left, and the solitary resident of this strange building still had some housekeeping to do. He worked on it until late afternoon, running back and forth with an ax. He needed a lot of firewood.

Outside the window, the forest loomed black. The trees had lost their primeval state and now looked despicable and uncomfortable. It was not the doom of old age; it was the helplessness of youth. The forest resembled an animal at a live lure training facility, its teeth and claws ripped out, being torn apart for someone's entertainment.

He heard a truck roaring by on the highway.

The stove had poor draft, and the room filled with smoke once the fire flared up. Water wanted to cook something for dinner and boil water for tea. He would then put out the fire for the night to avoid poisoning by charcoal gas. He could fix it tomorrow. Smoke hung in a thick cloud. Its stench, mixed with the fir tree scent, overpowered the smell of the old room. Water suddenly remembered he had a radio and tried to catch a signal, but it would not switch on—the battery was probably dead. He fiddled with the radio for a bit, then put it back into his backpack. It would've been more fun with the radio on. The water came to a boil.

Was he scared of sleeping here? No, surely not. The only thing he was scared of was water. In the early days of his adult life, he decided to try to understand his fear, to study it, but never to fight it. He believed he would conquer his fear of water by understanding it. So, he started that journey.

The body without water—that one was clear. It meant a definite death. Standing in the shower for hours was easy and not scary at all. But stepping into the water slowly, feeling the cold with your skin . . . One step after another. He could tolerate it and wade into the water up to his waist. He could probably venture even further. But when the transparent surface wavered with his every breath . . . When the body of water pressed relentlessly against his own weak body . . . It was unbearable. He wanted to scream and run away. But what if he tripped and fell? It would be the end. This was his biggest terror. He could not let that happen, no matter what. So, he would walk out of the water calmly and breathe again only once he reached the shore. Collapse on the ground, pressing against it with his whole body. Run away from fear toward love. Fall asleep on the shore, his teeth chattering, and walk on water in his dreams.

It took him a while to reach even this stage. At first, he found it hard to take a step. With each new attempt, he relied on his experience and muscle memory—until the body of water pressed against his chest . . .

It was important for him to enter the water without any clothes, not even underwear—pristine, nothing on, only like that.

He read books and watched movies. All books and movies he could get his hands on; research articles on the memory of water and its genetic code, even those full of actual madness and nonsense. But his brain craved even more information.

Later he decided to spend more time by the water, without breaking its surface. Spending nights by the water calmed him, while long walks along the river banks provided plenty of information. He walked along all the rivers in his region, from the sources to the places where smaller rivers merged with larger ones. Hundreds of miles, countless nights in the open air by the water. Hundreds of campfires, hundreds of sunrises. Even the sea. Water travelled to it in winter. The emotions he felt walking on the frozen surface of the sea became a radically new experience for him. Strolling on the sea, walking a fair distance away from the beach, feeling the ice under his feet, tons of hateful saltwater underneath it.

After these experiences, spending a few nights at the abandoned factory felt mundane. Rats scurrying around? So what? The fire was burning; the room was more or less warm, he was safe from the wind, and his sleeping bag provided good warmth, too. He had dinner and drank his tea—it was all good. Only the radio did not work properly, but he did not really care. Silence was his friend. On the second floor, the cell reception was choppy. Downstairs, he could probably only dream about it. The lake was close, too, napping under the ice. He felt awful in the water but fantastic near it.

Next day, Water got to work. He picked up the remaining bits and pieces and took them downstairs, leaving only the beds and some other junk upstairs. Mostly things he could not lift. There was so much garbage that he ran out of bin liners. Outside, cold wind blew. In lunchtime, it warmed up a bit. Snow started to fall, at first timidly, then thicker and thicker. Everything around him quickly turned white. The morning was bitterly chill. Water lingered in his sleeping bag for a long time but he couldn't stay there forever. He lit up the makeshift stove, and the room warmed up. The water in the bottles had frozen overnight, so he had to melt the ice to make tea. Then he just lay down, lost in thought. He had gotten used to smoke from the stove, which permeated his body. Fir twigs gave off barely any smell. It was afternoon when he went downstairs and saw a familiar car turning from the road toward the factory. The snow kept falling. There was so much of it that Water realized the car would not be able to drive up to the building. He went back upstairs to fetch his jacket and gloves to help push it through the snow. He had searched the factory for a shovel over those days but never found one.

# 003

The snow was almost knee-deep.

It might as well have been a fata morgana, a ghost. His clothes were coated in snow. He stopped and shook off his hat, then brushed the snow off his shoulders before moving on. He turned from the road into the field and stopped in front of the lake. Then he turned around and, keeping to the left bank, started to walk toward the ghostlike, barely visible building. He walked confidently, the route obviously familiar to him. Snow crunched under his feet. A car had recently passed through here, but the snow had already covered its tracks. On the ground, solitary snowflakes glistened. The wind caroused, blowing wherever it pleased, sweeping it all with snow. The lake vanished; the building vanished. His footprints were vanishing.

He approached the factory. An older man stood there, his face flushed from the frost. Deep wrinkles covered his face with rivulets. The man looked well over sixty. A shabby knapsack hung behind his back, along with what seemed to be a gun case the man kept adjusting. He could easily dissolve in such a heavy snowstorm. But the next moment, the man walked through the gate and became completely real. Another moment—and he was next to their cars.

Everyone was upstairs when the man entered the production facility and called out in a strong, deep voice: "Hello! Boys!"

He heard the stomping on the second floor. The four men hurried downstairs.

"Who are you?" Yuriy asked, confused.

"Uncle Vasyl," the newcomer responded calmly.

"And what on earth are you doing here, Uncle Vasyl?" Boss asked mockingly. He wanted to add something but stopped short after Yuriy glared at him.

Water lit a cigarette, while Hryhoriy watched the scene with surprise, without saying a word.

"Well, first things first. I walked for a long time and got cold to my bones. It would be nice to warm up," the man said, brushing the remains of snow off his clothes and backpack. "And then I can tell you many interesting things."

"Come inside," Yuriy told him.

In the room, the stove burned, oozing warmth.

"Would you like some tea?" Water asked the old man.

"I could really use it."

"Tea? What are you even talking about? What are you doing here?" Yuriy interrupted, boiling up faster than the kettle.

Uncle Vasyl took a pipe out of his pocket, spread out the tobacco wrapped in the newspaper on the table, and started to pack his pipe.

"You should expect guests tomorrow. Military, or maybe bandits. They came to the village this morning and asked folks about the factory—if someone works here, if anyone comes here. They seemed quite interested. This is exactly what happened when Snout wanted to butt in. But . . ."

"And what did people say?" Boss asked, cutting him short.

Water placed a cup of tea in front of the visitor.

"Just as it is. Someone comes and goes, they said, but they have no idea who that is. But they won't come here today for sure. They've been asking people in the village to put them up for the night. It's an awful weather. They just won't get here in a snowstorm like that. And then, Bereza has been drinking since morning. His grandson was born. And he's the one with a snow plough. They searched the whole village for him but no one knew where he went to celebrate. They would be here in the morning, I think. Not sooner."

"Why should we believe you, boss?"

Yuriy kept silent; Hryhoriy clearly had gotten scared. Water sprawled out on his sleeping bag, his entire demeanor indicating that this business had nothing to do with him.

"You don't have to believe me. Do as you wish." His pipe had gone out, and he lit it again.

Yuriy started to pace the room nervously. He had not anticipated such a turn of events.

"Might as well be too late," he muttered so quietly that no one heard him. "We have to get ready. Will build a barricade, and the hell will they break through. Come on. Let's get to work."

Yuriy, Hryhoriy, and Boss rushed downstairs. Uncle Vasyl unhurriedly drank his tea. Water threw a few logs into the stove.

"Water, take the chainsaw and the bag next to it!" Yuriy called.

"Will do!" Water yelled back. Then he turned to the visitor and said, this time quietly and respectfully: "Keep an eye on the fire, so it doesn't go out, will you?"

Water rummaged in his pile of clothes for the gloves. Uncle Vasyl shook his pipe out.

"I'll just finish my tea and join you."

Yuriy walked outside and looked around. The landscape merged into a white slush. But Yuriy did not worry about the weather. The old man who turned up at the factory to save them—this is what bothered him. Due to the problems with paperwork and the fact that the factory did not belong to him yet, Yuriy treated people's offers to help with suspicion. That someone could arrive to seize the factory was expected. That someone could turn up to save them—no. Yuriy wanted to shout at Water not to leave the old man upstairs alone but held back. He decided to take the risk. But if the old man did save them, he would have to take him in.

At first, they wanted to block the road. Only two roads led to the factory, along each side of the shore. One of them was barely even used by anyone other than forest rangers. With its ups and downs, it was quite unreliable, and you risked falling into the lake, which was slowly eating the road away. People took the other one. The men also came to the factory along that road. And it was the one they decided to block. The task was easy. On both sides of the road grew trees. Yet, these trees were not formally designated as a forest, so they could go ahead and cut them down. The trees were quite tall. Several more grew right next to the lake. They could fell them, and their trunks would block the road. An oak, not that old but strong and deep-rooted, was among them, too. It had still a long way to grow to reach any of those official anniversaries people invented for oaks, but it was tall and branchy. This oak alone could block the road well enough so no one could get around it.

Back in the yard, Yuriy suggested: "Let's just cut the oak down. It would be enough."

"No!" Boss shouted and then added, his voice calmer: "It's better to cut down the alders and aspen trees. Even all of them if you like. New ones will grow back a year or two from now. But it would be a shame to cut down the oak."

"A shame? Alright, whatever," Yuriy said with a nod. "Water, give me the chainsaw. Did you fuel it?"

"No. I don't know how to turn it on," Water said with a hint of apology.

"What about the generator? You didn't turn it on, either?"

Yuriy switched the chainsaw and walked toward a big aspen tree.

"Come on. I could use your help," he said.

The men followed. Meanwhile, Uncle Vasyl walked downstairs. The snow did not relent. The frost only grew stronger. A lucid sun hung in the sky. It had been a long time since such a snowstorm was last seen.

The buzzing of the chainsaw ripped the silence apart. One by one, trees lay down on the ground. Stretched across the road, tall white aspen trees were slowly getting covered with snow. The men dragged them one on top of another, building a formidable obstacle. Yuriy flailed away with such abandon that Uncle Vasyl had to stop him. They walked back to the factory, leaving several large snow-drifts behind. Black branches stuck out of them right and left. Behind their backs, a stout oak loomed amid the snowstorm. The tree looked majestic; it would have been a shame to cut it down, indeed.

They returned to the factory flushed and panting. It was growing dark. After a brief rest, they got back to work. Blocking the other road was impossible, so they were glad it was unnecessary. They focused all their effort on blocking the gates, the two main ones plus a smaller gate opening to the lake. They put to good use the bin liners full of garbage, metal beds, all sorts of junk, and any scrap metal they could find. There was no shortage of it, but the task took a lot of time and labor. It had long since become dark. Boss switched on the power generator and turned on the lights wherever he could. Water kept the fire alive. Uncle Vasyl proved even stronger than he looked—and not just in spirit.

Having finished the job—if a job like that could have ever been finished—they all gathered together upstairs. Water brewed tea and was now cooking porridge. Yuriy was making a shovel from a piece of plywood and an old handle, just in case. Hryhoriy frowned. He did not plan to spend the night at the factory, and yet there was no way he could return home now. The road was buried in snow. He was not just frustrated—he was frightened. He kept scratching at the scar on his face. Tomorrow's visit of armed strangers was not part of his plan. He was not paid for it, and volunteering for such an escapade was out of the question. He only hoped they would not kill him. Running away was too awkward: if things simply blew over, Yuriy would refuse to work with him.

"It will be funny if you just made it up to mess with us," Boss said to Uncle Vasyl.

"Then I wouldn't be helping you. I'd just watch you cut the trees down and lug them. The last time I worked this hard was like twenty years ago. You don't have to believe me, but for some reason, I'm here, right? Maybe I'm just an old man, and I was bored and wanted to get into a mess because I can't die in peace at home. And then, you know, even if I made it all up and no one turns up tomorrow, I won't run away too far from you, right? What with my old legs," the man chuckled.

"But there should be some reason. Maybe you want money from us?" Hryhoriy wondered.

"If I wanted money, I'd be screaming about it right out of the gate. If you want to get paid, name your price there and then, right? Let's get it straight. If you didn't believe me, why did you block the road? Ask Yuriy!"

Water fiddled with the fire. The men removed their wet shoes, putting them up by the fire to dry. On the stove, porridge simmered in the pot. They had dinner in silence. Yuriy was anxious. His mood affected everyone present, except for Water, perhaps. Water did not care. He was still captivated by the process of transforming the factory into a kind of a small fortress. He tried to remember every-thing he knew about cities and fortresses that had survived sieges. His thoughts flew far beyond the boundaries of a cramped room. For some reason, Jericho came to his mind. Water smiled. He would not want to see strangers with trumpets surrounding the factory tomorrow.

The men waited for Yuriy to say something; that conversation was long overdue. But he just sat there, texting someone.

"I don't have paperwork." Yuriy fired it off so fast that they all were left wondering whether they were hearing things. "That's true. I don't have the paperwork for this land and this factory. As of eight oh seven pm, this is not my property yet, and I also know for a fact that Uncle Vasyl is not lying."

He waved his phone in front of them. No one said a word. Hryhoriy abruptly turned pale. Water was the first to break the silence.

"Interesting," he said, flashing a weird smile, and then added: "It will be interesting."

"Right, very interesting," Yuriy said. "I'll get the papers tomorrow, but most probably, that won't happen by the time the visitors arrive. When I only started all that, they assured me that only some mere formalities were left, but now it looks like someone wants this land. Don't worry, though. Things will get settled by morning. This factory is already mine. They'll bring me the papers—if they make it through the snow, of course. Everything's going to be alright."

"So, there will be a fight," Boss perked up. "And it's cool, boss, you know?"

"Come on, you'll still make it. Both to the fight and into the grave," Uncle Vasyl said. "I didn't really look out for them in the village but I did see something. There are two dozen of them, not more. They're armed but without any insignia. They showed some papers to people but they might've as well showed them candy wrappers. I don't think they'll go for extremes, especially since they know who Yuriy's brother is. They'll just try to scare us away. That's it. Just make sure you don't piss your pants too early, or you'll freeze your legs off in the cold."

"How come you know about my brother?"

"It doesn't matter. I also have a gun." Uncle Vasyl pulled his rifle out of the case. "And three dozen cartridges. They'd better not even try to scare me."

"They'd better not," said Boss, placing a Makarov gun and two cartridge clips on the table.

"Oh, where did you get that?" Uncle Vasyl asked curiously. "Have you got the license for it?"

"It doesn't matter. I'm not going to whack anyone. Unless it's some kind of a force majeure. We'll see."

"Right. There's no need to shoot anyone. They'll bring me the papers tomorrow. Put your guns away. You can carry them tomorrow if you feel more comfortable with them. Just make sure no one sees it. And then we'll play it by ear."

Hryhoriy resembled a huge slab of chalk rather than a human.

"It's going to be fun." Water's eyes flashed with fascination. "Does anyone else want some tea?"

"We all do," Uncle Vasyl said.

Yuriy was tapping on his phone, text messages coming in one after another. It was after nine that he went downstairs and immediately hurried back up.

"It stopped snowing," he said, his eyes shining.

"What?" Boss asked, confused.

"Do we have any buckets?" Yuriy asked, as if addressing himself, and quickly answered his own question: "I think I saw a few in the basement. Put on your boots and let's go."

His plan was simple: to shovel away the snow, clearing up a patch in front of the barricaded gate, and flood an ice rink. To reinforce their defense even more. They found only two buckets, though, and a couple of big bottles. Water shoved the snow away with his make-shift shovel, flatly refusing to step on the ice. Boss cut a hole in the ice, nearly drowning his axe, and drew water in the buckets. The rest hauled them to the gate. They worked for three hours, before taking long breaks in rotation. The frost crackled, and the water quickly froze. The cold mercilessly stabbed their fingers and toes; they could not even feel their feet. At midnight, the men were so drained they could not work anymore. But then, there was not much sense to continue. Yuriy wiped sweat off his forehead, feeling his clothes, damp under his jacket, stick to his back. It would not be long before he caught a cold, and that was simply not an option.

"Let's go dry our clothes and warm up," he said.

The stove was emitting heat. The men took their boots and jackets off and spread them out to dry. Fatigue rolled over them, wave after wave, pushing their eyes close. Outside, silence rang, full of cold and snow. The generator hummed in the hallway, as if hinting that they would have trouble falling asleep.

"I don't think anyone would pop up here at night. But I can stand watch. I'm always having problems falling asleep in a new place anyway. A short nap would be enough. But you all should go to sleep," Yuriy said, his voice tired.

No one responded anything to that; they just had no strength left. Boss and Hryhoriy crawled into their sleeping bags, and Uncle Vasyl settled down next to Water on top of his larger bag. They went outside to the cars and brought whatever could be used as blankets. Warmth whiffed from the stove; the chill crept from the concrete. They turned off the generator. Silence became even more pronounced, filling the entire building in a mere second. It seemed that nothing would chase it away until the morning.

The men plunged into a dream. It enveloped them in a mirage, carrying them toward the warmth, toward the spring. Green fields spread around, and people crossed them in droves, singing, smoking pipes, preparing to sow spring wheat . . . A big yellow tractor appeared in the field, its wheels sinking heavily into the black soil, dragging a large plough behind it. The roar was so loud you could barely make out what people were saying. Suddenly, they vanished. The tractor's roar flooded the field, spread onto the forest and, having risen up to the sky, spilled over the whole room. The mirage disappeared, and the dream ran away, losing its boots. Uncle Vasyl snored savagely, pausing only when he rolled side to side. The tractor warmed up and headed back out into the fields . . .

For a solid two hours, everyone had trouble sleeping . . . But soon, it passed, too.

Water woke up first. Yuriy, who promised to stand watch, was blissfully asleep. The fire had long gone out. The cold was creeping in. Water lit up the stove. Food was half the trouble, as the boys had brought some supplies yesterday; the real trouble was coffee. By the time everyone else woke up, Water had already made breakfast, splitting it evenly.

Yuriy woke up last. He crawled out of his sleeping bag as the rest of the men already sat at the table, while Uncle Vasyl was packing his pipe. Boss, who had just started the generator, walked into the room.

"Morning, guardsman."

The men burst out laughing. Yuriy rubbed his eyes and looked at them with guilt.

"Morning."

The frost ran the show outside; the snowstorm still waned. Everything was frozen. The snow crunched under their feet. Despite their fatigue, they felt like walking on it for a long, long time. Walking deeper and deeper through the snow, listening to it crunching. Around them, the familiar silence reigned. In the cold air, their breath emerged as wisps of steam. Dogs' barking came from the village. The sounds traveled so far they could hear the door in the last house creaking open. The fortress was preparing to welcome its guests.

The men spent the entire morning waiting, and then returned to work. Water wielded the chainsaw like a small child with their new toy. He harvested so much firewood as if it was supposed to last them through the entire winter. The small aspen they had cut down to block the road never lived to witness the battle. The men decided to put together a small platform in front of the gate, using whatever they could lay their hands on—planks, all sorts of junk from the garage. The platform became the ultimate block; the defenders could now stand high and see what was unfolding beyond the gate. Boss hauled a barrel, and they made a fire in it. Waiting by the fire was much more thrilling. The sun had long climbed the entire height of a winter day.

Around three in the afternoon, they heard the growl of heavy machinery. The engine toiled away like there was no tomorrow, its roar frightening. A few minutes later, a big yellow tractor emerged at the edge of the village. It cleared off the snow as it went, tossing it right and left. Only two cars followed the tractor. Things went as expected. One of the cars stopped on the dirt road. The tractor kept pushing the snow aside, followed by a black mini-van with tinted windows. The rough terrain took its toll: the tractor kept sinking into the mud until it stopped. However, the mini-van continued to plough through until it reached almost as far as the gate.

The fortress defenders had long spotted the visitors. Noticing them, Hryhoriy opened his mouth for the first time since morning. He talked too much and off the point. He babbled about some money—how a counterfeit one-hundred bill had come into his hands last year—and other nonsense. Uncle Vasyl stood outside, holding his rifle, and smoked. Next to him, Boss pressed the gun, hidden under his jacket, to his chest. Water paced up and down with a long rebar rod, waving it now and then in the air. The frost was biting. Only Yuriy remained upstairs, the only place where the cell signal was up.

The men walked up onto the platform, where the fire burned in the barrel. The gate was almost chest-high, and they could see all around them. The sky was clear, an airplane's trail still visible on it.

Boss asked Uncle Vasyl: "Do you know the difference between the cock and the cockpit?"

"Why would you care about cockpits? A hullaballoo will start any minute now."

The black car had approached the barricade, but no one got out. Only Bereza was trying to climb out of the tractor. He struggled to open the heavy door; the tractor's right side had sunk in the mud and would not budge. He pushed the door frantically, but it would not yield. Bereza tried again and again, all in vain. Finally, he brandished his fist at the factory, resigning himself to his situation. He settled back into the driver's seat and after a while, when people stopped looking at him, dozed off.

Uncle Vasyl laughed heartily.

"I told you they wouldn't find him alive."

The others chuckled. Men in black uniform without insignia started getting out of the car, one after another. Seeing their guns, the men at the gate became nervous. Uncle Vasyl stared at the rifle next to his feet. Boss reached under his jacket to readjust the gun.

Yuriy hurried downstairs, shouting: "It okay! I'll be back soon. It's going to be alright!"

He jumped over the fence and ran along the frozen lake. It was white all around, save for this one figure running, adamantly refusing to dissolve in the whiteness. The figure pushed forward, without stopping, without slowing to a walk, running relentlessly toward the deserted road. Everyone stared at him. The people sitting in the car, which had stopped further away, hesitated about what they should do—run to intercept the runaway or drive after him. They just sat there, their mouths gaping open, staring after him.

On the walls of the fortress, where only four defenders stayed put, similar mood reigned.

"Now that's a trick," Boss said.

Their eyes followed Yuriy. He was clearly running toward a better world.

"We'll be fine," Uncle Vasyl said, trying to cheer the boys up.

"They'll kill us," Hryhoriy muttered, cheering them up in his own way.

"I hope you'll get to be the first one," Water said with a grin. "Yuriy said it will be alright. You've known him for years. And no one has even tried to kill you yet."

"We'll keep standing here. There's no escape, anyway. We walled ourselves up. And there's no way I can run across the lake. I'll just drop dead halfway through. So, there's no choice," Boss said.

Meanwhile, Yuriy had almost reached the road. He stopped, bending over, his hands on his knees, trying to catch his breath.

The new arrivals were impressed by the fortress with its barbed wire and walls made of concrete and ice. They had no clue how to assault it. One of them, probably the commander, spoke up:

"You have trespassed on the premises. It's a classic illegal take-over. Let's just do it the nice way. You leave the factory and get out of here. We'll even give you enough time to pack your personal stuff. Otherwise, we'll have to talk to you in a different way."

He adjusted the machine gun hanging on his chest.

The men on the wall remained calm and unfazed.

"Maybe you'll introduce yourselves first?" said Water. "What if you've come here to take it over, too? Where's your insignia? And come on, stop hiding, show us your pretty faces."

The men on the wall burst out laughing. Even Hryhoriy joined in.

"He has acne. That's why he's hiding his face," Uncle Vasyl said and coughed.

"So, you don't want to do it the nice way, huh? Alright."

One of the commander's subordinates wanted to come close to the gate but slipped and fell. When he finally struggled to his feet, he turned and limped back to the car.

The men's laughter could be heard as far as the road.

The commander did not speak anymore. He realized the ridic-ulousness of this whole situation. He had to make a decision. He pushed his balaclava under his helmet and lit a cigarette. Now they could see his face. Looking at him, you could think this man was a kind person. But it would've been a mistake. His subordinates were having a smoke, too, without removing their balaclavas, their backs turned toward the men. The commander whipped out his phone and wanted to give someone a call but was in for a surprise.

Talking to the fortress guards was pointless. The cold kept reminding them of its presence. The men on the wall were having tea, the steam swirling from their cups.

The visitors got back into their car, unable to bear it any longer. Only the commander was left standing. He peered into his phone, pacing up and down.

"You'd better just leave," Boss said calmly.

"Shut up. I know what to do. Just wait until they give me a go-ahead to kick your asses, and I'll see how brave you are. We'll tie rocks to your feet and throw you into that hole in the ice, and that would be that."

Boss frowned. He thought of intimidating his opponent with his gun but lacked the courage to follow through.

The commander shooed his men out of the car, and they stood there helplessly, smoking. Only the one who'd slipped and fell on the ice remained inside.

A car pulled up to Yuriy as he walked down the road, and he opened the door and got in. They set off toward the factory. The visitors' car—the one parked farther away—immediately made a U-turn and sped away. Having passed the tractor, the car stopped, and Yuriy got out along with a stranger in a coat. The man walked up toward the commander and had a word with him. The commander grew pale, jumped into the mini-van and, swiftly turning around, left.

Yuriy looked at his new guest with satisfaction and then extended his hand.

"Well, good luck. Enjoy your work," the man in the black coat said, and then added: "It's a nice factory."

The car left. The men on the wall could not understand what was happening. Boss shouted: "What was that?"

"Everything's alright. I made peace with my brother."

Yuriy showed them a white document folder. Everyone gasped with relief. The sun was slowly sinking. It was growing chilly. The forest did not remind of its presence in any way.

The fortress guard was taken down, the guardsmen sent home. The men returned to the factory, only Uncle Vasyl stayed behind.

"I'll go fetch that man from the tractor, or he'll freeze to death."

Now, they could finally go home. Bereza, the tractor driver, was free, too—they had no intention to take him hostage. He was granted freedom and a chance to finish his celebration since it was not every day that you had a grandson born. However, they did have to unblock the gates first, which took a while.

Water considered claiming the tractor as a trophy but then looked at its owner dozing on the backseat and took mercy on him. Let the tractor become a gift for his grandson.

Barricades always took longer to build than to dismantle.

# 004

The factory resumed its activity once the snow eased and started to slowly melt. The men made their comeback, one by one. Water arrived first. He'd grown attached to this place and wanted to return to it days ago. The middle of February now, the snowstorm was well in the past, and Yuriy immersed himself in handling practical arrangements. He and Hryhoriy ordered all types of spare parts. Boss even squeezed in the time to paint his car. Now, it glistened in the sun with its fresh dark blue color. Uncle Vasyl still stayed at home, smoking his pipe.

The factory was empty when Water returned. The most hardworking people on the planet would envy his gift for keeping himself busy. At first, he gathered all the garbage that was used as the construction material for the barricade and piled it on a heap. Then he decided to clear the roadblock. Friends with the chainsaw by that point, he cut all the logs in two days and lugged them to the factory. Then, he chopped them with an axe and stacked them against the wall. Alder and aspen trees made poor firewood but he could use them for other purposes. Bereza had yet to haul away his tractor, a heap of metal dying on the lakeshore. Water whiled away one of those days sitting by the lake, its surface still frozen.

When hardly any snow was left, the transformation of the factory began. Electric supply was the top-priority issue that Yuriy handled. A crew of electricians spent a few days on the task. Lots of people, lots of noise. It would be hard to describe in detail what happened over those few days. Yuriy was the only one watching the electricians work, and he was a man of few words. Water was busy, and other men had not turned up yet.

Finally, Water switched off the diesel generator never to switch it on again. This odious piece of metal with an empty tank, whose roar would haunt him in his dreams, finally shut up. That same day, Yuriy himself dismantled the stove chimney. Together with Water, they brought it downstairs. Yuriy wandered around the factory, glancing at the light of the lamps—they had hung way too many of them, according to Water—and touching this and that to check if it was real. Water had to get used to the electric space heater, or rather, to acknowledge that the firewood he had prepared for three winters ahead, proved unnecessary.

Yuriy brought some furniture. But where did he procure that GAZ truck he was driving? Water nearly rushed to meet the truck halfway with a rebar rod in his hands. For a moment, he thought that the story with unwelcome guests sprang back to life. But no . . .

The two of them lugged several second-hand desks and chairs, a few desk lamps and new DIY racks upstairs, along with some strange-looking crates and other things that failed to grab Water's attention. They had a hard time fitting everything into one, more or less habitable room, so they placed some furniture elsewhere. The rearrangements reached heights with a couch, which looked decent, even though clearly not new. Water's face lit up when he realized he could now sleep like a normal human being.

Water generally behaved weirdly, or rather, he did whatever he felt like doing. He often sat on the shore, just gazing at the lake. This resembled an ancient meditation with its unspeakable passion for the elements.

It was as if he could read the minds of the spring and the lake, sharing his secrets with them in return. So it was no wonder that it was Water who stumbled upon the well cover with a chain and a winch in the basement. It was shrouded with rust, hidden in the darkness. This discovery pushed him to the idea of a well. Yuriy had never mentioned one, but Water found it himself.

On the first night, when Water expected to sleep like a normal human being, he found a book inside the couch. It was incredibly thick, perhaps the world's biggest book about loneliness. He did not even dare to read it.

The next day, he observed an odd ritual, performed by Yuriy. With a confidence of a rainmaker, the man pulled out the tools. With slow, precise movements, he removed the old sign and nailed a new one, each gesture strictly to the point. This resembled a tea ceremony. People always found it easier to care for and protect what belonged to them. Water rummaged in the dark depths of his mind but could not find a different reasoning behind this thrill.

Once the ritual was over and its spiritual fires petered out and all known and unknown gods accepted offerings, Yuriy collected his tools and left.

The paint on the new sign glistened as brightly as if it was still wet. Now anyone who was not yet in the know could learn that it was again a private territory.

The next morning, the others arrived. Yuriy gave a lift to Hryhoriy. Water had not quite missed him and treated his return as a routine thing. Boss, however, burst into this carefree winter morning at full speed, on his freshly painted car, music blasting out of its windows. It was dramatic. Uncle Vasyl sat in the passenger seat. Their car was followed by a truck and a group of people, a familiar tractor driver, Bereza, among them. Sobered up after the celebration, he'd changed beyond recognition. The new arrivals found this place quaint. They stood in the yard smoking, grabbing at every chance to peer into the gaps in this mysterious building that snuggled up against the forest like a sleeping baby.

Water descended from his lodge like its rightful owner. Even Yuriy acknowledged deep down that Water had the first claim on this estate. A guard always knew what had been entrusted to him better than the one who trusted him to guard it. However, there was no one to guard the guards.

"Good morning. You're early," Water said, flashing his signature smile. "I haven't made breakfast, though. Not even coffee. Our home is not welcoming today."

"We've brought some food. I would've long dropped dead if I relied on you," Boss said and, turning off the music, got out of his car. "Uncle Vasyl took some stuff, too. We'll manage. I came to pick him up, but it took me a while to find his house. It was late when we dropped him off last time, and I couldn't remember the way. The old timer was weaving baskets when I arrived. So, we quickly put one to good use."

"Morning. No worries, I got coffee," Hryhoriy said.

Water could not understand why all those people turned up at the factory and what exactly they planned to load onto the truck bed with a crane. They did not hurry to explain it, either. But it proved to be quite simple: Yuriy decided to cut down the old equipment—all those huge metal crane-like constructions and other weird devices—and scrap it for sale. This would help them patch up holes in their budget. The men got to work. Metal beams and pillars fell one after another before being loaded onto the truck.

Uncle Vasyl helped eagerly. Boss and Water also joined. Only Hryhoriy and Yuriy just stood there, silent, and watched the men saw up a massive organism no one cared for any longer. This organism, whose importance they could not grasp, tumbled to their feet as useless pieces of metal.

When only a few beams were left, the inexplicable happened. The men were half-carrying, half-rolling a large beam. The next moment, it dropped on Bereza's hand, ripping off his little finger. Blood splashed onto the floor. Bereza screamed. Everyone stood in shock; only Water quickly found his bearings and dashed toward his backpack. He fetched a roll of gauze. Giving Bereza a painkiller, he bandaged his hand. Bereza growled like a wounded dog.

Yuriy and Water helped the injured man into the car and sped away from the factory. Despite the accident, Boss and Uncle Vasyl finished loading the scrap metal, and the truck slogged down the road along the lake. People scattered away; only the three men remained at the factory.

"What would happen to him now?" Hryhoriy asked. He placed the kettle on the electric stove and turned it on.

"Doctors are now so smart they can stitch his finger back," Uncle Vasyl remarked. He was laying out the instruments for his favorite ritual.

"Stitch it back? Oh, sure," Boss smirked and lit a cigarette, too. "His damn finger is lying on the floor of the production facility." He winced and then added: "And this happened just as things started getting back to normal. I only hope that cops don't come."

"What if they do?" Hryhoriy asked innocently.

"We should be fine, but Yuriy will get his ass kicked."

"It's too late now, but I did tell him not to call Bereza for help," Uncle Vasyl said.

The grimy kettle was coming to a boil. Out the window loomed the lake with the metal heap of the tractor taking root in its shore.

Later, Yuriy called and asked them to wait for him.

Dusk was settling in when Yuriy arrived at the factory. He headed toward the room where someone was smoking, and others were drinking tea. Hearing the stomping on the metal stairs, Boss shouted impatiently: "How was it? Tell us!"

When Yuriy entered the warm room, his whole body was shaking. It was hard to say whether he had been too worked up or too cold. His eyes darted around, searching for peace, consolation, or understanding, as if their owner was himself at a loss for what precisely he needed.

"They stitched it up and put a cast on it. He had two other fingers broken, too. They said he'd be alright. It could've been worse . . ."

"And where's Water?"

"What do you mean where's Water?" Yuriy's face shifted. "Oh. I left him at the hospital. It all happened too fast. I gave Bereza a ride home. Now, I'll have to take him to the hospital every day to have his wound dressed . . . I have no idea how we left Water behind. It's so weird. I even wondered why it was so quiet in the car, but then I figured we all were tired. I was driving; Bereza was sleeping, and Water . . . Well, he just wasn't there." Yuriy smiled as he spoke the last few words.

He immediately dialed Water's number only to be told that the recipient was out of reach.

"Don't worry, he'll come tomorrow," Boss said nonchalantly, as if this was a usual thing. "What about Bereza, though? He won't just let it go like that. He's a sketchy guy."

"He and I struck a deal. He told the doctors he got injured at home. It's going to be fine. They paid us handsomely for the scrap. And then, some of the orders have already arrived. I put them in the garage. We can start next week. Oh, and one more thing. We'll fix these rooms up a bit. This place should look decent, right? Okay, let's go now."

Boss turned off the electric appliances. The others packed their belongings. Uncle Vasyl finished his tea. Just before getting into the car, Yuriy asked:

"But how are we supposed to find Water in the city? He hardly ever sleeps at home, and his phone is turned off."

No one responded to that. The black eyes of the windows stared at the men. Concrete was slowly warming up. The walls had absorbed too much humidity. With the lights off, the factory resembled a corpse again. Finally, Uncle Vasyl broke the silence.

"He should here by morning," he said reassuringly. "You know how he is. I'm going to collect willow twigs in the woods tomorrow, and I'll stop by."

"Alright."

Leaving forest animals in peace, the cars departed toward human habitat, illuminating the lake and the trees with their headlights.

In the morning, the air grew warmer. Barely any ice was left on the surface of the lake. March was slowly approaching. The warmth proved to be misleading. It seemed as if it was embarrassed to even hope for spring. The forest was still in slumber. Wild animals chose alternative paths. People said there was scarcely any game left in this forest.

Two men could not believe their eyes. A roe deer emerged from the woods. Glancing around timidly, she headed toward the lake. They quietly watched this slender, gracious, long-legged animal. The roe deer gulped some water. Suddenly, she shuddered and galloped back into the forest, knocking the last year's leaves off the shrubs.

Water had stopped by Uncle Vasyl's house in the early hours. Uncle Vasyl stared at him in surprise, wondering how this odd young man managed to find his house. Nonchalant as ever, Water said that it was an elementary task—one's tongue could get one anywhere. Uncle Vasyl had nothing left to do but ask his guest to join him for breakfast, and then they headed to the factory together. He gave up on collecting those willow twigs. Uncle Vasyl packed a few things and picked up his rifle. He asked his neighbor, Nadia, to feed his dog while he would be away, even though he knew she would let him off the chain and bring him to her house. She always did that. It was no longer even clear whose dog that was—his or Nadia's. Uncle Vasyl did not keep any farm animals, except for chickens, but he had already stuffed their bodies into the freezer—they would be alright.

The two men walked toward the factory as if it was their home. How fast people get used to new places. They entered the building. Everything looked exactly as they had left it. Yuriy was worried someone might have taken advantage of their absence, even though there was little to steal.

Yuriy was supposed to return soon from the hospital, where he took Bereza every morning. It was bewildering why Bereza remained silent about the incident, especially for Uncle Vasyl who knew Bereza like no one else. They wondered what the price of his calm and silence might be.

Yuriy arrived in a while, his hands full. The men lugged the boxes upstairs. Yuriy offered Uncle Vasyl a ride home, but he refused. He said he would even spend the night at the factory. Yuriy quickly left to make it to the post office before the lunch break.

Water and Uncle Vasyl stayed at the factory alone. The morning was coming to an end. The new day breathed with warmth.

Later, the two men could be seen at the lakeshore. They sat on the bench at the water's edge. The silence rang around them, birds timidly trying to break it with their chirping. On the ground, not a trace of winter remained. Tall grass, trampled by the fishermen's feet, was reluctant to rise. The lake was alive, even though the shore looked unkempt. Someone left behind an empty can of worms. Water stared at the black soil in the can. On the trodden grass, many fishing tales of the yesteryear were written in a barely legible handwriting. The lake kept mum, although it could boast even more stories. The wind went into hiding.

"So, you're afraid of water? Is that true?"

"And I heard you're afraid of death."

Uncle Vasyl grinned as he tossed a pebble into the water. He did not hurry to throw another one; he knew he would run out of pebbles before too long.

"No, I don't think so. Death is not the worst thing that could happen to people."

"Funny that you say this. Everyone's afraid of it . . . And yes, I *am* afraid of water."

"Well, it's not the worst fear," Uncle Vasyl grinned again and looked his mate in the eye. "I'm afraid of snakes, but I love going to the forest. Just like you."

"Snakes? Funny. I don't think you look forward to the summer then, do you?"

"You don't have to talk to me so formally. We're friends."

"Are you sure?"

"Of course."

"We should get a fishing rod. Maybe there's fish in this lake."

"There's some, yes. I can bring a fishing rod from home. But it's too early. Let the fish spawn, and then we'll catch some pike."

"Is there pike here?"

"There's all kinds of fish here. There was some pike here for sure."

The old man had three pebbles left in his hand. He felt reluctant to throw them into the water. Ripples spread out across the surface. Solitary clouds and the sun reflected in the lake. One of the pebbles hit the sun, sending it in ripples.

"Shall we shoot at the cans with your gun?"

After a long pause, the old man said: "It's too early. Leave the birds alone."

They lingered by the lake for a long time. Uncle Vasyl tossed the last three pebbles into the water. It was growing warmer, and warmer, and warmer . . .

The next day, things started to roll. It was the first of March. Friday always made for an easy beginning, they said.

When Yuriy arrived, the boys were drinking tea by the lake. With his entire appearance, he made it clear that what had happened before was only a warm-up. It was time to raise the stakes.

By the time Boss and Hryhoriy arrived at the factory, things had indeed changed. An empty production facility, with its backbone of metal structures cut out, craved to spring to life. A long-forgotten yearning to create hung in the air—a yearning that had been blown out by the wind, lost among the footprints of rodents and unwelcome guests. It now permeated these rooms again, its sweetness enveloping the emptiness, bringing it back to the real world, bringing it back to life.

The process that was about to begin was not destined to be disrupted.

Again, they had to clear piles of junk and arrange the things they brought over the past few weeks. In this untidy, but already homely room, a workshop was being born. They moved the couch into the neighboring room. Water had cleaned it up immaculately. They arranged the desks and connected each workplace to electricity. Yuriy placed a computer and a printer on a separate desk. Each of the men received a new, comfortable chair.

White metal racks with wobbly shelves lined up by the wall. A high stack of empty boxes rose up. The men took the boxes away.

"Now this rat hole really looks like a workshop," Boss said, wrapping up their work. His voice was tired.

"Soon, it will look like home," quietly said Water who had found shelter inside these walls.

"It's still too long before it becomes a workshop," Yuriy remarked, wiping his forehead.

In the afternoon, even more boxes arrived. They dragged all of them upstairs. Everyone was weary; only Yuriy still ran up and down, his lucid eyes darting around, his voice pleading:

"Careful. Please be careful."

The more boxes they hauled upstairs, the faster the damp walls transformed into a full-fledged workshop, and the tighter the invisible cord tied Water to the factory. This feeling made him dizzy and urged him to run outside gulping for fresh air.

Humble kitchen utensils followed the same route as the couch. The room did turn into a workshop. Friday was over. When everyone else left, Water walked outside and stood beneath the star-studded sky, facing the lake and smoking a cigarette he had bummed off Boss. He rarely smoked—or rather, he rarely bought cigarettes. He never developed an addiction or desperately craved a smoke. He hated smoking when drinking, certainly not with a good drink in his glass. The smoke never complemented the taste, he said. But when someone he knew (and this was important) smoked next to him, he had trouble controlling himself.

The starry—too starry—sky covered the factory and the lake like a nightcap. Water decided to check in on his apartment next day since, judging by how the situation unfolded, he was soon destined to become the factory keeper slash hostage. He also wanted to bring over some of his belongings . . . On a night like that, you could let your thoughts go. Silence was a perfect soundtrack. Humans felt good by the water.

Yuriy returned from his hospital run. Water shared his plans of stopping by his apartment and heard no objections. A dense white fog descended on the ground as he walked along the shore. He had to keep to the opposite side of the road for fear of falling into the water. The mud squelched under his feet; wading through it felt satisfying. The village savored the silence. A group of people waited at the bus stop. Water joined them. When the bus arrived, he settled in his seat and squinted at the fields out the window. The women on the bus argued whether the spring had already arrived or if the winter had yet to bid its farewell. Someone was sharing the latest news, a whole barrage of it—a local newspaper with its two spreads could have been put to better use covering jars of milk. And yet, the spring, this hesitant spring remained the main topic of the conversation. Water would have witnessed the spring if he had not dozed off. More and more people boarded the bus. A young woman took a seat next to Water. She quickly drifted into sleep. When the outskirts of the city loomed ahead, the passengers fell silent for some reason. Outside the window, cars floated by and people hurried on the sidewalks. Stray dogs lay on the ground, their faces turned toward the sun. Spring knocked on house after house, staying like a guest or moving on if no one was home.

Water jolted awake, anxious that he had missed his stop. But he did not get off where he was supposed to. Water was too embarrassed to wake the young woman up and travelled all the way to the bus station instead. At one of the platforms, a sack of people must have come loose: a crowd of gardeners were getting ready to take their dachas by storm. After his stay at the factory, Water felt uncomfortable among this swarm of people, especially after he barely squeezed into the tram.

Screeching heavily, the old tram reluctantly rolled along the dilapidated tracks toward the suburbs. On his way between the tram stop and home, Water did not meet a single person he knew. He was glad he remembered to bring his keys . . .

The sky over the apartment block was overcast; no one sat on the bench by the entrance. Water ran to the third floor up the stairs that had been designed back in the day to allow enough space to turn a coffin when carrying it downstairs. He saw familiar graffiti on the walls. Water knew most of the authors of those scribbles, or the authors' parents. For the rest of his life, he was destined to return here and read this chronicle of unfulfilled dreams. A few 'artists' had long been confined behind bars; a few more died. But others stepped up and filled the gaps in their ranks, tools in hand.

Water harbored no hope that anything behind this door might have changed. Stuffy air hung in his apartment which felt cramped even though it had three bedrooms. Piles of second-hand rags which his sister, Svitlana, was trying to re-fashion into decent clothes reeked of dead bodies and old age. Two—or was it three by now?—munchkins, his nephews, darted between the piles, toppling the clothes to the floor. Water's mother left her room only when absolutely necessary. She barely even left the apartment, unless relentless heat drove them all outside. Tolyk, his sister's old—or new?—husband, was whiling his day away at work—or on a drinking binge.

Water's bedroom was locked, just as he left it. He always suspected that his relatives might want to occupy his room as their wonderful family grew. But they restrained themselves with their last bit of strength, which was especially hard when Water disappeared for days. This time, he gathered nearly all of his belongings and picked up a few books from the shelf. It took him a while to find the ones he needed, hidden safely under a thick layer of dust. Water stopped by his mother's room to say hello and give her some cash. Then he bummed a cigarette off his sister and ran outside.

This time, he did not lock the door to his room.

He spent the afternoon roaming around the city. Countless cafes beckoned to him. But Water headed towards his favorite pizza place. A small building was tucked among the apartment blocks. A gentle murmur of traffic was the only sound that reached it from the highway. Water knew Oksana well. She had worked here for years. At this restaurant, he could always enjoy a warm pizza—and a warm word. He could also down a pint or two of beer if he was in the mood for it. But that day, Oksana was not in. A young woman working the shift paid barely any attention to him. Unlike the pizza, the conversation did not turn out well. Music blasted from the radio.

Once his disappointment with this motley city crowd hit the bottom, Water took the old tram to the home improvement store. He strolled for a while down the endless aisles. He watched the forklift stack large pallets one on top of another. He wondered whether they had ever had any pileups. A scene reeled before his eyes with these endless aisles collapsing. Meanwhile, people around him peacefully shopped for necessary and often completely useless things. Water stocked up on them, too. Electrical tools caught his attention, but he only shopped around, checking the prices. In the end, he moved on—he would not scrape up enough money, anyway.

By the time he returned to the bus station, the last bus bound for the village had already left.

Water walked in the dusk along the highway hoping to hitch a ride. Cars sped past him on this cold Saturday night. The lampposts on both sides of the road enveloped it in the gentle light, running far beyond the horizon. Water remained alone at the spot where hitchhikers usually caught rides. He stood, shielding his eyes from the bright headlights with his palm. He tossed his backpack on the ground and straightened his back. The cars kept speeding past, the lampposts running away. People hurried toward their destinations. No one stopped.

He had been standing there for a good part of an hour when an elderly man driving an old cargo van finally picked him up. Throughout the ride, he told his companion stories about his large family. His daughter-in-law who twisted his son round her little finger. The hard luck of small farmers. The drawbacks of wholesale trade in dairy. The police tormenting the sellers. He provided his expert assessment of the condition of roads in the region, broken down by districts. Then, he abruptly shifted gears and turned to the political situation in the country. His conclusion was this: "It won't be the case forever." The old man wrapped up his tales by saying that he was disappointed in people because they lacked even a shred of an ability to listen. He dropped Water off at the edge of the village.

Water stood blissfully under the starry sky, with a heavy backpack on his shoulders. A young moon reflected on the crystal surface of the lake. As Water walked along the familiar road, the factory called out to him with the light streaming from the workshop window. Water knew that Yuriy was working late. He himself had assured Water that he did not need to rush. Finally, Water reached the building and disappeared inside the production facility. The starry night, the sleek surface of the lake, and the young moon reflected on it—all of them remained behind.

In the workshop, the stack of boxes grew significantly taller, as did the stack of unfamiliar—but even more intriguing—objects. As far as Water understood, important preparations were completed. Things were about to change. He was not afraid of the changes; he simply disliked them. There were too many changes recently.

Yuriy slept on the couch, so Water had no choice but to spread a piece of cardboard on the floor and lie down. He had not dreamed much lately. Sometimes, he dreamt of water—deep and dark.

By the time he woke up, Yuriy had already gone home. Sunday was a day off.

# 005

"Sunday's our rest day. The only one we get," Yuriy said, rocking in his brand-new chair. "But today's a big day. The very first one."

The men sat in the room, each at his new workplace, not that comfortable but their very own. The atmosphere had shifted over the past few weeks. The sense of expectation dominated the room which reeked of the dampness of concrete. They should've started by now.

"It's time."

Hryhoriy looked different. His pallor had vanished. Fear no longer existed.

Even Uncle Vasyl enjoyed himself, rocking in his chair. They resembled a bunch of people waiting for the train with a mix of eagerness and uncertainty about the upcoming journey.

"It's half past eight on a sunny Monday in early spring, and we're starting," Yuriy declared, rubbing his hands. He was clearly thrilled.

"A quite dramatic start, I'd say," Boss said. He leaned back, his hands crossed behind his neck, trying to shake off sleepiness.

Water only watched the others and waited. For some reason, he liked waiting. Uncle Vasyl, having rocked in his chair to his heart's content, went outside. Meanwhile, Yuriy was giving instructions in the workshop. Extremely simple and extremely unclear.

Water retrieved mid-sized white plastic boxes with silver buttons fastening the edges together. Their sides glistened, smeared with greasy substance that stuck to his hands. Each box was covered with a transparent lid, and inside lay a tightly coiled sealing ring wrapped in cellophane and screws that held the lid to the base. Water was instructed to dismantle the lids and remove the sealing rings. The boxes were supposed to serve as cases for the devices they would manufacture. The deadline, as always, was yesterday since in the afternoon, these beauties were supposed to be shipped away for laser engraving. They would come back sporting barcodes and other mandatory marks. Those marks never intrigued Water, but working with the cases was a whole different story.

Boss was cutting up cable. The process required hundreds if not thousands of pieces of a particular size and color. It was evident that he was frustrated by the task but tried to conceal it.

Hryhoriy, armed with a soldering iron and microscope, was soldering some circuit boards. Before that, Yuriy checked each one using a device that beeped unpleasantly, echoing throughout the workshop. Hryhoriy worked with such inspiration that it was impossible to take eyes off him. Only a thin wisp of smoke curled up from his soldering iron. Everything he anticipated came to pass. His eyes hurt a bit, having forgotten about this kind of work. He glanced up from the circuit boards now and then and gazed out the window toward the village as if searching for someone in the window of the outermost house. Then, he adjusted his glasses and focused on his work again.

For some reason, they did not speak. It appeared as if everyone knew what to do but it was far from the truth.

A model device, framed and under glass, hung on the wall behind Yuriy. The circuit boards of this very first test model sparkled in the morning sunlight.

The sound of hammering echoed from the yard into the workshop.

Work was in full swing; the spring was stirring awake, but the men paid no attention. Uncle Vasyl was making benches where they could stretch out during breaks, once every other hour, as Yuriy had said. Another nail pierced the old wood while the other men lounged comfortably in their chairs in the workshop. The nail drove deeper and deeper under the blows of the hammer, overcoming resistance. The wood deformed. Here and there, cracks appeared, and old green paint peeled off. Uncle Vasyl wiped his forehead and plopped down on the new bench. He made four of them, so they could sit snugly facing each other. He also planned to knock together a big table where their whole company could have lunch. For now, the choice was limited: they could either eat at their desks (but could you even call it "lunch" if you had to eat at your desk) or go to the lakeshore. However, this was inconvenient, especially for the cook, who had trouble carrying the pots and pans so far. And yet, it was on the shore that the table was set for their first lunch.

After an intriguing conversation with Yuriy, Uncle Vasyl said he was eager to join the team. Yuriy agreed and offered him a decent pay. But he did not need it; his pension had always been enough. The truth was, he felt lonely and bored at home. After his son's death, he made peace with loneliness. His daughter-in-law wanted nothing to do with him. He wondered what harm he had done to her. She lived in his apartment but never even brought his grandson over. Uncle Vasyl refused to visit them, either. Reconciled with his loneliness, he tried to manage on his own as best he could. Loneliness did not drive people to death, but it made them bored. The feeling of boredom gnawed at him like a worm gnawing the wood. He did not need anything from Yuriy but becoming part of a small team would do him good. Perhaps this would save him.

The men went downstairs for a break. They sat on the benches, their faces turned toward the sun.

"Why didn't you dig them in? We can smash our heads like this!"

Boss rocked the bench so hard that Hryhoriy nearly toppled over.

"There's no shovel," Uncle Vasyl explained, shielding his eyes from the sun. "Just wait until the sun beats down. You'll be the first one to grab that bench and run into the shade by the wall. I'll make a table, too, once it gets warmer. Then you can dig them in. If you bring the shovel, that is."

The break followed an old pattern: the smokers smoked; the non-smokers breathed in the smoke. The sky hung above their heads. So much was supposed to be said that day, but words stubbornly lingered in their throats. No one said a word. Then, Water broke the silence.

"Maybe we can grill some meat on Saturday? Celebrate the launch, so to say."

"And have a tiny sip of something, you know, just to rinse our mouths."

Boss kept rocking. Hryhoriy scooted over to Yuriy.

"But you're driving," Uncle Vasyl remarked.

"Yuriy will give me a lift."

"Am I a taxi or what?" The one who was supposed to speak first finally spoke up. "We'll just take the bus. Things should clear up by Saturday, so we might as well do a barbeque."

Hryhoriy appeared quite uninterested. In his imagination, he was still soldering circuit boards, finally making money. But he still asked the old man: "And what about you? Do you consume alcohol?"

The old man sprang to life. A thrilling debate was sprouting.

"I think I've already said that to everyone. There's no need to be so formal around me. I don't like this." He wanted to add that he was not that old but cut himself short. "I don't drink because it never ends well. But sometimes, you do need to look at the earth up close."

The wind scattered the men's laughter as the break came to an end. They returned upstairs, while the old man (who was actually not that old) went to make a fire. That day, he planned to cook lunch in a cauldron.

Yuriy took the cases away for laser engraving. Desperate need demanded, as always, either order or panic. Water continued to prepare the cases. Boss was not content with cutting up cable. He only calmed down when Hryhoriy entrusted him with cleaning circuit boards. Before long, Yuriy returned, and things gained a new shape and momentum.

Water only listened, absorbing the words that just recently meant nothing to him. His understanding of this world was so firmly established and stable that figuring out the purpose of all these resistors, transistors, power supply units, and whatnot became a new challenge for him. The boys knew it all, understood it well, and did not bother with explanations. They worked in silence.

Yuriy was implementing a program into a circuit board. The program he had been fortunate to find miraculously, thanks to old Schneider. Or, rather, he was fortunate to find a software developer who lived on a different continent or might as well, just like any developer, in a different world. The stars commanded it that way. Without this program, nothing would have happened; with it, it was all there. And he was breathing life into it.

They barely even talked about the device. Water could not possibly understand the purpose of all that hullaballoo and what might come out of it. But he was confident that someone else should know it. Turning over white boxes in his hands, feeling the smooth texture of plastic with his fingertips, he wondered about the arrangements in this place and what else might become his professional responsibility. Water could not imagine that he would learn the ropes before he knew it.

Uncle Vasyl ran behind with the lunch. He had spent so long fiddling with the cauldron that his face was flushed with heat. The hot cauldron he carried in his strong arms breathed steam all the way to the lake. Water watched this scene out the window.

They had lunch in silence. The men were so hungry they gobbled up the entire cauldron worth of food.

All afternoon, Water absorbed new knowledge. Uncle Vasyl

climbed upstairs now and then and called him for a smoke, luring him with a pack of cigarettes he must have bought for this exact purpose. But it would not look nice if he just slipped away, not when Boss, hunched over his desk, worked so zealously that you could shout yourself hoarse until he heard you.

And yet, he went down, and they smoked, stretched on the benches. Water found more and more things beyond his understanding; it was hard to imagine the end product, its purpose, how he would get used to the process. Those who cruised around for miles on their rolling chairs, who flooded their desks with their sweat despite the cool air, found it simpler. On that first day, they only started to know each other, but, as usually, there was barely any time for even that. Stupid choppy rhythm.

"We haven't even finished making it, and we already need to redo it." This is how Yuriy wrapped up that day.

Water stared at the starry sky that was absent in the city. A multitude of new universes whirred in his mind. How was he supposed to remember all that? And did he even need to? He tried writing everything down but lost the thread. Things would work themselves out.

A scoop of porridge was left in the cauldron, just enough for dinner. Too bad that Yuriy took his laptop home. Without it, their internet connection was useless. What with his antiquated cell phone . . .

Water picked up the book he had stumbled upon inside the couch. The manner of writing was so fascinating that he re-read the first page three times. But that was where he stopped. He struggled to fall asleep for a long time, scenes from the working day flashing before his eyes. His brain recreated a mishmash of words he managed to catch on the fly.

Circuit boards were ordered from abroad. But it was still necessary to solder some extra thingy onto them, just one term on the long list of unfamiliar words he had been hearing all day. A woman named Svitlana handled it. Yuriy chatted on the phone with her from morning to dusk. From what he said, it became clear that she worked at an actual plant, where they tackled the task. Then the circuit boards were brought to the factory where they checked and cleaned them with some gunk that stank so horribly he could barely sit in the room. Next, they soldered power units onto the boards, this time manually, along with the pieces of cable Boss was cutting. At some point between these processes, Yuriy implemented the program.

What followed was no less intriguing. The cases, which Water sorted so meticulously, ended up on Boss' desk, laser engravings and all. Boss worked on a lathe, making holes precisely beneath the buttons. Through the holes, he inserted four or five feet of cable with an electric plug at the end, fixing it inside the case with a plastic thing and a screw and rock-solid glue that made his eyes water. Then it was Hryhoriy's turn. He put all soldered parts inside, wired up the button, and—lo and behold!—green light came on. If something went wrong, the light was red. They took the device to the metal room where it remained on for one day and night. Afterward, Boss drenched it with glue, checked it again, and closed it with a lid. This time, the lid was not transparent but black, with a small hole in the middle for a light-emitting diode. Boss fixed the lid with glue and screwed it in so that no one could even dare to dismantle this miraculous device, so that no one saw how its insides operated.

After that, Water was supposed to step in, but he had to do serious preparations first. Uncle Vasyl helped him at these early stages—or would always help, who knew. They assembled the boxes that had been delivered long time ago and were now stashed by the wall. In a few straightforward maneuvers, a flat sheet of gray cardboard, without any marks or inscriptions, transformed into a neat box. Simple but quite intriguing. At the bottom of the box, Water placed a manual printed on a glossy paper and folded in half.

Then he wiped the device, which had been thoroughly tested

and sealed, with alcohol, rubbing off the remnants of glue and dust. He erased greasy fingerprints left by the workers and all other spots and smudges.

Water wrapped the device into the bubble wrap they all loved to pop as children.

Finally, just before closing the box and pasting a smiley-face sticker rather than a seal, he put a postcard on the very top. The postcard, printed on a thick piece of cardboard, had only one sentence: "You have just bought happiness."

Soon, people would come and take the boxes away forever. This device was like an extramarital child of electrical engineering and medicine. Yuriy claimed it would do miracles. Dozens of people signed up on a waitlist to test it.

It was Schneider's concept which Yuriy had to modify. The device was not cheap, but its effect was palpable. Customers would know what they paid for. Addiction was out of the question. It was just science, pure science.

Yuriy's modification, which Schneider had flatly refused to accept, was making the device unserviceable. Its operational lifetime was around a year, its warranty period—nine months. It was enough to justify the price tag. Yuriy came up with this idea so that no one could reproduce his device. The program was hard to read, and the design did not leave any chance to dismantle the device properly and figure out how it functioned. Yuriy resolved to secure himself a peace of mind right from the get-go. Troubles were galore, anyway. Electronic components were Chinese and American. Cases came from Poland. Electric plugs were made in Germany or Italy, and the cable was domestic.

All that came to Water in a dream. A lucid, fragile dream; a slightest movement or breath could destroy it. In his dream, a family with two children sat in a spacious, bright room with blue walls. Potted plants and bunches of flowers adorned the window-sills. The

TV was turned off; behind their backs, bookshelves loomed. If you looked closely, you could see that books were lined up strictly by alphabetical order.

The youngest, blonde boy, chased the cat who hid under the table. In the corner, a small box made of sleek, light plastic blinked with its green eye. A happily smiling family gazed at a boundless, starry sky. These people had bought happiness—and they felt happy now that they knew where to buy it.

The nights were still chilly . . .

When Water woke up, he heard someone's footsteps downstairs. He dressed in a flash and rushed into the hallway. Boss and Uncle Vasyl had already arrived. Boss's voice boomed out before he even caught sight of him:

"Water! You'd better make coffee now, or our morning won't be good!"

They had their coffee outside where a gentle breeze blew from the forest. Their higher-up was late, delayed by Bereza's hospital run. Unsure what to do, the men just waited for him, sitting on the bench. Despite the chill, they were reluctant to return to the concrete walls.

"It's strange no one's broken into the tractor yet," Boss said, sipping his coffee as he cast his eyes over the shoreline.

"What makes you think no one has?" Uncle Vasyl asked, lighting his pipe.

"Because I'm guarding this place," Water replied.

"With a guard like you, anyone could walk in and take whatever they want," Boss said with the confidence of an expert, leaving no room for doubt.

Water frowned like the morning sky—then brightened up just as fast.

"But I don't guard the tractor. I guard the factory."

"Some villagers might've tried, but they feel sorry for Bereza," Uncle Vasyl said. "It's strange though—no one's dared to profit from their neighbor's misery. Bereza spends his days drinking and whining, never able to keep his mouth shut, especially after a few drinks. But he hasn't let slip what Yuriy promised him. All he does is whine."

"Yuriy's staying quiet, too." Boss finished his coffee and dumped the grounds onto the grass—no one would be using them to tell his fortune, anyway.

The sound of a car rumbled up from the village road. A black Toyota was speeding toward them. The men stood up and went upstairs to meet their higher-up at their desks.

That day everyone was busy. Yuriy and Hryhoriy fiddled with the insides of the device. To an outsider, it might look like magic. There was no bigger magic than people engaged in what they love best—never had been. Boss prepared cases. He drilled holes in the right places. Using wire cutters, he removed unnecessary walls and other parts from the inside. Water was also assigned to this operation. His eyes shone cheerfully as he vigorously ripped out what was not necessary, admiring the results of his destructive work. He worked with such zeal that it was hard to imagine a better task for him.

But it was Uncle Vasyl who was assigned the most fascinating assignment. Water's desk had been fully cleared up and given over to him, while Water himself squeezed next to Boss as his temporary desk-mate. Uncle Vasyl folded manuals. Yuriy had picked them up at the print shop earlier that day and gave him a whole box. When the duct tape was cut, an aroma of freshly printed papers burst out from the box, overpowering the reek of stale air and strange smells of glues and lacquers. Even the old man who acknowledged only the aroma of tobacco yielded to these miracles of printing. His calloused fingers folded tender, pristine papers. Taking good aim, he tried hard to align the fold lines, but they ended up still crooked.

Lunch was hurried; Uncle Vasyl had been so absorbed in his work that they had to practically chase him outside to make it. By then, he was already seeing spots before his eyes.

In the afternoon, Boss was dispatched to meet with Svitlana and her people. Yuriy told him that starting from tomorrow, this would be his main task, while the desk assigned to him would be occupied by a new person. He should expect to be on the road a lot since Yuriy found it hard to shuttle between the factories by himself. Yuriy offered him the keys to his car, but Boss refused to take them. He would keep driving his buggy and would only ask Yuriy to cover the gas and some wear and tear. Boss left immediately and did not return until late afternoon.

Water took over Uncle Vasyl's tasks.

When everyone left, he decided to tidy up the workshop; others never even noticed how dirty it became in just two days.

Water struggled to fall asleep. Every now and then, he walked outside, shining his torch at the tractor whose dirty window reflected its warm light.

Since Boss' job now involved driving, a need arose to have someone else work at the desk. Next morning, they brought Dmytro in. Less than slender, he had trouble getting out of the car. Eternally round with a childlike face, he looked around him with curiosity. His eyes were very much alive, his thoughts lively. Just like Hryhoriy, he was bad at talking. His voice was so quiet as if coming from underground. Yuriy immediately introduced him to the team, but Dmytro did not demonstrate any curiosity toward people and remembered none of their names. He took his time slowly climbing the stairs. By the time he reached the top, his face was flushed, and he panted as if he had just run a marathon.

They showed Dmytro his new workplace, and he appeared content. He quickly removed his shirt, soaked with sweat, and put on a robe. The robe, though seemingly ordinary, was actually professional gear: it was designed not to generate static. The robe had seen better times but was clearly well cared for. The holes at the elbows were neatly patched, even if with a different fabric. As Water stared at the patches, Dmytro sharply said in one breath: "Let's see how quickly you'll wear a hole in your sweater against this desk."

He plunged into work. Someone tried asking him questions but without much success. It was almost lunchtime when he came back to life and embarked on the second round of introductions.

"So you go by what? 'Water'? Interesting."

He wiped sweat from his forehead. In the light of the desk lamp, his face glistened like a wet rubber ball.

"We need to protect you then. There's too little water on our planet."

"Not that little," Boss said skeptically.

"No, it's true," Dmytro insisted. "There's too little good water, and the rest . . . well, that salty slop is useless. The drinking water supply is dwindling fast. We might be in trouble sooner than we think. You didn't consider that, did you?"

Boss had no response. Dmytro continued.

"This problem is already on our doorstep, and we still can't accept it. 'We're not Africa,' and so on. It's all nonsense . . . "

Water stopped pretending he was not the topic of conversation and joined in.

"What else is there to say if forty percent of clean water goes down the toilet? Over a hundred rivers have dried up in the past few years. The situation might be even worse. I don't know the exact figures but . . . "

Yuriy cut him off.

"There's this river not far from here. It's a disaster how much it's dried up in the past ten years."

"That river's a poor example," Water interjected. He hated being interrupted but managed a smile this time. "If you walked a few miles upstream, you'd see it's actually quite deep. The beavers have come back and built huge dams. There's plenty of fish around those dams, and the beavers themselves are thriving. They're so large you might die of fear if you saw them. But people never go out there. They don't want the shrubs to prick their butts."

"We could shoot those beavers and make hats." Boss took off his cap and demonstrated how nice a fur hat would look on him.

Uncle Vasyl chimed in.

"You'd better stay away. Those beavers are so huge they'll turn part of you into a hat and gobble up the rest." The old man grinned. "Water is right. The river is thriving upstream."

"But beavers don't eat anything but wood, do they?" Boss asked, putting his cap back on.

"Forget that. Oh, by the way, I have beaver sausage at home. I'll bring some over on Saturday so you can try it."

Hryhoriy was not paying attention. He had just finished a meticulous manipulation. He adjusted his glasses and, rubbing the scar beneath the rim, stared at the window of the outermost house in the village.

Dmytro wrapped up the conversation with a mutter: "We need to protect our water."

Amid the excitement, Uncle Vasyl lost track of time, working alongside Water, and forgot all about lunch.

Later in the afternoon, still outside, Dmytro asked Yuriy if he would mind if he turned on the radio.

"Go ahead if everyone's alright with it."

Everyone was alright. Dmytro took out a radio from his fancy backpack and placed it on his desk. Music did what it could do best—livened up the room. The voices of anchors mixed with the voices of singers, ads, news, and weather forecasts. Hryhoriy grimaced as the noise disrupted his focus and he botched his work, getting an earful from Yuriy. He paled in comparison to Dmytro who was now scoring additional points.

Yuriy met Dmytro a few years ago. A friend from college, who was now teaching there, asked him if he had any job for the guy. Dmytro came from a dysfunctional family. He was sickly but sharp.

At the factory, his intelligence came out full force from day one, though it was to be assessed by those who knew nothing about all those resistors and transistors.

"I'm curious about that metal room," Dmytro said.

"I don't think you're the only one who's curious about it. They're just too embarrassed to ask. It's intriguing, right? I like it, too. I already told you about the specifics of our device, and you can find even more details in the manual. Schneider suggested using that room to prevent workers from getting an overdose of happiness from the device. As you'll see from the manual, it's not that good. The metal sheets in the room where the devices are tested are the only thing that can shield us from an onslaught of happiness. That room was here even before Schneider, if I'm not mistaken. It's also why we endure a twenty-mile commute every single day instead of just staying in the city."

"Maybe that room is why you fought so hard for this factory?" Hryhoriy asked.

"Maybe," Yuriy said.

Who could have thought that the presence of the radio would change it all so drastically. When everyone left, Water brought the radio to his room. He sat staring at it as if it was a miracle. Over the years, he'd spent many nights to the sounds of radio stations' lives. This always created a certain illusion of belonging to their world. A radio host talked like your distant relative or neighbor. You talked to him. You knew what was happening in the country. The ads tried to push you some junk. A local bar or school cafeteria invited you to rent their venue for your wedding party. How could you say no?

Since his radio broke down, a dark lake pooled in his soul, and nothing could fill it. The book about loneliness was too warm for this miserable spring . . . Books needed an appropriate backdrop, too. Meanwhile, the radio anchored you to the reality. The big city was drowning in traffic jams, and you knew about it immediately. You felt sorry for people who were running late to pick up their children from preschool. You could vividly imagine those kids, jackets on, faces flushed, waiting until their parents would finally pick them up.

Water would sit up and stare at the radio even longer, but the host had gotten tired and signed off for the night. The overnight music began playing, lulling him to sleep. Dreams gazed at him through the window.

With each passing day, Water resisted taking roots in this concrete with all his might. But spring had a different plan. He was stirred awake by the radio, and it was a pleasant awakening. A stranger woke up in the middle of the night, took shower and brushed their teeth with their eyes shut, and schlepped across the city on a taxi, listening to the weary blabber of the taxi driver. Taking the elevator up to the studio, this person realized they had put on their T-shirt backwards. And all that just for being able to yell into the microphone at seven am, after a couple of coffees: "Good morning, everyone! A special shoutout to all you drivers out there, and welcome to those of you getting ready for work. And if you overslept, you might as well go back to sleep—it won't change much anyway!"

This yelling woke Water up. Soon, he was drinking his coffee by the lake. Here, the chill felt double strong, a dark, overcast patch of sky hanging over the opposite shore.

"Too bad I can't bring my radio here," Water thought.

He had to keep himself busy; it would be another hour until the others arrived. He decided to go and check on the tractor. Nothing changed. A heap of metal sat intact. Up close, the tractor looked much more intimidating.

The day passed like any other. It was notable only for Dmytro nearly falling down the stairs. There was one other thing: in the evening, ten green lights switched on and burned throughout the night.

The first batch was ready for a Monday pick-up. A friend of Yuriy's brother expected it. He owned a large enterprise and wanted to test the devices in the field. Yuriy met this businessman at his brother's place, at the first formal meeting after the reconciliation. They sipped whiskey and talked about the device. The man liked the concept. However, he hesitated to bring it home. The businessman was weary about entrusting his precious health, not that strong anymore, to this machine. But he wondered: if this device is meant to help people relax and manage their household tasks efficiently, why could not he use this miracle to set his workers on the right path?

Yuriy liked this idea. But he gave him only five devices out of ten to test them on people. And he did not hurry to search for other clients. It would be great to see some actual results first. Yuriy did not expect favorable reviews, though—he would never settle for this. It was supposed to be a scream of delight, a hysteria in its most positive sense. And then, the price. The price was decent. He had already spent too much. This contract would pull them out of the hell of endless expenses and empty pockets.

They invested all their energy into it. The first batch was shipped for testing. The next item on their agenda was to create a small production stock. They could as well drink to that.

They drank to it on Saturday.

Saturday turned out extraordinarily nice. This time, Dmytro did a hospital run. It was quite epic: Yuriy got so absorbed in fiddling with his devices that he forgot to warn Bereza.

So, when Dmytro rolled up his acid-colored Daewoo Matiz to his house, Bereza forgot about the wound dressing and whatnot. But this passed, too.

Boss gave the others a ride. His car darted out onto the dirt road at full speed and later made a few funny twists in the yard. The passengers tumbled outside. Yuriy realized he would never trust Boss with his car.

Boss drove off to run errands, receiving strict instructions not to take too long and to buy all items on Yuriy's list.

Dmytro arrived later, but he might as well forget about work. Uncle Vasyl had been gathering wood for the campfire since early morning. The aspen which Water had cut down so much as if he had been preparing for a doomsday was a poor fit, just like the pine trees surrounding the factory. Armed with an ax, the old man set out in search of hardwood, nurturing hope to stumble upon a fruit tree. He had to salvage the situation, especially since he had left his beaver sausage at home.

The day did not entirely go to waste; the men upstairs did get some work done. Water packed the devices which the businessman was supposed to pick up on Monday. The others tied up the loose ends. First time on the job, Water slogged through the packing. He wiped each device thoroughly and then rolled the cable, tying the bundle with a small piece of slick black wire. They had bought a whole big spool of it. He paid extra care to put a manual and a "happy postcard" inside, even though this postcard meant nothing to the businessman. It could make a good impression, though. Water constantly caught himself thinking that the device indeed looked like an off-the-shelf gadget manufactured at a top-notch factory. It seemed especially convincing after he sealed the box and pasted the sticker. Water wondered how many devices and other daily necessities were manufactured in similar conditions? What else could be done in similar vein?

These musings did not benefit his work, slowing it down even more. The campfire was already burning by the lake. A thin wisp of bluish smoke was rising toward the sky, distracting Water. Uncle Vasyl shuttled back and forth, lugging bricks for a grill—there were enough bricks scattered around to build a house.

When Boss returned, Water was still packing. Instead of giving him a hand, the others only urged him on. Five nicely packed devices, brand-new, hot off the factory, lined up on the table.

The campfire lured people outside. Resisting this primeval instinct was useless. Boss took the food out of the bags. Their lunch, or rather appetizers, were modest and boring as hell. They had picked up some bread and vegetables to go with the meat, and cheese cuts were meant to make the wait more enjoyable while the pile of firewood, ablaze and shooting sparks into the air, turned to embers. Boss brought three bottles of whiskey, just as Yuriy asked. Uncle Vasyl apologized but flatly refused to drink. "Not today," he said, staying by the fire. His face turned red, and his mustache and beard seemed to have brightened up.

Dmytro was a non-drinker, and then, the mission thrust on his shoulders—delivering everyone safely home—demanded a sober mind and clear thinking.

This left the four of them. "Jack" joined the company. Boss opened a bottle of sparkling water, spilling it all over his jacket. That was his element: maximum movement, jokes, laughter. He threaded the pieces of meat onto skewers, wearing the expression of an expert who had seen it all in this predictable life.

"I'm glad that it occurred to me to fetch the skewers." Water helped the expert roll up his sleeves, which kept unrolling and getting in his way.

"I've got a few extra . . . " Water said, but Yuriy interrupted him.

"Come on, you can drink if you want to, but I'll be grilling the meat. This business needs only one pair of hands."

No one protested.

"I have a suggestion. Let's not talk shop today. We'll get back to it on Monday. For now, let's just raise the first toast to our business, and that's it." Yuriy uncorked the bottle, and Hryhoriy held up the glasses.

The meat was already on the grill as they knocked back their first round of drinks. Boss's face also flushed from the heat. The second round. Time to turn the meat.

Hryhoriy, unable to hold back, said: "We need to order more circuit boards. And look for other types of relays." He shook his groggy head. "I don't like these ones."

"Let's save that for Monday," Water said calmly.

"Monday? What difference does it make if I tell this to you on Monday? You don't know anything about it. So, just keep quiet."

"No, really. Let's discuss it on Monday," Yuriy said, pouring another shot.

They drank to love and all the usual toasts. The meat was served on the table. Boss plopped down on the bench, lighting a cigarette.

"I found a car for myself. Just the way I wanted. A model styled after a Coca-Cola bottle."

He burst into laughter. "You can find plenty of cars styled like this bottle, too," Uncle Vasyl grinned, pointing at the table.

"Come on, please, let him finish. I'm curious to hear more," Dmytro said, his eyes sparkling with interest.

"Don't you 'please' me," Uncle Vasyl replied with a smirk.

"It's a cool model. A Pontiac Firebird."

Silence.

"You've seen it for sure. They often show them in American movies. Any old movie will have one. It's a bit of a wreck, but I can fix it up. It's my childhood dream."

Hryhoriy, completely sozzled, worked up the nerve to ask: "How many miles on it? What year?"

"Not sure about the miles, but it was made in '67."

"Just like my mama," Dmytro said with a grin.

Everyone laughed. The meat tasted delicious if slightly dry. But no one pointed that out so as not to hurt the expert's feelings.

"Where did you find it?" Yuriy asked, placing another empty bottle on the ground.

Water gazed at the world glassy-eyed.

"Last week, a friend asked me to help him with his car. He'd just bought a new garage with a pit. So, we went there. It was a huge garage complex miles from anywhere. Thousands of garages. I'd never seen anything like it. But that's not the point. So, we were fixing his car and all. And then, I went for a walk searching for something I could snag. And I spotted this door open. An old man was rummaging about. I peeked inside and saw her. She was a beauty. The bird on the hood was partially scraped off, but that's no big deal. I asked him, "Is it running?" And he said, "No, but it's got all the parts." So I went, "It's a smash. Are you thinking of selling it?" And he was like, "No, I'm not." I checked it out. There's a horrible mess inside, but I'm buying it, you can have my word for it."

"But the old guy isn't selling it." Hryhoriy rested his chin on his hands.

"I'll buy it anyway."

Finally, Uncle Vasyl, clearly bored, spoke up.

"I'm heading out. Your company is nice, but being home alone is even nicer."

"Let me give you a ride. They'll still be here for a while," Dmytro offered, clearly relishing his role of the driver.

No one objected. His Daewoo Matiz sped off toward the village.

By the time he returned, the group had already suffered some losses. Yuriy had left, and Hryhoriy was asleep with his head on the table. Water spent an inhumanely long time explaining that Oksana, Yuriy's wife, had picked him up with a mix of screams and laughter.

Dmytro volunteered to take Hryhoriy home; Water and Boss dragged him to the car and shoved him inside.

"Alright, I know where he lives. See you later."

Boss expressed a desire to stay at the factory. He, Water, and a quarter of a bottle of whiskey—a cheerful, friendly company—went upstairs to spend time with the radio.

Dusk began to settle in.

And so it went: people came into their life every day, as if for a job interview.

# 006

On Monday, they came to work with joyful, refreshed faces. Only Hryhoriy was pale as a wall. He gave the impression of having been drinking all Sunday. His own explanation was very simple, though.

"I suffer for three days whenever I booze too much. Today is better. Yesterday, I was dying."

Yuriy brought a fire extinguisher and put it in the place of honor in the corner.

"Sorry I didn't think about it earlier. We work with machinery here. If there's a short circuit, we'll all burn to death. I'll also bring a well-stocked first aid kit tomorrow. Go ahead and start working as usual. I'll be back by lunchtime."

He picked up five boxes with the devices and drove off to meet with the businessman. It would have been a mistake to have him come to the factory, not with its unpresentable appearance. Their agreement demanded better. The factory's appearance had preoccupied Yuriy a lot recently. He seemed to be ashamed of it.

Water continued to pack the devices that had been tested. Boss went to the post office. Dmytro fiddled with the circuit boards, and Hryhoriy hissed, having burnt his fingers on the soldering iron.

Uncle Vasyl found a refuge outside, where warmth was still tentatively asserting itself. The old man lit his pipe, spreading out his bones on the bench by the lake. His joints ached, craving warmth, and he turned them toward the sun. It was slowly entering the spring mode. The trees, huddled together at the edge of the pine forest, were bursting into buds. Dark tall spruces had not changed even a bit. Uncle Vasyl wanted to clean up after the Saturday's picnic but lay on the bench instead, arms behind his head, gazing at the spring.

An hour later, Yuriy and Boss arrived. Water hauled a stack of boxes into the workshop. Their business was clearly off to a good start. The businessman accepted the first batch and promised to provide his feedback by Friday. Then they would consider different options of cooperation. They agreed not to communicate by Friday, not even on the phone, unless something extraordinary happened. Boss, however, had his own opinion on the matter.

"Or unless his factory burns down to hell," he said.

"If his factory burns down, ours might as well," Yuriy remarked.

A long, laborious process of unpacking followed. They invented a new task for Water. He was given a notebook. Water was supposed to take notes on the deliveries and check whether the numbers matched. He was to count everything but for smaller parts and circuit boards— those were Yuriy's responsibility; Water would not make sense of it. Meanwhile, counting the number of plugs, cases, and coils of wire did not require any special knowledge. He was also expected to record anything that Boss picked up. Anything he took for laser engraving. Yuriy explained that his intention was not to keep tabs on the team but rather ensure they did not forget or lose anything. In the future, he would be the one handling inventory, but at this initial stage, the process was quite straightforward.

The men got to work. No one even noticed how the day slipped away.

They set things on the right track, and they rolled forward. Days got longer. After work, Water was setting up house. He finally realized that these walls were becoming his home. He used to believe it was temporary, and he only had to wait it out. But now he understood he was there for the long haul. And this transformed his approach. Housing conditions were not the best, but he did not care. Cooking and storing food was no longer a trouble, not when a fridge arrived. Drinking water was no problem, either; he just had to fetch it from the well. An electric heater kept his room warm. The toilet was outside, a wooden, lopsided outhouse, but complaining about it would be a sin. Taking a shower and doing laundry was a trouble, though.

Water decided to knock together an outdoor shower. Wood was abundant, and no one was taking the chainsaw away. Its buzzing drew villagers' attention across the lake. Water quickly screwed together the framing, using the electric screwdriver he had already gotten the hang of. Things went smoothly, even though it was the first structure Water built with his own hands. He had purchased the supplies on the last day of his relative freedom. The only element missing was a bucket. Uncle Vasyl got him one. Water drilled a hole in the bucket and attached a piece of hose with a shower head at the end. It could even switch between several modes. He covered the frame with tarpaulin and tossed a wooden pallet on the ground. He also wanted to hang a mirror but could not find one at the factory. A pocket mirror he used for shaving would have to do. However, he did not shave regularly and saw his reflection in the lake more often than in the mirror.

Finally, he heated a bucket of water and took a shower. He only felt uncomfortably cold when rushing back to the building.

After the shower, he felt as if he had been reborn. Water listened to the radio for a while and then called a woman he knew on the phone just to hear a woman's voice. He wanted to invite her over but he knew she would not come.

The sunrise was phenomenal. The sun resembled a large onion that rolled onto the table, its sides glimmering. Water met everyone outside with the coffee. Its faint aroma wafted in the air, teasing people. There was enough for everyone; only Dmytro had no cup. He stared at Water, perplexed. The sounds of the radio drifted from the factory.

"I would've made coffee for you, too, but your cup was dirty. Sorry."

Dmytro hung his head, heaving a sigh. The enormous shadow his figure cast on the wall slumped to match.

"Okay, okay, I made it. It's on your desk."

The goliath of a man trundled upstairs, and the factory walls echoed his heavy panting. By the time he returned, the rest had finished their coffee. No one hurried up to the workshop, craving for springtime warmth.

Dmytro's face was red; he sat to catch his breath. He clearly enjoyed his drink. After finishing it, he thanked Water. From that day on, his cup never stayed dirty.

The workday began with computer glitches. Yuriy took the laptop home every single night. Now, the programming unit would not switch on. Yuriy sputtered and cursed, but no matter what he tried, the precious information—or rather the precious program—refused to transfer from the laptop to the circuit board through all the wires and circuits.

"Hryhoriy, come here and help me. Maybe you'll spot what the problem is. This thing is driving me mad."

Hryhoriy walked over. They both stared at the screen, but could not figure out what was wrong. After a long time of reinstalling, updating, and swearing, it finally started up again.

"Finally. It felt like some kind of mystery. This laptop costs as much as a decent car. I paid for all the apps, and there's a bunch of them here, I never install any hacked ones, yet it still doesn't work."

"Well, it seems like it's working now," Hryhoriy remarked timidly.

"It does, but . . ."

Each of the men already knew their responsibilities well. Another ten devices made it to the metal room. Yuriy often talked to Svitlana on the phone, and afterward, Boss would take a few boxes with circuit boards and spare parts over to her. Their cooperation had certain complexities, though. She occasionally had the elements soldered incorrectly, used the wrong paste, or cleaned the mold poorly, charging a handsome fee nevertheless. But Yuriy knew that without her, they would never have gotten off the ground.

In early evening, as everyone stood outside, ready to get into their cars, Uncle Vasyl, quieter than ever, searched for his pipe. Water took Yuriy aside for a word.

"We have to do something about the rodents. They're swarming all over the place."

"Are they sneaking upstairs, too?"

"They are. Well, I haven't seen rats in the workshop, but I did spot a little mouse scurrying across the room." Water smiled. "We need to do something before we catch rat fever. Maybe you could get some poison or traps. They're swarming out of the basement. We never cleaned it. Maybe we should clear out the junk one day and douse it all in chlorine. It won't be good if clients arrive, and we have rats jumping on their heads."

"I'll bring some rat poison. We should also make Uncle Vasyl our rodent hunter. He's just roaming around, bored. Let him have some fun," Yuriy said with a grin, and they left.

Water followed them with his eyes and then headed to the shore to watch the lake breathe.

The next day, Uncle Vasyl was sullen again. He ignored all questions and only responded with his very look that said he was doing just fine and would everyone stop pestering him and go nag at someone else instead. Despite his mood, he seemed to enjoy his new task.

"I must get rid of these devils of flesh and fur before they eat Water alive. Besides, I still need to borrow money from him."

The wheels were set in motion. He began with the most traditional method, sprinkling the poison around. But the rats would not fall for this banality. They were wild rats, not some domestic mice who could not wait until you fed them. They had grown up in much harsher conditions than a warm building. He had to strain his imagination to handle them. Cats would not do the job, either. Uncle Vasyl wanted to spare them, anyway. First, he needed to destroy the largest rats and only then he would bring a cat. A female would be best, he declared, since male cats, just like men, were too lazy.

Having scattered rat poison all over the basement, the old man was still far from satisfied. While the others continued to toil away, he shuffled back home, weaseling out of his cooking duties. His escapade worked in the team's favor, though, as they ended up ordering pizza instead. It was cold by the time Boss brought it to the factory, but once warmed-up, it tasted just as good.

The old man returned with his hands full. He carried several tools and some grain in his bag. Now, he had a chance to get creative. Grabbing a bite, he set down to work. Uncle Vasyl picked up a few boards and, cutting them with a saw, hammered together a few small crates with locking contraptions. He poured a handful of grain inside each one as a bait. Then, his eyes fell on a plastic barrel with a lid. He decided to refashion it as a trap, too. Drilling several holes in the barrel, he fixed a rebar prod to the lid, which he had cut shorter. Now that it was all connected, he filled the barrel with water. According to his design, rats were expected to climb the makeshift "plank" toward the lid where the grain was scattered. The lid would turn over, and the rats would fall into the barrel. The last thing the old man did was place the metal traps he had fetched from home all over the basement.

He wore himself out by the end of the day. Once his job was done, he sat on the bench and smoked. His usual cheerfulness was not coming back to him. Something clearly bothered him but he did not feel like sharing. He only warned Water:

"Don't snoop around in the basement at night. There's war going on. If they rush toward you, run away."

These words stirred Hryhoriy's imagination. He winced in horror. But Water was not frightened. He listened to the radio until midnight when the anthem played. At the crack of dawn, he woke up to the squealing of rats. It came from downstairs, but Water decided to stay put. The sounds of the radio enveloped him again, playing a song that was once his favorite and reminding him of a woman he once loved.

The morning was warmer than the last. When everyone gathered downstairs, Uncle Vasyl looked terrified, as if his old age—something they all tried hard to ignore—had caught him by the hand. His face was as black as soil. He did not speak and even refused his coffee. Instead, he headed outside to dig a pit. The others asked mockingly, "Why do you need a pit? You don't even know if there's anything to bury." He only muttered, "Ask Water if there's anything to bury."

Water simply nodded—they did have plenty to bury. Rats squeaked from every corner: smaller traps, wooden crates, and loudest of all, the barrel. Alongside the squeaking, a frantic splashing of water was coming from it. When they removed the lid, they saw a few dozen bodies, soaked wet. Many rats had already drowned. But a few still swam, desperately fighting for life, pushing aside the bodies of their fellow dead. Uncle Vasyl poured more water into the barrel and threw wooden crates inside. Then he finished off the rats in small traps. Afterward, he went outside to dig another, bigger pit.

There is a temple in India, in the state of Rajasthan. Dozens of thousands of rats live there. People adore and worship them. They believe these are the souls of young children who died too early. Reincarnation into rats gives them a chance to become human in their next life. If someone kills a rat on the temple grounds, they must compensate with a copy made of pure gold. Uncle Vasyl would have needed a ton of gold.

Upstairs, things went as expected. The men were busy with

their tasks, each at his desk under lamps they trusted more than the sun. Boss was clearly bored. He had to wait for Yuriy to gather the required spare parts to take them to Svitlana. Starting next week, she would be busy with other work and would no longer be able to solder their items. They had to modify their plans on the fly. However, Yuriy struggled to decide where to start and kept rummaging through boxes, hoping to find an answer there . . . Hryhoriy and Dmytro soldered the elements, cleaned the circuit boards, and applied varnish. Water packed the devices that were ready. He anticipated that he would need to assemble many more cardboard boxes soon, given the engineers' enthusiasm.

They heard the water sloshing downstairs, and an hour later, Uncle Vasyl finally returned.

"I've buried them all."

"How many?" Yuriy removed the eyeglasses he used only when working on very delicate tasks.

"The devil only knows. I started counting but lost track. Too many. I'll be outside. I need a break."

"Alright. Do you think there'll be more tomorrow?"

"Oh yes. I placed all the traps back."

They continued working. Water ploughed through packing. Dmytro panted heavily over the cases, sweating in his robe. Even though it was warm outside, they had to use a space heater in this concrete sack with windows. Yet they rarely turned it on, as it made the air too dry. Airing the room barely helped, since the only window that opened was next to Hryhoriy, and he hated sitting in the draft. Music cheered them up but only so much. Boss went to the post office. He was also supposed to bring pizza again. This new approach to the lunch menu was quite appealing.

Water walked downstairs to take a leak and breathe in some fresh air. A gentle breeze wrestled with the lake, raising the waves and tossing them onto the shore. The scent of pine wafted out of the woods and crept along the walls of the factory, eager to sneak inside. No one let it in, though. Water stared into the distance. Toy-like cars sped down the road, quickly passing the visible stretch. A car with the long-awaited lunch would soon follow the suit. Water loved pizza. Boss often brought too much of it, and he would get leftovers for dinner. Tonight, though, he would cook soup at the shore. His stomach needed a fasting day.

He turned his head right and left, searching for Uncle Vasyl to bum a cigarette.

The old man was not on the bench or in the production facility. Maybe he went to the basement? But why would he? He had set the traps a long time ago. He was not upstairs, either. Perhaps he headed to the lake? If he was sitting right by the water's edge, he would not be able to see him from this far.

Uncle Vasyl lay on the shore facedown. It took a while before Water spotted him. He bolted toward him. He wanted to shout for help but thought better of it; the workshop was too far, and no one would hear his shouting. He picked up the pace to cover that couple dozens of feet as fast as he could. But he immediately realized that of his excellent physical fitness, only a shell was left. Panting heavily, Water approached the old man. His breath pulsated in his ears. He could not hear a thing. Adrenaline rushed into his head, taking away the last hope for a cold head. He could not grasp what was happening.

Uncle Vasyl was alive. He was simply asleep, reeking of alcohol. The old man was drunk. His lucid eyes barely reacted, and his power of speech vanished. Water tried talking to him but without success. He lifted the man up and dragged him toward the factory like a catch that was too large to carry. Uncle Vasyl proved heavier than he thought. Back at the workshop, Water shouted for help.

"Guys! I need to carry the old man inside. Can anyone come down?"

Yuriy was the first to spring into action.

"What happened? Is he alive?"

"He is. He's just drunk."

"Drunk?" Yuriy sounded surprised.

"Uh huh."

They carried him into Water's room. Uncle Vasyl came around and started mumbling, but no one could decipher that primordial language. They laid him on the bed. Water rolled up his sleeping bag and instead spread out a few blankets that had been lying around since the cold spell.

As they left the room, Yuriy said: "Let him sleep. He can explain it later," then added: "I'm just curious where he found the time for drinking."

When Uncle Vasyl woke up, the whole workshop rushed to the noise. Water handed him a bottle of water, which the old man's hands groped for so thirstily. He looked at Yuriy, who stood there perplexed, and said, clearly and loudly:

"It's my son's birthday today."

Water built a fire at the lakeshore. No matter how warm it was during the day, the nights were still cold. The sky, sprinkled with stars, glimmered above, and the young moon hung over the forest, peeking timidly through the trees.

The water was slowly coming to a boil as he tossed ingredients into the cauldron. The light was more than adequate. A battery-powered tourist lamp illuminated the shore and part of the lake's surface. The lake radiated serenity. The silence hummed. His ears would have hurt if he had listened to it into the early hours. For a moment, Water thought he heard frogs croaking, but it was too early for them.

He craved a drink, but there was nothing at hand. Trudging all the way to the village seemed foolish. The soup turned out disappointing. Water dialed someone's number, but the call went unanswered. Once again, he found solace in the radio that rocked him to sleep on its waves.

The long-awaited Friday arrived. The rat burial continued, though they reaped a smaller harvest this time. Uncle Vasyl had come back to life, wearing a mask more of a hangover than sorrow. His flushed face only brightened in the afternoon. No one mentioned the previous day's incident. Yuriy wanted to have a word with him, to say that such behavior did not sit well with the team. But the old man did not need to be told that.

Boss could not help himself.

"Would you like me to bring you a beer?" He asked teasingly, his eyes sparkling. Boss took a pull at his cigarette with gusto.

"Let the kids drink beer. I'll go for milk."

A new workday struggled to find its place on the trodden path of workdays. The guys were all wound up. Nothing was coming out right. Water seized the opportunity and snuggled up next to his radio, listening to the music.

Yuriy stared at his phone on the desk. Now and then, his hand twitched toward it; he received a few calls—first from Boss, who was having trouble with shipments at the post office, and then from Svitlana about some practical arrangements. He was not satisfied. Something had to change. That very day. Once and for all. Anticipating the changes, he struggled to quell his thirst of expectation. The spring would come and go, but his life was about to change forever.

Dmytro and Hryhoriy worked diligently, inventing new tasks for themselves. They simply could not stand being idle. But soon, Dmytro grew frustrated. He walked outside, where the weather was so warm and pleasant. The wind cooled his face. Uncle Vasyl smoked by the lake, relishing the break. He had already buried all the rats and scrubbed the shovel.

Dmytro approached him. He was still getting used to the team. Yuriy was an old acquaintance, but he struggled to connect with the others. Boss spent more time in the city than at the factory. Water lived in his own world. Hryhoriy, his workmate, saw Dmytro only as his rival. He yearned for connection, for a sense of belonging.

"Tired?"

"A bit."

Uncle Vasyl scooted over so Dmytro could join him on the bench.

"There's something mesmerizing about this water."

"That's true. We grew up on this pond."

"We?"

"The entire village. The heat will drive crowds here. You'll see. People have always been swimming in this lake."

"So this lake has been here forever?"

"It has. For as long as I can remember. We'd go for a swim here all the time. No one ever chased us away. It changed hands, especially in the past two decades. But no one chased us away. At some point, we stopped swimming here after a woman from the village drowned. It was horrible. The whole village hoped she'd emerge from the water but only her body did. She was young, beautiful. People stayed out of it after that. Up until last summer. Five years have passed."

"What made them come back?"

"Well, they had no choice. There're ponds on the other side of the village, too. A whole cascade. They all used to be one fish farm, but now each pond has its owner. We all went swimming in one of them. The owner was nice, and the pond was great. A perfect swimming hole. Not too deep and yet not that shallow as others. And it wasn't too muddy. We all swam there. But when the old owner died, his successor didn't quite welcome our swimming gang. He didn't dare to kick us away, but last August, when it was so hot that asphalt was melting under our feet, he drained the pond. He said he wanted to fix the pipes or something. But people don't drain ponds in summer. That's the kind of thing you do in the fall. So, with that swimming hole gone, people remembered about this lake. There was just no other way out. The heat was merciless. And you can't drain this lake. It's fed by the springs in the forest. The water is cold but clear. It flows into the stream by the road and nourishes the swamp in the woods. I'll take you there one day. It's a nice place."

"And what was in this building before?" Dmytro asked, intrigued by the story and eager to learn more.

"The devil only knows. It was always some kind of a factory."

A telephone call shook up the whole room. Even the walls seemed to move, resonating with the rhythm of the ringtone. It was that coveted call.

A worried voice only said: "Come here. Now."

It was later, from Yuriy's story, that they learned how the meeting had gone. Yuriy recounted it with absolute rupture, throwing in a handful of seemingly unnecessary details.

He met the client at his office. He was immediately repelled by its gaudiness. Yuriy did not know much about interiors, but back in the day, Oksana had talked some sense into him. And she knew her way about it. The office resembled a gift shop whose owner had long been dead. Out of sheer respect for him, others did not dare to clear up all sorts of figurines, plates, spoons, cups, hats, and souvenir knives. It was all stacked into layered heaps covered with dust. At eye level, they kept the junk wiped down, but whatever sat higher gave a depressing impression. A large black sombrero embroidered with golden flowers reminded of a desert. Yuriy quickly remembered Oksana's words: if you wanted to showcase the number of countries you were fortunate to visit, you did not need to turn your room into a museum. Hanging a world map on the wall and marking places you had been to with pins would be enough. This would also serve as an extra motivation as you would realize that no matter how many countries you had visited, you had barely seen anything in this world.

The businessman, Denys Serhiyovych, cast a curious glance at his guest across the table, as if asking: "And what about you? Have you seen it all?" Yuriy, however, appeared genuinely worried. Denys Serhiyovych lit a cigarette, stroking his unruly beard to give it a decent look. He quickly noted that Yuriy could call him Denys, dropping the formalities.

"Would you care for a drink?" he asked, opening the doors of an enormous safe that, as it turned out, also housed a museum, just of a different type. This 'museum,' apparently, had many more admirers and visitors.

"I'm driving," Yuriy said, clearly nervous.

"I'll have one if you don't mind." Denys poured a glass of black liquid from an unusually shaped bottle—round and covered in intricate patterns. "Indian rum."

"No, thanks."

"Alright, let's get down to business." Denys theatrically sipped from his glass. "How many devices do you have in stock for now?"

Finally, they were getting to the point. Yuriy breathed a sigh of relief.

"Right now, if we don't count the ones you already have . . . "

"Yeah, don't count those."

"We have fifteen ready."

"I'll take them at the price you mentioned. I can pay for five devices today and the rest upon delivery."

Yuriy felt flustered—he wanted to be the one leading this conversation. He wanted to hear feedback and imagined the situation quite differently. But Denys Serhiyovych took him in a different direction.

"But . . . what's your overall impression of it? The device? What do you think about it?"

The businessman took another sip.

"I'll be honest with you. When we first met and you told me about this device, I thought it was just another gimmick, like that junk they sell on TV. But I needed to try it first. And after talking with those people, including your brother . . . You know what I mean. So, when we brought the first batch to the factory, I was skeptical and kept it to myself. I didn't want to look like a fool. And when those devices were switched on—I did it with my own hands—nothing happened. On the first day, there didn't seem to be anything unusual. But on the second day, some people started working better than others. Now that was interesting. Quite a few showed brilliant results. They were so efficient I couldn't even dream about it. Cheerful, energetic. Others performed poorly, but they never were particularly hard-working. Most of them had long wanted to quit, but I literally asked them to stay a bit longer because we had a big order from abroad."

Yuriy sat there and listened.

"Next day, all those who'd worked poorly the previous day came to my office and said they were quitting. You should've heard what they told me. I don't remember the last time workers spoke to me so openly and honestly. Some were unhappy with working conditions, which I'm afraid I can't improve. Others simply hated the factory and their job. A few wanted to start families, move abroad, or start their own business. They just wouldn't stay. And it all changed overnight. Of course, I was angry. I didn't know how to react. How was I supposed to replace them? And, even worse, where would I find new people? Honestly? I wanted to throw those devices in the trash. That's how I felt. But then I thought, 'Why would I keep people here against their will?' Why would I want workers who dreamed of getting out of here? Especially if it was affecting the factory's performance. So, on Thursday, we recruited new people. We receive many applications, thank God. And you know what I told them? I said the probation period was one week. I needed to play it safe. But in fact, I knew who'd stay and who wouldn't as soon as the next day. Guess how I found it out? They told me themselves. Your device is a miracle, and if it lasts for at least two or three months, that's just phenomenal. I'm ready to buy dozens more."

"It should last for nine months."

"That's even better. I have no idea what you've soldered inside, but it's kind of magic. I never expected anything like this."

Yuriy never expected it either, so he was at a bit of a loss for words.

"This is the money for five devices." Denys Serhiyovych placed an envelope with cash on the table. "Could you get us the rest on Monday?"

"Sure," Yuriy said, slipping the envelope into his pocket. He realized he should have counted the money first.

"Sorry. Someone's waiting for me. Let's talk more on Monday."

Denys Serhiyovych finished his rum. Yuriy counted the money as soon as he left the office. Everything was in order. He loved the idea of an old safe and alcohol stashed inside. However, something troubled him, though he could not put his finger on it. The factory was entering a new phase; they could soon operate at full capacity. If Denys went out for a night of drinking, the promotion for his device was as good as done. He was bound to brag about it.

In the car, Yuriy could not shake the feeling that he had been pressured into making a purchase rather selling something himself. However, the feeling gradually faded away.

He promised himself to prepare better for future deals. He should at least talk more, or he would not get very far. Ironically, Denys Serhiyovych owned a garment factory that had once belonged to Schneider.

On Saturday, Bereza came to pick up his tractor. His yellow Zhiguli rumbled heavily down the dirt road toward the factory. A group of men got out. They danced around the metal beast. Bereza occasionally broke from the circle to hop into the cabin, performing his personal rituals there, but without success. The tractor would not budge. Still, Bereza knew how to handle it. He was already back to his usual self, fully recovered.

A villager told Uncle Vasyl, who relayed it to the others, that Bereza had ranted about his life over a bottle, as was his old habit. He showed off his stump and claimed he could still feel his missing finger. Since then, people felt sympathy for Bereza and avoided messing with him, even though he asked for it. Now, he was fully absorbed in his heavy responsibility.

The men made a few more circles around the beast, yellow and crippled like its owner, before removing the battery and heading back to the village.

The next day, as the sun dipped behind the forest, the tractor belched out puffs of thick black smoke, its engine rumbling by the lake. Water watched the spectacle from the window. Once the tractor left, the lakeshore became deserted once more.

# 007

Everything was going according to Yuriy's plan. He went to Denys on Monday and kept coming back for more meetings. Each visit he was showered with glowing reviews and introduced to business ventures he had not even known existed. This small collaboration proved to be fertile ground for future grand deals.

Over time, one of the largest meat processing plants in the region saw a marked increase in the number of happy employees. More happy workers appeared at other enterprises and in various industries. Yuriy's brother promoted the device through word of mouth—primitive yet effective—and the sales increased even more. They achieved great results without much difficulty, advertising the product to a broad audience in a quiet, informal, yet productive manner.

A certain distinguished farmer even tested the device on his cows, but his bold experiment failed.

The more Yuriy talked to business owners, the more he realized how different they all were. They spoke of what had led them into their industries with varying degrees of reluctance. Denys, for example, did not hide (though he did not publicly disclose either) that the circumstances had practically forced him into buying a garment factory. He needed to legitimize some cash and invest it somewhere before he had a chance to squander or drink it all away. He did not know anything about sewing but was convinced that it mattered little in business.

"Business is all about management," he'd say, a glass of wine in hand.

The farmer who tried the device on his cows also had stories to share. He had worked abroad in Europe in the 90s, still fresh out of school. First, he went to the Czech Republic, then Germany, and finally England, where he decided to stay. How he managed to enter the country in the first place he did not mention. He landed a job on a farm in the idyllic county of Somerset, where he quickly adapted to the nuances of his new occupation. It was a quiet place, with low chances of deportation, and yet . . .

It did not last long. He missed hustle and bustle and yearned to be among people. So, he bid the farm farewell and moved to London to work on a construction site where he knew some guys. Handy people are always in demand, so they took him in. Everything was going well, though he had to be more cautious of immigration authorities. Still, it was more fun to be among people than alone on a farm.

One fine evening, the farmer decided to visit a popular British pub. He had never been before, but the guys from work invited him to watch a football game. He ended up punching some Russian fella and causing both of them to be deported since, as it turned out, neither was in the United Kingdom legally.

He returned home with some cash. Tired of construction, which he had never enjoyed anyway, he found his only other skill was looking after cows. He started small. The first few years were spent in anticipation of record-breaking milk yields, but mostly it was his pockets that were milked dry. Then things got better. The scale of his enterprise was proof enough of that.

With more customers came more work at the factory. Uncle Vasyl got his hands on every task. Chores took a back seat. Rats were no longer an issue. The final offensive on their positions was continually postponed.

Boss spent all day behind the wheel. In addition to the post office, Svitlana, engravers, and various stores, he now had a whole list of delivery addresses. The car, loaded with devices, darted from one company to another. He had little time for work in the factory but still helped out here and there.

Yuriy, Hryhoriy, and Dmytro often stayed after official work hours, tinkering with circuit boards and microchips.

Water became absorbed by the packaging. The same repetitive tasks every day required no thought. It was a strange transformation from a man with minimal skills to a human machine. In the evenings, he would sit by the lake to clear his head and see cardboard boxes, instructions, and devices float past him. After two weeks, Water noticed that his sweater was fraying at the elbows.

None of the customers had seen the factory yet because Yuriy was embarrassed by its appearance. He tried to make the gray walls look decent, but it all came to naught without a proper remodeling. The workshop looked terrible, and the concrete floors constantly gathered dust. Despite Water's best efforts, it never seemed to stay clean. The kitchen was no better—so bad, in fact, that they were embarrassed to offer coffee to visitors. Finally, Yuriy decided it was time to start renovating.

The spring warmth made it possible to work outside, but the damp concrete walls of the factory had not yet warmed up.

That was when Ivan Oak arrived. He was a short man of about forty, who inherited his last name from the tree but none of his name-sake's sturdiness. His bald head gleamed in the rays of the spring sun. Childishly lively Ivan was a jack-of-all-trades. His hands were tasked with doing everything necessary so that the owner would no longer be ashamed of his factory.

Oak lived in the same town as the rest, except, of course, for Uncle Vasyl. His house was right next to Water's, but their paths had not crossed. Later, Ivan would claim he had known Water since child-hood, and after a drink or two, he would even say he had seen him being thrown into the river. But Water insisted he did not know him and had not seen him before.

Ivan was skilled at all kinds of repairs—tiling, plastering, painting, assembling furniture. In other words, he could do anything. But he liked working with wood best of all and had been assisting his father in a carpentry shop since he was a kid. Many years ago, when a new residential neighborhood was being built nearby, Ivan and his father made balconies for several houses. Now, as he walked by those buildings—which he always did when he was feeling down—he counted how many of their balconies remained. He promised himself that when the last wooden balcony was replaced by metal and plastic, he would stop going there.

After his father's death, Oak could not bring himself to work with wood for a while. Eventually, he returned to work to keep his skills sharp and to pass on the craft to someone else. He got some tools and found a place in an industrial park, but they kicked him out after a few years. So, Ivan moved the equipment to his dacha, where he set up a workshop, warehouse, and home all in one. That place always smelled of wood. Ivan and his small family—his wife Sofiia, whom he married three years ago—lived off carpentry and were always shuttling between the city and the workshop.

Sofiia reignited his drive, helped him at work, and insisted on buying a car, even though it cost all their wedding money. Soon, she became his apprentice and eventually pushed the master himself off his unshakable pedestal. Ivan had no choice but to remind everybody that he had taught her everything.

But he came to the factory without his wife because his mother-in-law had broken her leg and needed someone to look after her. His relationship with his mother-in-law was one of the things Oak did not like to talk about.

Ivan knew the factory well, so he immediately went up to the second floor and asked Yuriy:

"No repairs in the production facility and basement for now?" He smiled, knowing the answer as he had already heard it from Yuriy.

Oak wanted to head to the workshop, but Yuriy invited him to a different room. He looked at the cracked walls.

"We need to install windows everywhere because they take up too much space in my house, and I'm sick of moving them around. We had put them up on the first floor back in the day, but there's no trace of them now."

He was referring to the windows that old Schneider had ordered. Besides the windows, Ivan had kept other materials from Schneider's factory that he was hesitant to use elsewhere. He had been patiently waiting for Yuriy's call.

They entered a small room cluttered with various boxes.

"Let's start here. This will be my office," Yuriy said.

Oak took out an old, slightly torn notebook from his pocket. "It's been a while, but yes, I still have some tiles that'll fit here. There's also everything for the wiring. There should be enough tiles for all rooms. That is, for the entire floor. You might need to buy one or two packs if you can find the same kind. We have no glue. I already mentioned the windows. There's no putty. There's stuff for the ceiling, unless the mice have finished it, but I don't think they have . . . Everything is clear here, more or less. What about the kitchen and the workshop? Has anything changed there?"

"Nothing's changed, but we'll start in this room. Have a think and write down what we need to buy."

"Sure thing, I'll make a list. Is there any cement in the basement? Even if there is, it's probably frozen . . ."

"We had cement in the basement?"

"Two pallets."

"Wow."

"I need to go to the dacha and see what I have there. I can't tell my stuff from yours anymore, so I don't touch any of it." Oak laughed and put the pen behind his ear. "There's definitely some paint there somewhere; I remembered about it recently. And what will we do with the doors? We didn't agree on doors back then, and I won't have time to do everything at once."

"We'll just buy something cheap."

"I'd recommend repairing this one." He pointed to an old door with a large piece broken off at the bottom and a broken lock. "But if you want cheap, that's fine. And what about the corridor?"

"Leave it as it is. We had no plans to remodel it back then either."

"I'll replace the window and that's it. But the wiring will be visible on the ceiling. And you need some lighting here."

"That's okay. For now, I just need a decent-looking office, a workshop, a room for Water to live in like a human being. Maybe a kitchen too."

"There're many issues with the kitchen. Plumbing needs to be installed and other utilities. We didn't buy materials for this. Where do you get water now?"

"From a well. Drawing it with a bucket."

"I see."

They approached the metal room with green lights flashing in the darkness.

"What will happen here?" Oak asked.

"Let it remain as it is. I like it. No one else has a room like this. We'll clean off the rust and call it a day."

Oak examined the rooms on his own, measuring and remeasuring things with his tape. He checked the numbers against his old notes, and when he saw that everything matched up, he asked for coffee.

"Make enough for everyone, don't be stingy," said Uncle Vasyl. Water ran to put the kettle on.

"So, are we having renovations? Renovations are necessary but expensive," said Hryhoriy, tearing his eyes away from the microscope for a moment before looking back through it into the boundless world trapped in a small circuit board.

They drank coffee outside. The treacherous spring sun had hidden behind the clouds. Everyone had already gotten used to the warmth, and now a cold breeze was blowing.

Oak went home.

Orders were plentiful, so they could not afford to take long breaks. Over the next few days, the weather turned sharply colder, and spring seemed to have vanished without a trace. On the eighteenth, white smoke billowed from the Vatican, and everything else turned white too.

In the morning, Water woke up to the radio host talking about snow. At first, he thought it was a dream, but when he went downstairs in his underwear, he saw fluffy snow falling from the sky. When did it even start?

By the time the first cars appeared on the snow-covered field, Water had already been outside for a while. The snow was not letting up; it was only getting heavier.

"If it keeps falling like this, we'll be chest-deep in it by evening," said Uncle Vasyl as he planted his boot into the snow.

"If it keeps falling like this, we'll be stuck here," Yuriy said.

Hryhoriy grimaced, remembering the long nights he had spent at the factory.

"Maybe it will stop."

"Yeah, don't count on it." Dmytro pointed to the sky, though it was hard to see anything through the blizzard.

"Call Boss and have him bring you sleeping bags and some provisions," Water said, descending the stairs with a cup of coffee in his hand. "And your coffee is upstairs; it's warmer there."

"Where's my coffee?" red-cheeked Uncle Vasyl asked as he prepared for his tobacco ritual.

The frost had set in the night before, and by morning, the

temperature was as low as twenty-three degrees. As thick smoke curled from his pipe, the old man handed Water a pack of cigarettes. Water realized he was the only one smoking from this pack.

These two had no intention of working. While they stood around, the snow covered their footprints. The lake and the forest had disappeared underneath the white blanket. The upstairs was warm, but outside they could continue lazing about.

"I don't remember a March like this," Water said, flicking away a cigarette butt.

"Nothing can surprise me anymore. Let's go warm up."

"Let's get to work."

Not much progress had been made in the workshop either. The dry warmth from the heater had enveloped the room in a hazy film.

"This snow is going to cause a lot of trouble," Hryhoriy said, tearing himself away from the table.

"Why's that?" Water asked.

"Well, any unforeseen event causes trouble, mainly financial . . ."

"On the contrary—we should see it as an opportunity," Water said, sipping his tea. "Look at it from a different perspective. Most people, yourself included, buy winter clothes on sale at the end of the season. So, everyone has already bought their jackets and coats, and now they have a chance to step out into the snow in a brand-new outfit. Forget about soiled collars and sleeves that won't wash out. Seize the moment."

Water looked into his cup, as if not believing it was empty. He glanced into it again and set it on the table.

"I'll stick with my old jacket," Hryhoriy said firmly and turned back to work.

Dmytro was listening to the radio. His favorite host was speaking, and her voice was so enchanting that Dmytro's imagination conjured her as an angel. He was ready to run before this angel and adjust the clouds to make her walk easier. For now, though, he simply listened to her beautiful voice reporting that the snow had snarled all traffic, and that the city had not seen such chaos since the Barbarian Invasions. No one had been prepared for such a storm.

Uncle Vasyl was folding user manuals. It was the only contribution he could make at the moment. They had already folded several years' worth of them, but he enjoyed the task. The spines became straighter, and the corners more symmetrical. His hand kept reaching for the inner pocket where he kept his tobacco, which provided a perfect excuse to go downstairs and see how much snow had fallen.

"People will manage, but birds will be in trouble. The storks have already arrived," he said, closing the door behind him.

The snow showed no sign of stopping. The roads were invisible, making the escape impossible. How Boss would get to the factory was also unclear. The wind was picking up, blowing snow into the production facility. Yuriy kept dialing Boss, who clearly had more pressing matters to attend to.

After a while, Water and Uncle Vasyl heard a honk. They could not see the car, buried as it was in the snow. They dug it out, inch by inch, until evening. At one point, they were about to give up, but Boss persisted. Everyone was drenched and calm. Only Dmytro was uneasy because he had never spent a night at the factory. Fortunately, the car was relatively light; otherwise, they would have breathed their last before pulling it out.

Wet and exhausted, they went to dry off. The rumbling of a tractor came from the road— Bereza was trying, in vain, to clear the path. His Sisyphean battle with the snow continued for hours, with no success.

Boss brought provisions and warm clothes, so neither cold nor hunger threatened the crew. The isolation provided a good opportunity to catch up on work.

Bereza continued his rescue efforts until late into the night.

The frost was biting. Snow had piled up in rooms with broken windows as much as outside. It was everywhere.

After dinner, everyone called home to check in and make sure their loved ones were alive and well. Those who had no one to call listened to the radio. There was a sense of calm; news broadcasts had long ended, radio DJs had left the studio, and the music seemed indifferent to the snow.

Even by morning, the blizzard had not stopped. So much snow had fallen that leaving the production facility was a challenge. Only the forest remained visible. Fragile silhouettes of fir trees poked through the endless white wall like long spears of an enemy host.

The guys tried to work, and some even managed to make progress. Yuriy was so preoccupied that no one knew if they were following the plan or just trying to catch up, so they worked as if they were racing against time. With all trips canceled, Boss joined the work effort.

Uncle Vasyl went out to battle the elements. He might have succumbed to the snow if Water had not been sent to help him. They were clearing paths to essential communication facilities, but their efforts seemed futile given the constant snowfall. From a distance, it looked as if they were standing in a lake up to their chests, using cups to pour water over their backs— though Water would never willingly dive into a lake.

A pleasant voice on the radio urged people to stay home, avoid the streets, and assist those who could not care for themselves.

Water returned to the familiar ritual of packaging: wipe the case with alcohol to remove any streaks, wrap it in plastic, throw in a manual, write down the number so Yuriy could print a warranty card, place everything in the box (don't forget the postcard), close the box, affix the label—only then would the happiness be ready for sale. Water always referred to the device as "happiness", even though no one else shared this sentiment. He was packing someone's happiness, happiness meant for someone.

Meanwhile, Uncle Vasyl continued to battle the snow until fatigue and cold drove him upstairs for a hot tea.

"We have a problem, guys. One might even call it a disaster."

"What happened now?" Yuriy asked, his eyes fixed on the monitor.

"How should I put this . . . I ran out of tobacco."

He poured the remnants onto the table to pack his pipe.

"And you can't do without it?" Yuriy asked.

"Can't." Uncle Vasyl lowered his head. "I packed a bag for the trip but left the tobacco on the table."

"You can smoke cigarettes," Hryhoriy interjected.

"Let *them* smoke cigarettes," Uncle Vasyl pointed to Water and Boss, "and I'll go back for my tobacco."

Dmytro got up and walked around the room to stretch his back and loosen his legs. Within about forty seconds, he was puffing like a blacksmith's bellows.

"Did you hear what they said on the radio? Don't go outside without necessity," he said.

"But that host got to the recording room somehow, didn't she? That was a necessity. And this is a necessity too, for me."

"Okay, a necessity . . . Drink some tea. Water will finish with the packaging, and the two of you can go," Yuriy said before turning his attention back to his work.

"And if something happens, it's easier to find two people than one," Boss added with a smile, standing by the window with a cup.

When Uncle Vasyl and Water stepped outside, it was already close to one o'clock. Both were bundled up, but the cold laughed at their efforts. It felt as though the entire world around them was made of snow. Its whiteness rendered them almost speechless. Any words they managed to utter were immediately whisked away by the wind, like crumbs from a table, and carried off into the middle of the lake. Snowflakes drifted into their mouths and melted on their faces. They clung to the forest like a lifeline until it ended.

In the eerie haze behind them, tall spruces loomed. They stopped near an oak that stood alone but was considered by everyone to be the edge of the forest. It was better not to stop, but they needed a rest. The journey had been arduous, and their strength was almost spent. The only consolation was that the hardest part was behind them.

Water glanced back, as if in response to an unspoken call, but there was nothing there. Then, suddenly, right near the edge of the forest, he spotted a bird.

A stork was watching Water, waiting to be noticed. At first, Water did not recognize it as a stork. Its feathers against the snow appeared not so white but rather yellowish. The bird shook off the snow, glanced at the travelers once more, moved its red beak, and tucked its head under its wing.

Water wondered if it was a hallucination or a strange vision. But when he realized the bird was real, he saw several more—more than ten in total.

"We need to get them out of here," he called to Uncle Vasyl.
"We will."
By the time they reached the old man's house, they were completely worn out. The bag of tobacco lay on the table. Uncle Vasyl turned on the gas stove. They removed their jackets and hung them up to dry. Water's hands were extremely cold, and the warmth began to make his fingertips tingle. He rubbed them and managed to warm them up. Water made himself as comfortable as he could in the unfamiliar kitchen while Uncle Vasyl searched for something in another room. They settled in the middle of the kitchen, drinking tea and smoking. Water noticed that he had already smoked more than half a pack. It was getting warmer, and the small kitchen quickly filled with smoke.

"And where will we put the birds?" Water asked, leaning back in his chair.

He could feel his hands again. He watched the red flame from the poor-quality gas struggling to warm them up.

"Upstairs, I think. They'll freeze in the production facility. The concrete there is cold, just like bare ground."

"Should we ask Yuriy first?"

"Do you think he won't understand?"

The question was rhetorical.

"They'll need something to lie on—it's not exactly summer in that room."

"I was just about to bring that up. Here's a simple solution. We'll gather some hay, stuff it into sacks, and haul it to the factory," Uncle Vasyl said as he finished his tea and began putting on his boots. The boots were warm but damp.

"We'll die on the way."

"No, I've thought it through. We'll pack a few sacks tightly, load them onto the sled, and drag them through the snow. There's no other option."

"We can drag the sled. But what are we going to feed them? Bread? I've heard you shouldn't feed birds bread, not even pigeons in the park. It's bad for them."

"We'll boil some potatoes," said Uncle Vasyl, who was not in a hurry to go outside. He took off his boots again and started packing his pipe. "It's simpler with animals, especially small ones. Whatever you find, you can feed it milk. But birds are different . . . I still have some meat. We'll defrost it—a few chickens. And fish. I caught some in the summer, cleaned them, put them into the freezer, and then forgot. I'll sacrifice a broiler for our birds. Though will they eat their distant relatives?"

"Don't tell me you act this calm when a kite steals your chicks . . ."

"Well, a kite's a different beast," Uncle Vasyl looked up as if to show how high those birds can fly.

"A stork isn't a simple creature either," Water remarked as he placed the old, soot-covered kettle back on the gas stove. "They'll eat anything. When I was sent to my grandma's village for summer chores—and I was a good worker because I enjoyed it—we had an incident. A hen hatched some chicks. There were about five of them; she laid the eggs herself. Four of the chicks were red. When you held one in your hand, it looked like you were holding a flame. But one was black. I loved watching them; they were so funny. And Grandma told me to keep an eye on them—first to make sure the magpie didn't take them, then to protect them from the weasel, and later from the neighbors. One day, Grandma poured some millet for them and accidentally stepped on the black chick. She crushed it a bit, and it stopped moving. She tried to revive it with water. From the side, it looked like she was trying to drown it after one already unpleasant death."

"Get to the point. We need to get moving, or we won't find the birds before dark."

"Alright, here's the point: after her efforts, she threw the chick onto the manure heap. I kept watching over the other chicks. But after a while, the black chick came back. I yelled down the street that our chick had risen from the dead. Grandma came out and couldn't believe I was telling the truth. But the next day, while we were picking early cabbage for holubtsi, a stork stole it right from under our noses. It descended from the sky like an angel, grabbed it, and flew off with it in its red beak. Maybe it mistook it for a frog; the chick wasn't very pretty. So, the point is—they'll eat the chicken."

Uncle Vasyl laughed.

"If they'll eat it, they'll eat it. And I could eat something too, but there's nothing. Let's go."

Water went to the barn to gather hay. There was plenty of it; it had been lying there for several years. Uncle Vasyl said he had offered it to the neighbors, but they did not want it. The old man handed him a metal hook to pull the hay, but Water could not manage it. The hook got stuck. Water ended up pulling the hay with his hands, picking up what was on the floor. He had to pack it down with both hands and feet to fit more into the sacks. By the time he finally filled six sacks, he was sweating heavily.

Uncle Vasyl returned with a wooden sled—the kind anyone, child or adult, would love to ride down a steep hill, though it had not been used in a long time. They placed the sacks across the sled and tied them tightly with rope. The structure seemed more or less stable. Uncle Vasyl handed Water a pair of warm mittens. He gathered all the necessary supplies and a rifle. He checked ten times to make sure he had not forgotten the tobacco.

"Let's go, or the birds will fly away," he ordered, locking the door behind him.

The snowfall had nearly stopped. Somewhere nearby, a yellow tractor roared. It was getting noticeably colder. In the village, the road was not yet covered in snow after Bereza had cleaned it. The light sled glided smoothly over the white surface. Beyond the village, the highway posed no significant challenges. They followed the tractor, but it quickly disappeared around a bend.

When they turned onto the field road, the snow was knee-deep, seeping into their boots. The cold returned, and the sacks of hay came undone. The entire load fell apart. Water took off his mittens and began untying the knots he had made. His fingers quickly grew numb from the cold. Finally, he managed to gather everything back together.

They continued on, but the sled kept tipping over. It was very difficult to pull, so Water carried the sled with the sacks, lifting them over his head. Such method of transportation required frequent stops. The snowfall had completely ceased. For a while, it was quiet and windless. Massive dark clouds, fluffy like Icelandic horses, loomed from the west.

They arrived at the factory exhausted. So much snow had drifted into the production facility, it was as if they had been gone for a week. When they began carrying the sacks upstairs, everyone came out of the workshop, watching them with puzzled expressions.

"What's this?" Yuriy asked in confusion.

"Can't you see?" Uncle Vasyl was breathing heavily.

"There are birds. Storks freezing in the forest—we're bringing them here, or they'll die out there."

"Storks? Bring them in, but you'll have to clean up after them yourselves."

From behind Yuriy, Hryhoriy's head appeared.

"You're trying to save storks in the factory, while in ancient times, they'd be shot and eaten."

"So, should we eat them now?" Water was clearly irritated but quickly calmed down.

"You should at least eat something," Yuriy said, this time kindly.

"No time," Water said as he cut the sacks open with a kitchen knife, unable to get the hay out any other way—it was packed in so tightly.

Boss agreed to go with them.

The storks were still in the same spot, standing with their heads tucked under their wings. Catching them was not difficult—the exhausted birds offered no resistance. There were fewer of them than it had first seemed—seven in total. Six of the birds were caught easily and carried one by one. The men could feel their warm, beating hearts. When only one bird remained, it was up to Water to catch it. The stork resisted, trying to escape and wasting its last bit of energy. All it managed to do was peck Water on the finger. It later tried to strike with its wings when Water picked it up, but it had no strength left.

The new guests were given water and food. The crew hoped that rest and warmth would save the weak birds. They had struggled so hard to get here that it would have been unjust to let them die in the snow.

The guys in the workshop had been working hard too. "The key to the work process is its continuity," Yuriy liked to say. The number of devices was slowly increasing. The dream of forming a stockpile or at least some reserve no longer seemed so unattainable.

That night, the snow began to fall again and did not stop until Friday. The work did not halt. The guys got used to the barracks-like conditions. They had little choice, as the snow level reached halfway up the factory doors. The tunnel that Uncle Vasyl and Water had dug to fetch water was not much help for escape.

The storks acclimated quickly and, within a few days, were walking around and inspecting the entire upper floor. They clattered loudly with their beaks and tried to stretch their still-weak wings. Sometimes they kept the men up at night with their noisy calls to each other. But everyone grew accustomed to them. The birds, however, were slow to grow accustomed to people, allowing only Water to approach them and greeting him with friendly hissing.

By Monday, the snow began to melt, and water flowed in from all sides. The lake spilled over into the fields, and green grass started to peek out from under the snow. The basement flooded, adding another problem. Later, when the roads were cleared and a pump could be brought in, they pumped out the water. It poured out like a dirty black river, flowing toward the forest. A lot of dirt and debris were carried out of the basement by the water. The long-postponed task of cleaning the basement became more urgent than ever.

One fine day, when the storks finally dared to step outside, they cleaned their feathers in the thawing snow and immediately became snow-white. They flapped their wings, showing they were ready to fly. And they did. For a few days, a pair of storks tried to build a nest on an old, unused power pole, but they clearly didn't like the spot because, after a few days, they flew away for good.

# 008

"My father used to say that the key to success is honest work. Work honestly and diligently, and eventually, someone will notice you and take you under their wing. That's what happened to me. And now, here I am."

The warmth gently lifted tender shoots of green grass, still flattened by the recent rain. Here and there, patches of swamp were visible, left behind by turbulent streams. The forest was alive, its breath carrying the scent of pine across the lake, where Dmytro and Water sat on the shore.

"And what's next? More of the same strategy?" Water asked.

"I don't think so. I'm content here for now, but who knows what the future holds. I'll pay off my car loan if things keep going well. I really screwed up with that loan. As soon as I started earning some decent money, I decided I didn't want to walk anymore and bought a car—big mistake. Now I'm working my ass off just to pay for it. There's no time to think about anything else," Dmytro said and turned toward the factory where his Matiz was parked.

"Would you want something different?" Water inquired.

"You always want something better. Look, I'm working here now, and it's fine, but what might change in five years?"

"I don't know," Water replied.

"Probably nothing. I'll still be sitting by the radio, soldering microchips, and that's not enough for me. I haven't worked much in my life, but a job like this—this is the kind of place where you hit the glass ceiling on your first day. What potential for career growth is there? None. You solder on your first day, and you'll be soldering until the day you die. I'm not even talking about the money—the pay is good enough—but I want more in terms of the work itself, in terms of development. Yuriy can't offer me that. I'd like to join a company where I can grow, aspire to a managerial position, even if it's just a workshop supervisor. That's what I mean."

"What if we expand?"

"Maybe we will, but no one can guarantee that."

"Have you ever tried getting into a bigger company?" Water pressed.

"Not yet. I'm afraid I won't make it, but I'll try."

"You should."

The sun shone brightly, reflecting off the water. Everything returned to normal as soon as regular communication with the city was restored. Boss became hard to pin down once again. Uncle Vasyl was as happy as a child because the soil had soaked up plenty of water this year. In his joy, he decided to plant a garden, something he had not done the previous year.

The phone calls increased. Yuriy never let go of his phone, constantly listening to a torrent of praise from yet another businessman. Every day, there were more and more happy people.

Hryhoriy, who had bravely taken on the main burden of the production process, tried to take advantage of the recent lull. From time to time, he would step outside to feel the spring and rubbed his eyes, which watered from exhaustion.

Soon, Oak arrived and brought some construction materials.

The lake struggled the most. It was breaking free from the icy grip it had not expected this spring. The wind drove waves crashing against the shore. Near the water, spring had yet to make its presence felt. But in the evening, if you tuned the radio down, you could hear the frogs conducting the first tentative rehearsals of their chorus before the grand spring concert.

After Oak delivered necessary supplies for the renovation, he wandered around for a while, unsure of where to start. But eventually, the work began. The key was not to scare it off and to watch over it, like a housewife tending to rising dough.

It was getting warmer. The frog chorus performed harmonious concerts, and the fish began to spawn. Thousands of carp crowded in the shallows, rubbing against the duckweed and each other. You could scoop the fish with your hands—just lower your hand, and you would catch a plump carp. The locals came to the lake to watch the fish, but no one dared to catch them.

Nothing passes as quickly and subtly as the first warm month. Uncle Vasyl planted his garden. Oak laid the wiring and poured the screed in the office. Slowly, he moved on to the walls. Boss's car had already broken down three times and had been repaired three times. Many years had passed since his father had placed him on his lap and let him steer. So much had happened since then. Boss had had plenty of chances to end up as a metal cross on the side of the road. But somehow, he had always made it through. He lived in cars, often having to sleep in them.

When the need arose to repair his car, Boss decided to set up his own space so he would not have to rely on anyone else. He cleared out the garage, getting rid of all the junk. The pit he was so eager to reach was filled with old tires. For a few days, or rather weeks, when the factory was empty and Water spent all day sitting by the lake, Boss prepared his nest. He even made it up to the second floor, where there was a room suitable for living. Since it had not been used in a long time, it smelled strongly of dampness and rat droppings. Boss drove his car into the garage for repairs. Later, he moved here all the tools he had managed to acquire through honest—and not-so-honest—work.

The warehouse was gradually filling up, and the list of buyers had outgrown the second page of the notebook. Amid coniferous trees, green grass and shrubs thrived. The sturdy oak made it clear who the master of the place was, and the slender spruces had to yield.

Before Easter, everyone had relaxed a bit. On the holiday, the factory was closed, taking a break from people. Everyone had left, and Water stayed at Uncle Vasyl's. The old man insisted that Water sample the juniper-based moonshine he had bought from a neighbor as a special treat for his dear guest.

After the holidays, everyone was reluctant to return to work. Oak was the first to arrive. His presence was overwhelming—he seemed to be everywhere and doing everything. Here he was carrying something upstairs, and there he was pouring coffee by the bucketful. Here he was arguing with the host, bent over the radio, and there he was running around in his colorful work overalls, splattered with all sorts of fillers, paints, glues, and other mixtures.

By evening, as the last rays of the sun touched the lake, Oak joined the others by the shore. They were already getting ready to leave. Dmytro was to take Hryhoriy home. Yuriy stayed by the shore, watching the cold wind whip the waves. Twilight was settling over the thick green grass that seemed to have grown overnight. Water remained at the factory.

"It's cold," Oak said, sitting down on a bench.

"Then go home and warm up," Yuriy said, pulling his neck into his coat and hiding his hands in his pockets. "Everyone's left, and I'll be heading off soon too."

"I'll head home, but it's empty there, and it feels lonely. My Sofiia is at her mother's."

"Is something wrong?" Yuriy asked.

"Her mother's been ill for a long time, and now she's also broken her leg."

Oak pulled out a stalk and twisted it in his hands.

"Maybe you should get an advance on your pay?"

"No, that's not necessary. Money is not a problem for now. The only thing that bothers me is Sofiia's absence. An empty apartment feels like a stranger's place. I don't even want to go there."

"How do you get along with your mother-in-law?" Yuriy shifted restlessly, seeking a more comfortable position to escape the biting cold.

"She's a good woman. She's worked hard all her life and helps us out. But we've never really understood each other. She wants grandchildren, but that's been tough. For our family and for Sofiia's sister, too. We're undergoing certain treatments. We've already spent so much money . . . The doctors say we need to keep trying."

Suddenly, a light came on on the second floor. Water had misplaced something again. It happened sometimes.

"My mother-in-law lives alone; her husband passed away a long time ago. The girls were still young then. She has a big apartment. She wants to leave it to someone. The children don't need it because they've made their own way, so she wants to leave it to the grandchildren. Whenever she came to visit, she'd step into the apartment and immediately say, 'With children, the house is a fair; without them, it's a cemetery.' And she said that every time. I stopped talking to her, but Sofiia won't abandon her mother. She and her sister have always helped her and took turns sitting by her bedside when she was seriously ill. Her sister is abroad now, so Sofiia is there alone. Her mother keeps asking about the grandchildren and accusing us of not providing any. Sofiia calls me crying, but I don't intrude into their relationship. And the home is so empty that I can't bring myself to go there."

Yuriy's phone rang. He pulled it out of his pocket, squinting at the bright screen.

"Alright, I'm heading out; my wife's calling. You'll be here tomorrow, right?" Yuriy stood up and rubbed his numb legs.

"I will."

Yuriy walked towards the factory, and Oak remained by the lake. He tossed the broken stalk into the water. The waves played with it and washed it up on the shore, but Oak did not see it. The moon did not appear that night. The cold drove Oak away from the lake.

Water watched the car from the window until it pulled onto the highway, flashing its headlights into the sky. It was warm inside. The sounds of the radio drifted through the room.

The next morning, rain fell on the thick green grass.

In May, the work routine remained unchanged. The guys in the workshop continued as before. Boss was now assigned more complex tasks as the number of contacts in his notebook grew. He followed routes plotted by Yuriy. In the evenings and on Sundays, he stayed in the garage, initially working only on his own car, then changing the oil in Yuriy's and checking Dmytro's Matiz for strange noises. He grinned like a Cheshire cat as he emerged from the pit with dirty hands.

Dmytro was probably dealing with spring vitamin deficiencies, as he had been in a sour mood lately. He had become withdrawn, as if the ground had fallen away beneath him. He performed his tasks precisely but showed no interest in other aspects of life. The radio had become his best friend, as it always had been.

Hryhoriy still occasionally paused his work to check what was happening at the window of the outermost house in the village, but he also developed new ambitions. The management of the factory was gradually shifting into his hands because he was always on site and aware of what was available and what was lacking. The increased responsibility had given him more confidence, which he relished.

Uncle Vasyl disappeared in his garden and had not been seen at the factory for over a week. Water often visited him. However, for the past few days, Water had been going through a rough patch. He had learned to package so quickly that he had to be given other tasks to fill his hours.

He was entrusted with soldering resistors. Hryhoriy had explained it all—two resistors with different values needed to be connected with solder and thin wire. The resistors differed not only in value but also visually, though it was hard to tell, especially if you had never worked with them before. Hryhoriy had anticipated this and helped set up a conveyor where Water soldered one resistor and then the other. But Water ended up mixing things up and making a mess.

It was a heavy blow for him. He said he would never touch unfamiliar objects again and would stick to what he had been doing before.

No one scolded him. Everyone forgot about it, except for Water.

For several days, Water wandered around in a daze. Every evening, as everyone left the factory, he spent more and more time by the shore, sometimes waking up in the morning to watch the first rays of sunlight reflect off the lake. It was on such a morning that he found a bicycle—and it was the end of all his troubles.

The night before, Water had heard some noises but decided he must have imagined them. In the morning, he found empty bottles on the table, trash scattered by the shore, and a forgotten bicycle in the grass. He waited two days for the owner to appear, but when no one came, he decided to visit Uncle Vasyl. No one in the village recognized the bicycle either, so Water had no choice but to keep it for himself.

On a warm day, when everyone preferred basking in the sun and enjoying the gentle spring breeze to working, he returned from the village. Water too decided to draw health from nature's gifts. For several days, he had been going to Uncle Vasyl's neighbor to fetch milk.

The newly minted cyclist emerged on the lake's shore, his wide grin stretching from ear to ear.

"I'll never believe that someone lost or forgot such a bike," said

Boss, lounging on a bench with one leg draped over the other. His entire demeanor was trying to convey that he was not keen on being exiled to the post office today.

"Then don't believe it," Water replied, riding into the factory and soon reappearing at the door. "I always had good luck."

"Yeah, sure, we believe you. Did you tie something to the owner's legs? Uncle Vasyl says there's enough depth in this lake for everyone."

"Too much, I'd say," Water said with a smile as he poured milk into Boss's cup.

"And where's Yuriy?" Water asked.

"He went to a meeting," Boss replied. "Some young business-woman is interested in our device."

"And then you'll be happy to deliver the device to her home, right?" Hryhoriy was unusually talkative today.

"Yuriy is a responsible family man; he only paves the way to the doorstep. The rest is up to me."

"Yeah, keep telling yourself that. No one will even let you as far as the doorstep. They'll take the package at the gate and bid you good day. Is Dmytro by the radio?"

Footsteps were heard from above.

"Grab a cup and have some milk," Boss called out.

Moments later, Dmytro appeared, clearly excited by the offer.

"Thanks," he said, wiping his plump lips. "Did you really find that bike?"

"Yeah," Water replied, clearly tired of the question.

"You must have lost something valuable yourself," Dmytro said, settling comfortably on the bench and making it clear he was now part of the conversation.

"I don't think so."

"Then you will. It's never the case that someone finds something truly valuable without losing something in return. I, for one, have never found anything, although I have lost some cash," Dmytro said and looked into his cup, which still held a little milk.

"I haven't found anything either. But there might be something to that theory. I had an acquaintance who found two hundred euros back in school. It was quite a fortune then. The whole class was taking a walk outside, and she found it. She had enough sense to keep half for herself, and the rest we squandered. She bought herself a leather jacket. We were all green with envy. The jacket was like something out of a poster. But then she lost it. She said it was warm in the morning, so she took off the jacket near the house but didn't want to go back. She was in a hurry as usual, and going back was bad luck. She put the jacket on her arm or hung it on her bag. At the stop, there were so many people. It was only in the bus that she noticed the jacket was gone. She got off at the next stop, went back, and was late to a class. The jacket was gone—she must've dropped it somewhere, or maybe it was stolen. Sometimes going back isn't such a bad idea. I don't know if she had lost or found anything else since then," Boss said.

"Was she beautiful?" Dmytro asked.

"Why 'was'? She's still beautiful."

They basked in the sunlight. Water poured the remaining milk into cups and threw the empty bottle into the trash.

"After this milk, the bottle will be useless, and soon there won't be any more milk because Nadya is gathering cream and cheese for a wedding," Water said, almost as if to himself.

"Well, my time here is up. I'm heading to the post office," Boss said, getting into his car as his phone rang. "Water, bring out one device; we have a buyer."

Water disappeared into the factory and returned with a cardboard box. Boss carefully placed it on the front seat. The car kicked up dust and disappeared around the corner with the loud roar of an old German engine.

"I once lost money too, but it was real magic," Hryhoriy said.

"My mama gave me fifty kopecks to buy some water. I clenched the coin in my fist and ran to the store. I didn't open my hand until I got to the store, and when I wanted to look at the coin, there was nothing in my hand. Real magic. I haven't lost or found any money since. It's just wrong to find things—you should earn them, and then do whatever you want with them."

Everything was bathed in warmth. The white clouds seemed to beckon to be touched. Yuriy had not returned. After lunch, Water went to the village. Boss had returned from the post office but was busy maneuvering the car into the garage and clearly was not in the mood for conversation. The pair was indulging in the fumes of solder, the aroma of various solvents, glues, and other chemical substances permitted by current legislation. The radio was playing, but Dmytro had no desire to share the music with anyone.

Water pedaled along. The lakeshore was overgrown with thick grass, with only a few visible nests trampled by fishermen. Near the far shore, a large gray heron was measuring the depth.

Uncle Vasyl was at home, chasing a dog that had run off to the neighbor's. The old man was not in a hurry to return to the factory, even though he had finished the work in his garden. Neat rectangles of garden beds stretched out beyond the metal gate. There, they silently yearned for warmth and moisture. The old green hose extended to the garden, and a small pump in the well was humming laboriously.

"God bless you, good man!" Water called out in a solemn voice.

"It's you again . . . " said Uncle Vasyl. "Have you finished the milk?"

"*We* finished the milk."

"You lot would've finished even a bucket."

"A bucket, yes, but not of milk. You can't have too much milk."

The dog, which had been put on a chain, did not even bark at the guest, only whimpered plaintively.

"Why is he upset with you?" Water propped up his bicycle against the wall and walked over to the old man.

"He wants milk, just like you do—or maybe a woman's touch. She doesn't tie him up, but if I don't, he'll end up guarding her house instead of mine."

"You're wasting so much water."

The ground could not absorb the moisture quickly enough, forming dirty puddles on its surface.

"There's still plenty left in the well."

"That's what you think. In some countries, people are fined for wasteful water use. For such watering like yours or for washing cars."

"We're not Africa," the old man said as he sat on the doorstep. "We have enough water to last generations."

"Again, that's what you think. In ten to fifteen years, everything will change fundamentally. And in fifty years, we'll have to buy water. Water is also a resource with limits, and it's not as abundant as we think."

"I'm not planning to live that long, and you all will figure it out somehow . . . It's your head that will hurt over this, not mine."

The dog whined in the kennel. The ground was slowly absorbing the water, and a cuckoo was calling from an apple tree.

It was the first time this spring that the cuckoo had called. If anyone had asked it to predict their fate, they would have been sorely disappointed—a frightened cuckoo took off and flew to someone else's warm nest.

Oblivious to the spring, Oak was finishing the office. Yuriy had cheered up, now able to host visitors there. The first visitor was Denys Serhiyovych, who came for new devices. He walked around the factory with his mouth agape, examining everything around him. Oak continued with the renovations.

The sun blazed mercilessly. People who had praised its warmth a few months ago began to complain. Before the guys flooded the workshop with sweat, Yuriy decided to head to the village and save everyone. The sun hung high, and the air-conditioned car offered much-needed relief from the heat. He drove along the lake, where the dense grass on the banks was lush and reaching upward. From the highway, Yuriy could see fields where people were hard at work. The first haymaking of the season had just begun there. An old tractor with a rotary mower was cutting the grass, occasionally disturbing large molehills. Small clumps of earth and dust swirled into the air. Meanwhile, inside the car, it was pleasantly cool.

The wooden village shop did not heat up as much as the brick walls of the factory. The saleswoman with large brown eyes was preoccupied with thoughts of Valka from the neighboring shop. That devil . . . The tax office had already paid Valka a visit, and now they were knocking at her door. They had just opened, and these unwelcome officials were coming to her shop so often you would think they had found a spring with holy water here. To make matters worse, the district police officer was also present, moving about with an air of sternness and suspicion as if this was a torture chamber and not a village shop. Who would be next? The health inspector? Firefighters? What a devil Valka was after all . . .

"Hello. Could you pour me some kvass, please?" Yuriy looked around the shop that had not been fully furnished yet.

The large, spacious room smelled of fresh paint and wood. The owners had divided it into two zones: the light-filled area by the windows was cluttered with cardboard boxes of goods, while the darker side remained under construction. In the corner, wooden boards were stacked somewhat neatly, surrounded by various tools.

"Kvass?" She perked up a bit and held her breath. "A glass?"

"Five liters."

She finally exhaled.

"Are you going to drink that much by yourself?" she pressed lightly, a smile appearing on her face.

"There's several of us."

"You're lucky I have a lot of empty bottles. I see you have come empty-handed."

The dark drink filled bottle after bottle. The white foam rose to the top, and cold drops ran down the bottle. The stifling heat from outside did not penetrate the shop. The foam kept growing.

"The barrel is empty," said the saleswoman. "Will you help me get a new one? We just ordered a few. But it's so heavy I won't carry it all by myself."

"Sure thing."

While Yuriy helped, a tall, thin man entered the shop. His young face was drenched in sweat, and his wet shirt clung to his body. He carried a black leather folder that must have heated up in the sun. He immediately placed it on the counter.

"Pour me some kvass, or I'll die," the man said, wiping off sweat from his forehead with his sleeve.

"Don't you know how to greet people? That's no good," Yuriy chimed in, though the district officer seemed to ignore his words.

"It's a dreadful day. It's scorching, and those shitheads with the cards . . ."

"I'll pour it now," she said, turning pale for some reason.

Yuriy stepped outside with a bag in hand. On his way to the factory, he was stopped by the head of the village council, who invited him to a celebration next week. In the heat, Yuriy did not catch everything clearly and asked the Head to come to the factory the next day to discuss it further. He promised to help. He would have promised anything just to get back to his car.

Later, after all the kvass was consumed and everyone had dispersed, Yuriy stayed late at work.

"You say the Head stopped you? They have Village Day on the twenty-second. They're planning a festival at the stadium."

"He mentioned something about patronage. Now I understand."

"He's always asking for help. People here like him; I've only heard good things about him. He's been in office for many years, and everyone's satisfied, except for Uncle Vasyl."

"We can help. We'll all go and enjoy the festival a bit," Yuriy said. "And how do you know all this?"

"The answer, almost like in a joke, is I have a bicycle," Water grinned.

"Got it. Will anything interesting be happening there? We don't know anything about them."

"They know a lot more about us. There's always something interesting happening in the village. Yesterday, some kids were playing cards. One of them was the son of the pig farm owner. He either lost or had a gold ring stolen that his dad gave him for his fifteenth birthday."

"What a nightmare . . ."

"Today, the district officer was searching the entire village, gathering witness statements and writing up reports. No leads. Even the Head has a headache over this case. The district officer is said to be quite inept. They also say he can't find anything except the saleswoman in the shop."

"In the new shop? I saw him there, but she seems much older than him."

"Older and married. But to each their own . . ."

"And the husband?"

"They say he's a decent man, very kind. Too kind for this world. He's a doctor who works in the city. In the evenings, he tidies up the shop."

"And he stays silent?"

"He says everything will pass. They've been together for a long time, and he believes her."

"That's their business. The Head will come tomorrow. And I'll bring fans or else we'll roast here."

"You should go for a swim."

After Yuriy left, Water went into the lake, which had warmed up throughout the day. The water felt like hot milk. He waded in up to his chest, his breathing growing heavy, but he kept control. Mosquitoes bit his face, but he ignored them to avoid sudden movements. The water was his fear—and he was entirely immersed in it.

The next day, the Head arrived, and two days later, the ring was found. It had apparently rolled under the bed, though everyone said the thief was scared and discarded the stolen item. No one bothered to investigate further. That was the last anyone heard of that story.

# 009

The day was splendid. Sparse clouds drifted across the clear sky, causing no interference with the sun's primary function—blazing heat. From the moment everyone had woken up, it was clear the celebration would be scorching. It was a triple event—summer St. Nicholas Day, the anniversary of Taras Shevchenko's reburial, and Village Day all rolled into one. Although this year the anniversary fell on a Wednesday, the Head of the village refused to move the festivities to the weekend.

As a result, the preparations for the celebration proceeded swiftly despite the heat. The factory was at a standstill for the day, and judging by Water's frantic running around, it seemed it would remain deserted. Water was busy preparing for the festival, while the others had not even arrived. Dmytro had requested the day off, and Boss was supposed to bring Hryhoriy. Water assumed they must have been at Uncle Vasyl's since early morning, but that was not the case. Yuriy had asked everyone not to overindulge before the festivities began, as it was all too easy to do so in the heat. He was to arrive with his family directly at the village. Water was washing up, shaving, and searching for clean clothes. When he realized he had no shorts, he decided to go in jeans and a Deep Purple T-shirt.

He locked up the factory and rode his bicycle to Uncle Vasyl's. The main event was to take place at the stadium right after the church service. The factory delegation was invited for two o'clock.

The area, or rather the stage, had been prepared the previous evening. They had initially planned to hold everything in the center of the football field, but the football team opposed it, and besides, in such heat, no one would last even ten minutes. They decided to move everything into the shade under the trees, a few hundred feet from the stadium. They mowed the grass, quickly built a stage, and set up benches knocked together from poles and planks gathered from around the village.

Early in the morning, local vendors were setting up their stalls and seeking refuge in the shade. A large pot was brought from the restaurant for making millet porridge. The entire community took part in its preparation, collecting groats and other ingredients from various shops. The official part of the event would conclude with the porridge meal, and the informal festivities were to continue wherever one wished.

The restaurant also supplied a barbecue for grilling meat to sell. A large pile of firewood had been delivered from the forestry the day before.

Nearby, a saleswoman and her husband set up their pop-up stall, selling beer and snacks, kvass, and ice cream from a small freezer.

Another shop set up a table, but instead of ice cream, their freezer was stocked with vodka.

Near the stage, in the shade of the largest tree, the local paramedic was stationed with cold water, a small first aid kit, and ammonia. A few feet away, a girl sat. She was from this village but had lived and worked in the city for a long time. No celebration was complete without her, as the locals flocked to her for a new kind of fun—face painting. She painted cheerful designs on children's faces, which transformed them into amusing little creatures.

A web of wires was tangled across the clearing. Near the stage, someone was setting up equipment from the local community center. A young sound engineer arranged his workspace by the control panel. The only spot he could find was under the direct sun. Someone brought him a large beach umbrella to shield him from the heat. After setting up the sound and adjusting the microphones, he turned on the music.

The musical interlude did not last long. Someone ran up to the sound engineer with a message from the church, and the music had to be turned off.

When Water arrived at the stadium, a few young boys who looked like school students were hanging a net on the goalposts. They were helping each other onto their shoulders to attach the net to the hooks welded to the crossbar. The boys had brought only one net and, while the adults were at the service, decided to have their own celebration. Scoring a goal with the net was a whole different thrill.

Water sat on a bench in the shade, observing the boys. Their small figures flickered against the backdrop of the vast green field. The oldest one constantly kicked the ball towards the goal, occasionally passing to the other two. For them, each pass was an absolute surprise. The youngest had been assigned as the goalkeeper, thereby missing out on any chance to enjoy himself. So, out of the four, only one was playing the role of a real footballer. He was wearing a white jersey with the number seven and the name Ronaldo on it. The local Ronaldo kept aiming for the crossbar. No matter how valiantly the small goalkeeper jumped, he had no chance. Water loved football, but he was not particularly interested in children's games. Still, he did not know how else to pass the time. It was either this or watching the young sound engineer sit under the umbrella, guarding the equipment entrusted to him.

One of the players missed the ball with a clumsy kick, sending it flying towards Water. He had no choice but to kick it back. Water caught the ball and sent it towards the boys. It wobbled slightly off his foot but went where it was intended.

Boss approached the bench at a leisurely pace.

"Hey, I knew you'd be around here somewhere."

"Hi. Well, I wouldn't be in church, right? Where's Hryhoriy?"

"He'll be coming with Yuriy. And where's the old man?"

"Somewhere there probably. Did you leave your car at his place?"

"Yeah. I'm thinking of staying there tonight. There's going to be a disco here. The girls are pretty and hot-blooded."

"In this heat, everything is hot," Water laughed.

"It'll be nicer at night."

The ball rolled back to Water. He got up from the bench, picked it up, and kicked it towards the goal.

"Nice kick," Boss smiled. "Have you ever played as a goalie?"

"A long time ago."

"Maybe we should join the boys, and I'll take a few shots at you to test your technique."

"Alright, let's go."

The boys reluctantly cleared a spot on the field, but little Ronaldo was excited about the chance to shoot at an adult goalkeeper. Since he was the decision-maker, Water was allowed to take his place between the posts.

"I'll just focus on technique, not strength, so I don't break your fingers," Boss laughed.

Water nodded. He caught the first few shots easily, thanks to his well-chosen position. Then Boss began to shoot harder. One shot was so off-target that the ball flew high and far. Water went after it.

"You've got a nice field here. Do you have a football team?" Boss asked young Ronaldo.

"This year, we've assembled a team for the district championship for the first time, and my dad's the captain," the boy boasted.

Boss aimed for the top corners. On his fourth attempt, the ball grazed the crossbar and went into the net. The boy applauded. Boss aimed there again. Water made a superb save. He knew how to play as a goalkeeper, but the heat was taking its toll.

"Let's go to the shade, or I'll collapse," Water said, panting.

"Alright. By the way, why did you never mention that you used to play football?" Boss asked.

"You never asked, and it was a long time ago."

As they moved a few steps away from the kids, young Ronaldo called out to them:

"Come watch our football games! We practice every evening."

"We'll come by sometime," Boss replied, wiping the sweat from his face.

"I know you! You work at the factory," one of the boys shouted.

On their bench sat two men, identical in appearance—same gray hair, weathered faces, and rotten teeth. The only difference was the color of their shirts, which dispelled any suspicion that they were a hallucination. The men were a bit tipsy, though in this heat, that was hardly surprising.

"Hey guys, would you like to play for our village in the district championship?" they asked almost in unison.

"Sure," Boss replied, while Water simply nodded.

"I'll talk to the Head today. He'll tell us what we need to bring— like a photo and a copy of your passports. Then you'll be officially added to the team."

"What kind of team is it, anyway? Is it any good?" Boss asked, smiling.

"We're just in our first year. The boys play well; they've been competing against neighboring villages. His dad plays too," the old man pointed to young Ronaldo.

"I know."

"To be honest, he's not much of a football player, but he's a great organizer. He got everyone together. We used to have a team, but it fell apart. Now it's all self-funded, no sponsor. We won't pay you, but there'll be drinks and snacks after the game. And I see you're not married." He smiled with his rotten teeth. "You'll find it interesting."

"And what about your friend? Is he mute? He hasn't said a word," his twin brother asked Boss.

"Oh, I talk," Water smiled. "Don't you already have a goalie?"

"We do, but not one like you."

The service was likely over as the sound engineer under the umbrella had come to life. Folk music started playing. A large crowd of people streamed toward the stage. Along the way, men stopped to down a few cold beers, trying to shake off the smell of incense and juniper from their clothes. By the stage, activity was in full swing, and girls with script copies and event checklists were darting back and forth. One of the schoolteachers responsible for organizing the event was searching for some Oksana. Members of the church choir were drinking beer until the deacon rounded them up and reminded them of their upcoming performance. Many of the choristers were also wedding musicians and could have kept the celebration going all night if needed.

Yuriy arrived, and with him came Hryhoriy and Dmytro.

"You said you'd bring the kids. Looks like you weren't lying," Boss smiled.

"You're quite the comedian, aren't you?" Dmytro mocked. "If you're so worried about the kids, why don't you buy them some beer?"

Boss turned around and walked away.

"You did actually say you'd bring Oksana and the kids," Water said.

"I didn't expect it to be so hot. The kids have been splashing in the inflatable pool all morning, and I don't know where to find a SWAT team that would dare to pull Oksana out from under the air conditioner. Besides, she didn't want to leave her writing. She's a writer. Not sure if I've ever mentioned that."

"You haven't," Water blurted out, scanning the crowd for Uncle Vasyl.

"So I decided to bring them instead," Yuriy nodded toward the guys who had gone over to Boss. He was standing by the stall, waving at them.

"But Dmytro took a day off," Water remarked.

"Yeah, he did," Yuriy smiled. "He wanted to do nothing under the fan in his apartment. I stopped by his place, and he was watching some nonsense on TV. Here, at least, he can watch people and drink some beer."

The guys returned with cold drinks. The driver was allowed some kvass.

A delegation led by the Head emerged from around the corner. An older man in a light blue short-sleeve shirt and light-colored trousers walked confidently despite the sweltering heat. The celebration was unfolding according to his plan. If anything were to go wrong, he would handle it himself. He had led the community for many years, and there were rarely any surprises. The Head liked to emphasize his devotion to his family—his wife walked beside him. She was a petite woman with dyed blonde hair and an exceptionally kind face. Next to her was their daughter, a young woman of no more than twenty, the only and very late child in the family. She resembled her father but was thin and delicate, with bright blue eyes. Her long, loose blonde hair fell over her shoulders. Her name was Oksana.

As the procession reached the factory workers, the Head detached from the group and went to greet the guests. He smiled from afar and opened his arms as if to hug everyone at once.

"Hello, boys," the Head greeted each of them with a handshake. "It's scorching today, but that shouldn't spoil our mood. I'm glad you all made it."

The twin brothers, already quite drunk, appeared out of nowhere, shouting over each other as they made their way to the Head.

"Hryhorovych, we need to get these two on the team. They're

the right kind of guys. We'll finally have a decent goalie, and Kolya can play out on the field like he wanted."

"Tomorrow, boys," the Head said.

"Tomorrow? We need to do it now."

"Alright, we will."

Uncle Vasyl arrived at that moment.

"What are those evangelists shouting about?"

"Evangelists?" Yuriy inquired.

"Marko and Ivan."

"Oh, they're recruiting Water and Boss for the football team."

"Good. Stop by my place; I'll give you some cleats," the old man said to Water.

The festivities were starting on stage. The hosts, the best-looking couple from the senior class, said a few words about the event and kicked off the ceremony by thanking and awarding certificates to the patrons and benefactors. The Head stoically shook hands with everyone and handed out certificates. They went to all the shop owners, the owner of the wedding hall, and the paramedic, who had already revived several fainting people. The district officer received a certificate; he thanked everyone for their trust, professed his love for the village, and especially for the Head. Many more people took the stage. The director of the community center spoke about the importance of culture and invited everyone to the evening dance. The priest talked about sin and repentance, frequently wiping sweat from his brow as he struggled to endure the heat in his black cassock. Yuriy also received a certificate, but he was not one for words—he simply thanked everyone and expressed his hope for future cooperation.

After this, the hosts recited a few poems about their love for their homeland and invited the choir to the stage. While the choir sang, the paramedic tended to the hostess, who had fainted.

Somewhere in the background, the twins were drinking beer,

despite their belief that one should never follow hard liquor with weaker spirits.

"People are dropping like flies."

"Tell me about it."

After the choir, there was a dance performance. The pride of the village, Olenka, had been driven by her mother twice a week for years to attend dance classes in the nearby town. The girl had won prizes at various dance competitions, including international ones, and danced in an ensemble. But the conservative audience received her performance rather coolly.

After Olenka, the women sang sorrowful songs. The audience swayed gently in the waves of May heat.

Then a boy took the stage, introducing himself as Petryk. He grabbed the microphone, set the stand aside, and walked across the stage, reciting his own poems. The listeners did not fully understand his texts, but the overall effect was mesmerizing. As they say, with a voice like that, Petryk could have read a phone book, and it would still have sounded impressive.

After the young poet, the stage was once again taken by the men's choir, who sang traditional folk ballads. The heat gradually subsided as the sun retreated. The Head's daughter, Oksana, then stepped onto the stage. Young and delicate, when she began to sing, everything fell silent. Resisting the magic of her voice proved impossible. Everything that came after Oksana's performance felt meaningless.

When the festivities ended, the organizers finally breathed a sigh of relief. The paramedic also sighed and collapsed into a chair.

One large collective celebration splintered into dozens of personal ones.

In the Head's office, all the patrons, staff, the district officer, and a delegation from the factory gathered. At first, everyone caught their breath and enjoyed the evening coolness. The conversation flowed naturally, like water.

"We're bringing these guys onto the team. Tomorrow, I'll stop by for their photos and passport copies," the Head said, pointing to Boss and Water.

"Oh, now we're in better shape," exclaimed the father of little Ronaldo, Captain Serhiy.

But the Head did not hear him and continued, "And finally, Kolya will be able to play out on the field like he wanted, because now we'll have a proper goalkeeper. I haven't seen him play, but the twins said he's solid. I don't trust the twins much, but if it's about football, they won't lie."

Water pretended it was not him they were talking about—his favorite way of blending into a new group. But no one paid him any attention anyway. They started discussing football matters. Noticing Yuriy's indifference to the sport, the Head took him outside to continue their conversation.

Boss simply vanished into thin air—no one even noticed when or how. He was eager to escape and join the younger crowd.

A tipsy Hryhoriy was deep in conversation with little Ronaldo's father—they seemed to strike up a bond.

Dmytro, at the far end of the table, was almost passed out, but the district officer would not let him sleep, constantly asking questions and trying to engage him in conversation.

Meanwhile, Kolya would not let Water go.

"I'm so glad we found you," Kolya said.

He and his wife owned the new shop. They were selling goods at the festival. In addition to that, Kolya worked at the clinic. In the village, he was known as Kolya, but there, at the clinic, he was Mykola Viktorovych and wore the white coat.

"Was it really such a problem?" Water asked.

"I'm not much of a goalie. And the rest are too scared to even try. If I'm absent, it's like we're playing with an empty goal. Now we'll have some options." Kolya sized Water up. "The uniform will fit you, and I have gloves. They're cheap, but better than nothing. As for the shoes, that's up to you."

"I haven't played in a long time, so I don't have any gear left. I'll find shoes, and thanks for everything else."

"Well then, I'm off because I don't drink, and I'm already bored."

"Good luck."

Kolya carefully slipped out the door, ensuring no one could pull him back to the table.

Yuriy was trying to round up Dmytro and Hryhoriy to leave because it was time for him to head home and they had had enough of the festivities. The guys tried to resist. Yuriy apologized for leaving so soon as he slowly retreated toward the exit.

The Head had cornered the new goalkeeper and was telling him about the football plans for the season, the main competitors, the key matches, and how hard it was to balance the role of village head with that of the team's head coach.

"People will come to the stadium—you'll see who you're playing for," the Head finished.

Outside, it had long since grown dark. Frighteningly loud noises were coming from the community center—they were blasting music. Water stumbled down the main street, barely able to see. He had a lot to drink but was determined to return to the factory at all costs. He did not want Yuriy to later complain that he had not returned to the factory after Yuriy had left him in charge. Water always preferred to avoid unnecessary conversations. He feared that someone might have already broken into the factory and stolen the equipment and tools. People passed by him on their way toward the music.

When Water arrived at Uncle Vasyl's, the house was dark. Water thought the old man was unlikely to be asleep at this hour. Maybe he was not home? But the door was open. After several attempts, he finally managed to turn on the kitchen light. The old man's voice came from the bed.

"I thought you wouldn't manage it," he said warmly.

"It might seem like a simple task, but look at how well I did it—didn't knock a single thing down."

"Oh, you're on fire today. Simply outstanding."

"Did I mention that they invited me and Boss to the football team?"

"You did, and I promised you a pair of cleats. Did you forget?"

"I have a good memory," Water said, sinking heavily into a chair.

"Are you heading to the factory? Maybe you should stay?"

"I have to go. Yuriy won't understand. A drunk guard is better than no guard at all."

"That depends on how you look at it," the old man laughed. "Just make sure you get there in one piece."

"Yeah."

Water asked for a cigarette. The old man always had some on hand for him. He sat and smoked, letting the ash fall to the floor. The old man fidgeted on the bed. He did not like these kinds of festivities. Since his son's death, he had been avoiding large crowds. The factory was the only place that still drew him in a little.

A radio played softly on the table. As Water left the house, a song he had known since school was playing. It stuck to him like resin, and he hummed it all the way home. In the village, Water passed by people and thought he heard someone calling his name a few times, but he ignored it. Moving away from the noise and light, he wheeled his bicycle beside him.

He left the main road and felt a sense of relief. He tried to look for footprints to see if anyone had broken into the factory after all, but it was too dark. Finally, he sat down on the bench by the lake, leaving his bicycle where he had first found it.

The lake was calm, and half of the sky was covered with clouds. Water gazed at the stars. Across the lake, life seemed to be in full swing. Far on the horizon, lightning flickered, but the storm passed them by.

He undressed, gathered his courage, and waded in. The water was warm, but fear made it hard to feel that. He only went in up to his knees and could not go any further. Angry with himself, he quickly found excuses: alcohol and water do not mix, even if you can swim, and for him, it was just plain foolishness.

He returned to the shore, gathered his things, took his bicycle, and hurried back to the factory. He walked quickly, not even noticing the fresh graffiti on the fence.

# 010

He was parched. Everything around him was cloaked in red dust. The infernally hot sun hung high in the sky. The corn in the fields wilted and fell helplessly between the rows. Weeds, just sprouted from the earth, had turned yellow and withered. A cloud of dust rose as a car drove down the road.

The little boy watched his sister's husband at the wheel, then his sister and his mother. The boy could not understand why he was so small. Everyone was thirsty. Bottles lay scattered on the ground, but not a drop of moisture was to be found. The large, heated vehicle moved toward the unknown. The metal was so hot it was impossible to touch. Salty sweat and tears trickled into his mouth. The boy felt dizzy. He could not tell if the dust was outside the window or inside his skull. Why were they leaving home for this hell? What would become of them? Would they find a river to quench their thirst and save their weak bodies? Would he burn like the corn under the sun? And why was he so small? The thirst was unbearable . . .

Water woke up. The age-old question—why is the hangover so bad in the morning?—troubled him. The radio on the table crackled and popped. A few empty water bottles stood by the bed, but there was not a drop of life-giving liquid. He finally found the much-needed water in the workshop. His whole body itched from mosquito bites. Outside, the sky was gray, and mist lay over the lake.

When he was woken up again shortly after, Water could not

understand why he felt so terrible. Boss stood over him, and Uncle Vasyl was in the doorway.

"Did you drink everything? Feeling dry, boy?" Uncle Vasyl asked, then disappeared into the workshop.

"Get up, let's go have some coffee," Boss said.

"I don't think coffee is a good idea," Water said, rubbing his eyes and trying to find a good angle to see the world again.

It was not scorching outside yet. The start of the workday was postponed indefinitely. Angry Oak had arrived and silently gone upstairs. Within minutes, the sound of him tearing out old window frames from the workshop echoed through the building.

The mist over the lake had dissipated. The air was pleasant, and it was nice to breathe.

"What happened yesterday?" Uncle Vasyl asked, grinning. "I know both of you were invited to the football team."

"And was there anything else?" Water smiled. "I came here right after that. It was a long walk, but I made it."

Uncle Vasyl offered him a cigarette.

"There were some wild times," Boss scratched his head.

"And that's it?" Water asked.

"It wasn't just any regular wild times. The last time I partied like that was at graduation from the vocational school. Only then, I ended up with a black eye . . . "

"And did no one try to give you one yesterday?" the old man asked, lighting his pipe.

"That's the thing—people did try. It would've been a sin not to. I would've tried myself. Some shady guy, drunk, dancing with the most beautiful girls—well, with the most beautiful girl . . . And not at all worried about getting his legs or ribs broken."

"So how come no one took a swing at you?" Water asked, puzzled.

"Well, the musicians on stage announced that the guy in the red shirt was off-limits because he's on the football team. And that was that."

"They love football players."

"Wait," Water coughed loudly. "With the most beautiful girl? You danced with Oksana?"

"Yeah."

"And did no one say anything to you about that either?"

"Just told me to score two goals on Sunday."

"And that's all? What about her?"

"She's a marvel."

Oak was looking down at them through the broken window on the second floor. The rest of the crew did not show up.

When Yuriy later brought those unfortunate souls, it was clear that no work would be accomplished. Boss yelled from afar that he was not going anywhere today, no matter what. Yuriy was in a great mood because some businesswoman had ordered ten devices. He had to deliver them himself, while the rest were allowed to waste time as they pleased.

Loud thuds and the clatter of a perforator echoed from the workshop. The trio of newly minted members of the wild hangover club went to the lake to cool off their weary faces. Water and Uncle Vasyl shuffled into the village. They stopped at the shop for some kvass, and the saleswoman was still doing everything she could to chase away the district officer.

"I'll get him someday," she said as the officer scurried toward the village council building like a frightened bird.

"And where's Mykola?" the old man asked.

"In that damned hospital. He just says, 'I trust you,' and disappears there." She kicked an empty kvass barrel. She stood behind the counter, knowing that as soon as the customers left the store, the officer would return.

The streets were deserted. A hangover is an intimate affair; it's best to endure it at home. The old man's dog had once again broken loose and run off somewhere. The wooden house still retained a hint of coolness.

"Why bother with football?" the old man asked.

"It's just that Boss wants to be around people, and I can't fault him for that. He spends days visiting businessmen who treat him rather condescendingly. He's always complaining about it. But here, he's close to real people. And you can see he's got some skill; he's pretty fast . . ."

"And you?"

"What about me? I've always wanted to do what I enjoy. Why not start with this?" Water replied.

"I've got all sorts of things here," Uncle Vasyl said, opening the door to a room.

The room was filled with an assortment of belongings.

"All my life is in these boxes and on these shelves," the old man said, sinking heavily into a chair.

"So much junk," Water remarked, not realizing he might be offending his friend.

"This 'junk,' as you call it, is all my life. See how beautifully it's arranged?"

Water was silent.

"This is all that will be left of me . . . But now, we need those football cleats," Uncle Vasyl said, forcing a smile.

He pulled out a cardboard box that was standing nearby, so he did not need to get up from the chair. Inside were many pairs of shoes—some worn out, a few pairs of decent-looking shoes, worn sneakers, and several pairs of cleats. Uncle Vasyl picked up a pair of "Predators" in excellent condition and handed them to Water.

"Try them on."

Water sat down on the floor in the center of the room. The cleats fit as if they were made for him. He stood up and paced the room back and forth. They were a good model—now completely retro, and in such great condition.

"Where did you get them?"

"Bought for my son."

The room, already gloomy, grew even darker. Water realized it was time to leave.

"Thank you," he said as sincerely as he could. "I should probably go."

"Go ahead . . . I won't be joining you today."

When Water stepped off the road and reached the lake, the guys were nowhere to be seen. There were two possibilities—either the heat had driven them indoors, or Boss had led them on an assault of the shop. The only one at the factory was Oak, who continued installing windows and paid no attention to the newcomer. The radio had not been moved to the workshop that day—it played loudly from Water's floor.

Thursday turned out to be tough. The air outside was stifling, making it hard to breathe. The storm that had passed the day before was now closing in. Oak kept on working despite the oppressive heat. Everything around him seemed frozen in place. Water, an ordinary man, weak by nature and prone to temptation, settled peacefully on the couch. He listened to the radio until he drifted off to sleep.

No dreams came.

Oak woke him up. First by slamming the workshop door, then the car door.

Thunder rumbled, so loud and close that it could have woken anyone. Water quickly got out of bed, unplugged the radio, and rushed to the metal room to turn off the devices that were being tested. He checked the workshop windows to make sure they were closed. Finally reassured, he headed downstairs. The air outside carried the scent of the approaching storm.

Thunder struck again, louder and closer this time. Lightning slashed through the sky. Rain poured down as if someone had turned on a faucet. Water stood in the doorway, staring at the wall of rain. Whatever was happening in the world beyond the storm no longer mattered.

Then Petryk appeared, with nowhere else to hide. He stood in the doorway, soaking wet, water dripping from his long hair. An unzipped backpack hung from his shoulders, with spray cans peeking out.

"Can . . . can I . . . can I wait out the rain here?"

The confident voice from yesterday's stage performance was gone.

"Come in," Water said.

"It's raining buckets," Petryk remarked.

"Want some tea?" Water asked, heading up the stairs to the second floor.

The curtain of rain still lingered outside.

"Yes, please," the guest quickly responded.

It felt cozy in the workshop. Rain drummed against the brand-new windows.

"So, your name is Petro?"

The boy nodded.

"But everyone calls you Petryk, like you're a little kid?" Water smiled.

"Petryk is my last name. I'm Petro Petryk," the boy said, a bit calmer now.

"Interesting."

"My mama came up with it." The boy took a sip of hot tea, still shivering in his wet clothes. "And now guess what my patronymic is?"

"Petrovych?"

"Yeah. Petro Petrovych Petryk."

"And what brings you here, Petro Petrovych?" Water asked, a bit too formally.

"I . . . I . . . I was out walking."

He spat out the last words quickly, as if shooting them from a gun.

"I see," Water said, gesturing toward the backpack. "And I was wondering who the artist behind the new graffiti was . . . "

"Well, I'm learning. I like art. Everything in the city is already painted, but here, there are so many untouched fences."

"I don't mind. I actually like it. But what Yuriy, the owner, will say, I don't know. And something tells me he hasn't seen your artwork yet."

"I'm just learning . . ."

"I'm telling you again—I like it."

"Do you have any work available?"

"I'm not sure. Do you want a job?"

"Not right now, but maybe later, just a part-time thing. I'm staying with my grandma for now, preparing for the new national tests that they use in university admissions. But soon I'll take the tests and come back here."

"So you finished school already?"

"Last year. I didn't do well, so I've spent all this year studying— getting ready to go back into battle. I was actually ready last year, knew all the material, but I couldn't control my nerves. I got anxious and messed it all up. Now I'm working on staying calm, and graffiti helps me with that. This year, I have to pass. I can't put it off any longer."

"What about the army?"

"They won't take me because of a mole on my head. They say a helmet could rub against it and cause problems."

"I see. We can talk about work once you're done with your tests. And if you want to paint, do it where I can't see you. And no obscenities. And make sure it's not visible from the road."

"Okay."

"It's raining so hard you're not going anywhere soon, so drink your tea."

"Why do they call you Water?" the boy asked.

"Because I love it."

"Maybe it's because you're afraid of it? I know." Petryk smiled.

"Then why do you ask? Besides, you can love what you fear. Was it Boss who couldn't keep his mouth shut?"

"I've only seen him once at a disco. I just spend a lot of time at the lake."

"But I haven't seen you there."

"Maybe you're not the best guard," Petryk smiled.

"Drink your tea."

When the rain finally ended, Water was left alone at the factory.

On Friday, everyone returned to work. The previously miserable souls, now cheerful, arrived in Boss's car. The trio had spent the night at Uncle Vasyl's, and judging by their smiling faces, they had finally caught up on sleep. Yuriy was late, but his relaxed demeanor from the day before had vanished. He herded everyone into the workshop. After loading the car with equipment, Boss received additional instructions and headed into the city. Dmytro bent over the radio, preparing parts. Hryhoriy and Yuriy conducted an inventory—or rather, searched for a box of screws. In the process, they unexpectedly ended up doing a full inventory and realized they were missing everything. They decided to postpone the debate about "how we got into this mess" until the evening. Yuriy got back in the car, trying to make up for lost time.

Hryhoriy had no choice but to work on the device parts. He was making some adjustments.

"Can you take a look? Something's not working here," Dmytro said, distracting him.

"Later."

Dmytro clung to the radio. Neither Water nor Uncle Vasyl

could help him. Water was cleaning the finished devices with alcohol, packing them in plastic, and placing them in boxes. Uncle Vasyl was collecting manuals for him.

Oak was drinking coffee outside. Then, with little enthusiasm, he carried the equipment into the kitchen. Friday passed quickly. In the evening, Boss arrived to pick up the guys. Water was once again left alone.

On Saturday, things were calmer, but Water spent the entire day waiting for work to end so he could go to his first football practice. However, just as he was about to take out his bike, the sky erupted with lightning, and a downpour flooded everything, including the football field.

Water spent the evening in his room, listening to music and watching the raindrops stream down the window. The next morning, when Uncle Vasyl arrived at the factory, Water was already waiting for him by the lake. Yuriy did not like leaving the workshop unattended, so Uncle Vasyl was forced to spend the entire day at the factory. Yet it was evident that the old man knew exactly how he planned to spend his time. He brought several bamboo fishing rods with him.

"Hello. Are these the rods you promised to bring back in April?"

"Not those," the old man smiled. "I'll bring those another time. Now get out of here. I've taken over the post."

It was a pleasantly warm summer day. Whiling away with a fishing rod by the shore was not a bad idea at all.

"Then I'll be off."

"Go ahead," the old man said, then added, "Don't slack off today; people are counting on you."

"Is Boss not there yet?" Water shouted from a distance.

"Not yet."

At the meeting point, no one had shown up yet, save for the team captain and, by coincidence, the owner of the establishment.

"Kvass on the house?" he asked.

"Thank you, I won't refuse."

He returned with two glasses, covered with a frosty haze.

"The main thing is to make sure everyone shows up because the opponent's team is serious. Last year's bronze medalists."

"And how many people are usually on our team?"

"It varies. Sometimes we can't fit everyone on the bus, other times there's no one to play on the field."

"I see."

Water tried calling Boss, but his phone was turned off. Kolya arrived and handed Water a bag with a uniform and gloves. Boss arrived soon after. He saw that only three people had gathered, and he turned around and went somewhere.

Gradually, football players started to arrive. A small bald man immediately approached Water.

"Was it you who found my bike?" he asked.

"Yes. You can pick it up at the factory."

"I don't need it yet. You can keep it for now."

"Are you, by any chance, Bereza's son?"

"No," he smiled, "I'm his son-in-law."

People continued to arrive. Some were already dressed in their kits, while others looked bewildered, as if questioning why their mothers had brought them into the world. When Boss arrived, it seemed like everyone had been waiting for him. Music was blaring through the street, and the car owner was already mingling with people. Water was wondering how he managed to already know everyone and why they were so friendly with him.

Head ran up, counted the players, and confirmed that the team was all set.

"There won't be a bus today; we're going by car. We'll cover your fuel, don't worry," he said to Boss.

He ran off somewhere, then returned in an old Audi, with

Oksana, the district officer, and another man inside. The officer was beaming since they were going to play against his village.

The team piled into the cars, making sure not to forget their kits in the bar. Little Ronaldo jumped into his dad's car. Boss and Water remained standing there.

"Follow me; the road is easy to get lost on," the Captain advised Boss.

The evangelical brothers were running toward them.

"Is there room for two more, boys?"

"Yes."

"Then we're coming with you."

The caravan of cars rolled westward, kicking up dust.

The stadium was decent. The young footballers had just marked the field with sawdust. Fans had turned out in large numbers, filling the benches like swallows flocking to electric wires.

The party that arrived was small but mighty: eleven football players (a full team with no substitutes), the Head, the district officer, Oksana, the evangelical brothers (one of whom was immediately assigned as a linesman), little Ronaldo (who was made the second linesman and tasked with signaling the referee from the other end of the field), and the referee himself—Yaroslav Semenovych, a school physics teacher whom the Head trusted immensely. The teacher officiated all the away matches.

The team spilled onto the field, warming up and taking shots on goal. Water, in a slightly oversized kit, looked like a goalkeeper from a bygone era. The team was disoriented—too few spectators on their side, too few players. The officer quickly made his way over to some group of people, demonstrating that he knew everyone there.

Warm-ups ended, and the final line-ups were confirmed.

"Hello to the opposing team!" one side shouted.

"Hello to the opposing team!" came the reply.

The whistle blew, and the game began, although it would have been better if it had not . . .

The car slowly trundled down the road, away from the field. The players' earlier enthusiasm had completely faded. Boss kept the music off, and despite his smile, remained silent. On Water's flushed face, a painful grimace was breaking through. He retreated into himself like a hermit crab into its shell.

Even the fact that he had learned to distinguish the brothers by their tattoos (Mark had a lion inked on his forearm, while Ivan sported an eagle) did not offer him much comfort. Mark kept insisting:

"Guys, don't worry, it's not your fault. Without you, the team would have been utterly humiliated."

"And now it's been humiliated with us," Boss interjected.

"We played okay. Last year's team won bronze, and we only just signed up. What more could we hope for? Don't take it to heart. You played well," he said to Water but got no reply.

"My brother and I didn't call you here for nothing. It'll be alright," Mark reassured him.

"It better be," Water replied.

"It will be. Football is a great way to forget your worries, to feel needed and happy. Every Sunday for years, we put on our kits and go play, even though we know we'll never become professionals, that we'll never be seen or picked up by some league. We go because we enjoy it. And when you step onto the field, nothing else matters. We, the fans, also get a piece of your happiness. We have nowhere to run. Maybe you'll still run away, but we can't run anywhere, not even off the field," Mark said, glancing at his brother Ivan, who was peacefully sleeping beside him.

The happy district officer did his best to console the Head. Meanwhile, the Head was contemplating where to drop off the officer. Oksana was cheerful but tried to hide it from her father.

They had lost today. They had been thoroughly beaten. Water

had conceded six goals in his debut match, miraculously not letting in more. None of the goals were his fault. Even the opponents felt sorry for him (which was particularly disheartening), and even the opposing fans praised him. But six goals were still six goals.

Only Boss was pleased, having scored two goals, just as he was asked. Despite the defeat, the team had gained new players. As they say, there's always next time.

When Water and Boss arrived at the factory, Uncle Vasyl understood everything at a glance but remained silent. Boss took him away, and they headed to the village.

Water stayed at the factory. He went down to the lake and stood there, watching. The water was clear and calm, and the sky was unblemished. A hawk was hunting near the forest, gliding effortlessly on the air currents. After a defeat, the only remedy was sleep.

Petryk sat by the shore, reading a book.

"It's not the worst outcome," Petryk smiled, closing the book and setting it down beside him.

"You know already?"

"Everyone knows, but it's not as bad as it might seem at first glance . . ."

"Are you here to paint or what?" Water asked, irritated.

"No, I'm reading a book . . ."

"Preparing for the national tests?"

"No, just relaxing. It's Zhadan's *Voroshilovgrad*." He showed the book to Water. "Let classics rest, and I'll read about Herman for a bit. Just a way to unwind."

"I see. I'm going to rest now. We'll see each other later."

"Good night," Petryk said and immersed himself in the book.

A few hours later, Petryk was back to practicing his painting. No one disturbed him. The forest stood aside, not interfering with anyone's business, rustling peacefully with its leaves and glistening with its pines. Soon summer would come, and people would have nowhere to run.

# 011

The next few days everyone was hard at work. Oak was absorbed in the final stages of the renovation, and no one paid him much attention. The radio created the ambiance of a lively world—greetings were exchanged, songs were requested, and the hosts were late for their morning shows. The workload kept increasing. Water was constantly preparing new batches of devices, packaging them one after another. Other guys were sorting through parts that had arrived by mail. Boss was torn between the city and the village, practically living at Uncle Vasyl's place. He was stopping by the garage frequently, trying to turn it into a workshop. The first customers from the village were starting to arrive.

The next home game, played in front of a packed stadium, ended in victory. The initial moments were tense and unpromising, but they managed to score three goals towards the end and finally breathed a sigh of relief. Boss scored once more, and even Kolya managed to head in a corner kick. He was overjoyed, celebrating like a kid as he ran the length of the field to kiss his wife. She was serving beer to everyone and embraced Kolya with her cold hands.

But the real hero was Water. In the first half, he saved a penalty that should not have been given in the first place. Everyone signaled this to the referee, but he officiated as if he were blind. This was Water's true initiation into the team.

After the game, something remarkable happened—the Head treated the brothers to drinks for bringing in the new players. Elated and drunk, they wandered around the village, telling everyone what great recruiters they were. They were on the brink of tears one moment and laughing like children the next. According to them, they had not been this happy since they last played on the field themselves. Everyone reveled in this triumph as if it were an ocean. The field smelled of freshly cut grass.

On Monday, Uncle Vasyl started helping Water with the packaging. He wiped the devices with alcohol, saying, "You can't drink them, but don't they smell great?"

Yuriy's client list expanded to new pages. Somewhere in the dusty summer city, Petryk was taking his national tests. The nights were warm and starry. The stars sparkled like grains of sand at the bottom of a gold panner's sieve.

Everything was going as it should be, until . . .

The gold panner gathered everything he had sifted and went home. The workshop's morning calm, set to a soundtrack of summer melancholy by the radio, was shattered by a phone call.

"Brother, I'm coming to see you." The voice on the other end was calm.

"Alright." Yuriy's voice trembled.

He had fallen out with his brother two decades ago. There was no clear reason for it, or perhaps it was hard to remember it now. Two similar temperaments refused to yield to one another. When Yuriy tried to take over the factory, he had not even considered reaching out to his brother. But someone was always trying to get their hands on the building. His brother found out about Yuriy's aspirations and helped him. They had met three times in the past year but had barely spoken. Even after the winter blockade, when Yuriy thought they had finally reconciled, nothing changed. And now, this call.

"Do you guys want to go on a picnic in the woods?" he asked the men who were sheltering from the heat in the factory's shade.

"What about the work?" Hryhoriy inquired.

"It can wait for today. My brother is coming, and I'd like to talk with him privately."

"We can just continue working in the workshop and be quiet," Hryhoriy persisted.

"No, that won't work."

"I know a place," Uncle Vasyl said.

"Then let's go," Boss commanded.

Water packed food and drinks. There was still a case of beer in the fridge that some customer had brought a while back.

"Oak, you'd better come with us to the picnic. The tax officer is on his way and will hassle you if you don't," Boss joked.

Water loaded the car, and the men squeezed into the vehicle. They did not drive far. Once out of the car, they continued on foot. The hot June sun filtered through the high branches of the trees. Dense green grass, which covered the entire path, bent underfoot. Many trails were overgrown, but that would soon change. Foragers would cautiously carve out the first routes, followed by women and children with plastic buckets in search of berries, and the paths would become more defined. By fall, a steady stream of people would flow into the forest, filling it with voices, children's laughter, and desperate cries for help—if someone got lost.

Near a short, carved post, the group veered off the road. They walked on a soft, leafy carpet that cushioned their steps. A swarm of gnats quickly made it clear it would not be an easy walk. Signs of wild boars foraging were visible on either side of the forest road. In the shade, spiderwebs glistened on the bushes.

"We're here." Uncle Vasyl pointed to a clearing overgrown with tall grass. "The young folks celebrate Kupala Night here."

"We could hide in the grass, and good luck to anyone trying to find us. Great spot. I suspect there's even a bench around here somewhere," Boss said, pointing to the tall grass.

"There is," the old man replied, "but not there."

They walked to a tall tree casting a shadow over the clearing. There was no grass under it, only a carpet of leaves, a table, and benches. They sat in the shade.

"Will Yuriy be able to reach us?" Hryhoriy muttered as he checked his phone. He nodded to himself. "Yes, there's service here."

"Interesting, I thought this forest was all conifers," Dmytro said, looking around.

"No, the conifers are only at the entrance. Further in, there are oaks and younger trees. On the side, there's a birch grove, and there were beeches, but nothing's left of them. There used to be more oaks, but they were cut down. What was planted didn't take because no one cared for it. And over there is a ravine," the old man explained.

"A ravine?"

"Yeah, if you follow the grass, you'll fall right into it—it's quite steep," Uncle Vasyl replied.

"That's not very considerate of Yuriy to send us here," Hryhoriy said.

"Don't worry. Just enjoy the gnats biting you and drink the beer while it's cold. As for everything else—what's destined will come to pass; it was determined long ago. We can only accept it and wait," Boss said.

A pause hung in the hot air for a while.

"So, you think nothing depends on us?" Dmytro asked.

"What could depend on us? We're too insignificant for that," Boss replied.

"What about religion? 'And it shall be rendered unto him according to his deeds . . .'" Dmytro continued.

"What religion? Christianity? Live however you want, repent at the end. Where's the justice in that? Didn't manage to repent—that's your problem. Brilliant," Boss said sarcastically.

"There's always hope for repentance," Dmytro countered.

"Hope? What a great concept. I sit here doing nothing because

I have this damned hope that everything will turn out fine, or that someone else will handle it for me. Is that how it works?" Boss snapped, his patience worn thin.

"Maybe," Dmytro conceded.

"One should believe in justice but work hard to earn an honest living," Hryhoriy said quietly.

But Boss was not to be stopped.

"Whose justice should I believe in? Yours or mine?"

"The only religion I believe in is nature," Water responded. "Repentance and all-forgiving God don't suit me. They corrupt people. No matter what a person does, they still have a chance to get away with it. Nature doesn't work that way. Pollute a river—there's nothing to drink; cut down a forest—your house gets flooded. All your rot is reflected in the water around you—the water you drink, bathe in, and wash your children with. Perhaps cruelty is nature's last hope. I believe that," Water said, drawing obscure symbols in the dirt with a stick.

"We should've brought the radio," Dmytro said, trying to steer the conversation anywhere else.

"We don't have batteries," Water replied.

"Regardless of what you believe, you'll still have to face death. I believe death isn't such a bad outcome. Even God died . . . " Uncle Vasyl spoke up.

Everyone fell silent. The sun had shifted to another tree, and the forest trembled with the summer breeze. Beyond the ravine, the buzz of a chainsaw echoed, its sound carrying through the woods. Ants marched in the leaves, seemingly on a mission. A shiny beetle crawled across a mossy patch. Wild cabbage grew nearby.

The men sat quietly. Neither food nor drink was appealing. Summer had just begun and already promised to pass quickly. High above the forest, a kite was hunting, and an owl slept in the hollow of an old tree.

Yuriy seemed to have calmed down a bit. He had managed to sort things out with his brother, and everything had returned to its usual rhythm. He and Denys spoke not of work, but of their families and their elderly parents, whom they planned to visit together for the first time in years. His brother was in the midst of a divorce and sought support where he had not found it before.

The summer days began to blend together, like a praying mantis on a green leaf. The heat drove people indoors, forcing them to camp by fans and air conditioners. Life-giving moisture evaporated in the afternoon, only to fall from the sky, which had burned red the day before, in the evening. The clouds lost their density and drifted in ragged patches across the blue sky. The unmowed grass lay at their feet, turning yellow. The lake was losing water, and a dark stripe appeared at the edge of the reeds. Everything living along the highway was withering. Only the snakes still warmed their flexible bodies in the sun, causing Uncle Vasyl to watch his step more carefully. Occasionally, he would forget his fear and walk boldly, as the snakes slithered away from him.

It was the snakes who brought the new crowd here. This happened on another Monday, after a tough game. In a fierce battle, the team lost. Although Water only let one goal slip past him, it was enough.

An old Zhiguli trundled into the forest and came to a stop. The sun attempted to warm its metallic raspberry body. Two people, carrying backpacks and thin sticks, got out and ventured into the woods. From the factory, only the car was visible, but it did not draw much attention—people had driven through here before. The area attracted many fishermen eager to try their luck in the forest.

Uncle Vasyl arrived. For several days he had been mowing the grass with a trimmer that Yuriy had recently bought. He still had a small patch of the lakeshore to finish. Occasionally, Uncle Vasyl had to let his new companion—the trimmer—rest, as it overheated quickly. He gazed at the shimmering surface of the calm lake, where the sun danced playfully, like a child. Around noon each day, the heat drove him to retreat to the factory's coolness, leaving the trimmer behind.

The snake hunters arrived by car. They emerged from the forest with their live catch. They carried long sticks with tongs at the ends and canvas bags with wriggling contents. After tossing their gear into the trunk, they attempted to start the car, but it refused to cooperate. The starter turned a few times, then fell silent. The hunters popped the hood and inspected the car before heading to the factory. Several pairs of curious eyes had been observing them from the factory for some time.

"Greetings," one of the snake hunters addressed the crew. He was an older man with glasses in a thin golden frame and a bushy mustache. His much younger partner remained silent.

"Our battery is dead. Can you jump-start us?" he continued.

"Good morning. No problem," Boss replied before asking, "Did you catch anything?"

"We did, but we had to go quite far. At first, we only found grass snakes, but further in, we came across a few of the ones we were after," the snake hunter replied calmly.

"Are you catching them for a serpentarium?" Water interjected.

"Yeah, sometimes also for orders. The demand keeps growing every year." The snake hunter removed his cap, sat on a bench, and lit a cigarette.

"What a curious job," said Uncle Vasyl.

"It's just a job, really," replied the young snake hunter. "Better than working as a warehouse loader."

"Will you jump-start us or not?" the older snake hunter steered the conversation back on track.

"No problem," Boss said and went to retrieve his old Volkswagen Golf.

Everyone watched as Boss's car pulled up alongside the Zhiguli, how he fumbled with the cables that resembled snakes. They saw him explaining something to the snake hunters, how the old engine roared to life, and how the car, swaying on the uneven ground, made its way toward the highway.

"That old wreck runs on pure faith," Boss said when he returned.

The smoke break dragged on. The sun was determined to drive everyone back into the workshop.

"They said they'd come back. They'll bring tents, camp by the lake, and I'll see what I can do with that car," Boss added.

"Will they pay you in vipers?" asked Uncle Vasyl.

"I'll sell them to you at a fair price. Are you interested?"

"Yeah, I'll buy a whole bag. And don't try to short-change me!"

Whether it was the democratic prices or the lack of other options, people kept coming to the garage, and each day brought more cars. Boss stayed there late into the night, feeling more content than he had in his courier job. The skin on his skilled hands had taken on a familiar tan.

He was not relieved of his previous duties either, so he had to juggle both. Oak made minor repairs to the room above the garage, and a bed was moved in. Boss was torn between his main job and the auto service, where he was his own manager.

The week ended quickly, but the work never seemed to end. On Saturday, Petryk arrived. Water spotted him by the lake. He was in good spirits, having completed the national tests and now awaiting the results. He returned to his painting, which went unnoticed by everyone except Water.

On Saturday evening, rain began, followed by thunder. It poured until morning. The next day, the downpour turned into a light rain and then resumed again. Even Uncle Vasyl, who was supposed to take over Water's watch, had to drive by car. Despite the weather, the football match was not postponed.

No one was in the mood, and victory seemed unlikely. The stadium was covered in puddles, and the goalkeepers stood almost knee-deep in water. The grueling match ended in a scoreless draw.

On Monday, Yuriy was the first to arrive at work. Dmytro was supposed to bring Hryhoriy, who had taken a few hours off for personal errands. Boss was still asleep in the village after yesterday's outings. Water was sitting by the lake, sipping coffee, when Yuriy approached him.

"Do you drink coffee here every morning?" Yuriy asked, sitting down on the bench.

"Yes. I've only recently learned not to scald my hands while carrying a full cup here."

Water was still sleepy and yawned widely.

"And why are you here so early?" Water asked Yuriy.

"Well . . . I couldn't sleep."

A thick mist lay over the lake. Two figures were completely engulfed in it. A large fish swam near the shore, its back glistening.

"I see."

"How do you like it here? We never really talked about it."

"I'm used to it now. It's good."

"We need to let Boss go . . . "

"What do you mean?" Water asked.

"Don't you see how passionate he is about his auto service? It's only going to hold us back. He's afraid to admit it, lacks the courage, but I can see it."

"He's got a lot on his mind."

"But unlike the rest of us, he knows what he wants to do."

"Maybe."

"We should let him do his thing. We'll manage on our own somehow."

"And when will you tell him?"

"Today, I think."

"Then we need more people. Petryk asked about a job. He's a good kid."

"Is he the one who read poems?"

"Yeah."

"Let him come. Dmytro will be driving to the city a lot, so you'll need to cover for him. Uncle Vasyl and Petryk will handle the packaging."

"But I don't know how to do it."

"You'll learn."

Water was not thrilled with this, but he had no choice. The thick mist was slowly dissipating, and small carp were leaping out of the water and splashing back down loudly.

"You said only Boss knows what he wants to do. What about you?" Water asked.

"I don't know either. I'd like to go somewhere else."

"To another country?"

"I don't know."

Water stayed by the lake. There was still over an hour until the start of the workday. Yuriy got up and was about to leave.

"I'll bring you a companion tomorrow. He wants to live in a tent by the lake. We'll stay together, at least for one night, because he won't stop pestering me."

"And how old is your companion?"

"He'll be five soon."

"Alright. We'll go fishing."

That same morning, Yuriy made Boss happy. He decided to stay at the workshop for one more week. But something had changed in him. He moved around the garage with great enthusiasm and excitement. For a modest rent, Boss gained what he had longed for but had not dared to pursue before.

Water was slowly adjusting to the new tasks. Dmytro used all his pedagogical skill to teach Water new techniques. But the only thing Water managed on the first day was to burn his fingers with the soldering iron.

Hryhoriy walked around with a gloomy expression, displeased with the prospect of having such a partner.

Only Uncle Vasyl seemed unfazed.

They stocked the warehouse as best they could. New clients popped up like mushrooms after the rain. The old ones returned as well. They had grown so used to the device that they admitted more than once they could no longer imagine life without it.

The radio stayed on its frequency, breaking up thoughts with music, music with news, and news with advertisements. It reminded everyone of the vast world that stretched beyond the lake and never seemed to end.

Water was anxious. Adapting to his new circumstances quickly was a challenge. He managed some tasks without problem, but delving deeper into the technology behind the device was far from enjoyable. He had already grown used to the factory, the forest, and the lake, even to the bicycle. He even considered buying his own someday, as he would need to return this one to its owner, who did not seem too concerned about its fate. Water made some minor repairs to the bike but was reluctant to invest much in someone else's piece of metal. Every evening, he sat by the lake, reassured by the thought that he could stay here for at least another year.

The next morning, when the thick fog filled the valley like a deep bowl, Yuriy arrived with his son. Woken up early, the boy was still uncertain about what was happening. He remembered his father had promised him a camping trip, but morning memories are always different from those in the evening.

Yuriy left him on a bench by the lake and spoke on the phone. From the snatched phrases, it was clear the conversation was work-related. The boy rubbed his sleepy eyes. The valley was shrouded in mist, and he stared at it without blinking, though it was hard to focus on the fog. He took a deep breath and exhaled heavily.

"What are you doing here, young man?" Water asked.

"Breathing." The boy inhaled and exhaled again, filling his growing lungs with the morning air.

"And how does it feel to breathe?"

"It's good. I just want to sleep . . ." The boy yawned and continued breathing.

"Why did your dad wake you up so early?"

"We're going to live in a tent by the lake."

"And what's your name?" Water asked, though he already remembered it from Yuriy's stories about his children.

"Mykhailo."

Water decided not to pester the boy with the usual questions—how old he was, what his family's names were, when he would start school, and so on. Adults often ask such questions, treating children as if they weren't as complex as themselves.

"Do you like it here?"

The boy nodded.

"And where is your tent?"

"In the car. Dad's busy."

"Don't worry, he'll come soon," Water sat down on the bench next to the boy.

They sat in silence for some time.

"I need to live by the sea," Mykhailo said in a serious tone.

"Why's that?"

"That's what the doctor said." The boy shrugged, and his bright childish face took on a more mature expression at the mention of the doctor.

"And your dad?"

"He needs to live by the sea too, and so does mama and my little sister."

A small carp jumped out of the water in front of them. Ripples spread across the surface.

"Nobody knows why the fish jumps like that," Water said.

"Maybe they want to look at us. I'd be curious too if I were a fish."

Yuriy returned and said they would set up camp in the evening. The boy did not seem too thrilled. Water understood everything without words. For the next few days, his work would change drastically. Yuriy brought breakfast, and they ate by the lake. The boy was silent, breathing deeply and watching the mist rise from the lake. After a while, he got up and ran across the damp grass to watch the fish jumping on the opposite shore.

"Just don't fall in the water," Yuriy called after him.

"When are you moving to the seaside?" Water asked.

Yuriy said nothing, only smiled, but there was a lot of pain in that smile.

"How old is he? He chatters like an adult."

"I told you—he'll be five soon. He started speaking late, but now he won't stop . . . You'll keep an eye on him until evening?"

"I've got it."

"You don't need to come to the workshop."

The sun decided to shine a bit, but a band of clouds interfered with its infernal efforts.

They sat by the lake for a while longer. The boy ran in circles around the lake until a large butterfly distracted him. He chased after it.

"It's a good thing Uncle Vasyl mowed the grass. Otherwise, we'd never have found him in the tall weeds."

Water chased the boy, who was oblivious to all worries. His little legs scampered along the shore, eager to dart into the forest and uninterested in hiding in the shade of stone buildings. Later, Water made him a bow from willow branches and arrows from reeds. They all hid to avoid having the young Robin Hood accidentally shoot them. The arrows quickly ran out, but there were plenty of reeds.

By noon, Water was more tired than usual. They agreed to venture into the forest, but only a short distance. The boy spotted a squirrel and ran in circles around a large tree, observing the little animal. The squirrel muddled its trail, leaped to another tree, and disappeared.

"Are we going to fish?" the boy asked as they emerged from the forest.

"If an old man brings us fishing rods," Water replied.

"Will he bring them?"

"He will," Water said, though he was not sure, but he also wanted to catch some fish himself.

In the workshop, everyone labored with their heads down. The radio broadcast personal messages and greetings from callers to their relatives. The boy wandered around the factory with little interest and soon fell asleep on a bed, clutching his bow.

After lunch, two luxury cars arrived at the factory. The people from the first car went upstairs and locked themselves in Yuriy's office. The occupants of the second car stepped out to stretch their legs. Water was downstairs, sitting on the bench by the wall and observing the people in black suits. He immediately recognized them as security. Among the guests, he spotted a familiar face, trying to recall where he had seen him before. Then he remembered.

"You're back? Did you like it so much the first time?" Water asked.

"I did. This time, you see, we pulled up right to the doors," the guest replied.

It was the commander of the group that had trying raiding them in the winter.

"So, you changed jobs?" Water asked, genuinely curious.

"No. I'm working where I worked before."

"And are these the same guys?"

"Yeah," the guest smiled.

"Are balaclavas only part of the winter uniform?" Water joked. The man remained silent.

The guests loaded two cars with devices and disappeared toward the city.

By evening, the fish were biting slowly. The boy caught a few small carp and played with them in a bucket. Conversation resumed.

"Those were some serious people," Yuriy said.

"I figured that out. They've been here before," Water replied.

"How do you know?"

"I recognized the commander."

"I see. They invited us to join them on crazy conditions."

"Did they try to scare you?"

"On the contrary—they offered mountains of gold."

"And you?"

"I said not now."

"Where would you have to work?"

"Anywhere you want. They have enterprises almost in every region."

"Does it have to do with the device?"

"No. They bought them as a gesture of goodwill."

"So, what do you think?"

"I don't know yet. I haven't decided."

The boy caught a few fish. Behind them, a tent was set up, and a fire was kindling. Heavy clouds drifted westward. It was warm. In the houses somewhere far off, happy people were settling down for the night.

# 012

The next game was against the current leader of the championship. Their team was young and skilled. Several patrons had invested generously in it, providing excellent facilities and decent prize money.

Water had been informed that this team was interested in his modest goalkeeping skills, as it was one of the few poorly staffed positions. But in his typical reserved manner, he had declined their offer. So, at the beginning of the match, he got his head split open. Whether it was intentional or not would remain on their conscience. Water finished the game with his head bandaged, and after the match, Kolya stitched up the wound. Kolya said it was nothing serious, only two stitches. But with this turn of events and the sour mood, any hope of success evaporated. After an uneventful first half, Water conceded three goals in the second half, and the game ended.

On his first day at work, Petryk eagerly absorbed information. But there was so much of it that he struggled to keep up. Water taught him how to package devices, while Yuriy tried to spark his interest in other important tasks. Petryk was unusually bashful and stammered more than he typically did. Everyone noticed his discomfort, and both Water and Uncle Vasyl tried to reassure him.

"You'll get the hang of it quickly. I'm old, and even I managed to catch on, so you'll do just fine with your sharp mind."

Petryk was indeed trying hard. He was genuinely interested in the workings of the device. At the first opportunity, he asked Yuriy about it. He read the instruction manual twenty times. It seemed strange to him that the device was intended for private homes and apartments, yet at work, it was discussed only in the context of enterprises. He really wanted to ask about this but was too shy.

Yuriy had asked him not to tell anyone details about the device. This left Petryk with the challenge of explaining to curious people—of whom there were many—what he was working on.

When he packaged the devices, he twisted and turned them in his hands, trying to examine them closely. He studied the instructions thoroughly and was impressed by the quality of the paper and the design. The illustrations of a happy family were particularly intriguing.

Petryk was curious about the initial reaction of people opening the box. What did happiness mean to them?

Boss did not know what to do with himself now that he had been freed. He felt as if a stone had dropped on his head. That day, he was not at the factory, and neither was he for several days afterward. The factory continued its routine, and no one minded the empty garage.

Every day, Petryk arrived on his bicycle before work started to have his morning coffee with Water by the lake.

In the summer, many people, both old and young, flocked to the lake. First, they came alone, and then in crowds. Everyone wanted to dive into the clear, cool water. They took advantage of Yuriy's permission to relax there, unaware that he had no legal right to prohibit them. Yuriy, however, was aware of this. The only rule was not to litter, and everyone followed it.

After the first few days, Petryk adjusted to the new place. He was drawn to the forest, but he did not dare to go there alone, and Water did not want to join him on account of being busy.

Days trickled by like grains from a leaky sack, as they always do in summer.

The next game ended in a surprising loss. All forecasts had

predicted a victory, but Water conceded two goals. Boss, in particular, played poorly. It was clear that something was bothering him, and he was not in the mood for football.

On the third day, Boss finally returned. He was in high spirits, though no one knew why. He was beaming but remained tight-lipped, only making jokes and saying that everyone would find out soon enough. The workshop buzzed with speculation, and everyone came up with their own theories. Only Petryk and Water were unfazed by his mysterious behavior.

"You have quite a collection of names here. Boss, Water . . . Do you also have Pip and Friday, by any chance?" he asked.

"I don't know who Pip is, but I liked Friday as a child," Water replied.

"Then you should know that he died . . ." said Petryk.

"Died? How?" Water was astonished.

"At the very beginning of the second book."

"There's a second book?" Water was even more surprised.

"Yeah."

"Can you bring me *Voroshilovgrad*? I've read my own books countless times. Will you bring it tomorrow?"

"Okay, but you must return it to me after you finish. Books aren't money; they need to be returned."

In the workshop, Boss was the only topic of conversation. The crew's idle speculations might have continued endlessly if a truck had not arrived the next day, turning off the highway and heading toward them.

When the truck neared the factory, everyone went downstairs. Water exclaimed:

"I knew it!"

The tow truck carried a car covered with a gray tarp.

"Here we are!" Boss shouted, jumping off the tow truck and smiling broadly.

Finally, he brought the car he had been after. The entire workshop watched the unloading process. While everyone else had figured out what was happening, Petryk looked on in surprise.

"What's this?" he asked Water.

"It's a Pontiac Phoenix."

The tow truck drove off, and Boss took his time removing the cover, despite the impatient spectators urging him on.

"Wait a bit, let me catch my breath."

"Did you steal it?" Dmytro asked.

"No. I haven't stolen a car in a long time. I bought it."

"But you said the old fella didn't want to sell it," Hryhoriy said.

"And he didn't sell it. He's in a bad situation now. His grandson sent him into exile to a distant village. He had just married, and his grandfather quickly became the third wheel in a small apartment. So, he sold the car for a pittance to make room in the garage for his own junk. It's without documents, so you can consider it sold for scrap value—maybe a bit more. Now it's mine!"

"And why do you want it without documents?" Petryk asked.

"I'll repair it, then I'll sit here," he sat down on the bench by the wall, "and look at it."

"Enough with the speeches; you're not on the podium. Show it," urged Uncle Vasyl.

"I don't need to be rushed; I'm not a cow. I'll show you in a minute."

When he finally removed the cover, everyone's jaws dropped. The car was in a rough shape—missing several windows, with a battered body, serious dents, and flat tires, and covered in rust. It was ugly, yet somehow beautiful at the same time, with its unique geometry of lines and effortless boldness. They do not make them like this anymore. Together, they shoved it into the garage. Boss finally sighed with relief:

"Now it's mine."

"And the spare parts? Where will you find them around here?" Water asked.

"Don't worry, I've been preparing for this for a long time. I've got some things."

"You said you were an orphan. Where did you get the money for all these cars, tools, and spare parts?" Hryhoriy asked, a hint of envy in his voice.

Boss did not answer, only smiled.

Then the magic began. No one was allowed to enter the garage. Sometimes Boss would call on Water for help, especially when something heavy needed lifting. He disassembled the car down to the last screw, staying late into the night, practically living in the garage. He worked as if he were racing against something. When Uncle Vasyl teased him, saying, "Don't rush, or God forbid you actually manage to finish," Boss just kept silent.

While he worked on the Phoenix, his old Volkswagen Golf broke down. Boss started using it as a radio. He would sometimes forget to turn off the music before heading to the village, leaving it to blast across the entire valley until the battery died.

In the evenings, Water sat by the lake with a book. When the sun set, he stripped down and waded chest-deep into the warm, clear water. The evening sky hung above him.

For a whole week, Petryk tried to adjust to the new job. He was not sure if he was doing well or poorly. He received only a few minor comments, nothing critical. But there were no words of encouragement—none of the praise he had hoped for. Petryk was always a talker, and it seemed like he had a daily word quota to meet. But the only person he could chat with was Water, and that was only during breaks. Petryk could not seem to connect with Uncle Vasyl; they were just too different. As for Oak, who rarely showed up, nobody could talk to him—not even Yuriy. Oak had taken on a big apartment renovation and was running around like crazy, trying to handle both that and his work at the factory. But Petryk craved conversation.

"Where are you planning to apply?" Yuriy asked him over tea.

"The Department of Philology. Maybe I'll turn out to be a writer. They say that's the only way to make it in this field," Petryk replied.

"Do you have a good chance of getting in?"

"This year, I do," Petryk said, a bit shyly.

"Because of the national tests?"

"Yes. It's the best thing they've done for young people. If any-one ever abolishes it, that'll be the greatest crime against our future. Although, when things go wrong, sooner or later, it's the children who get sacrificed—whether by families or by the government. The only thing that can save us is good education. Everything else is easier to fix," he said, as if he had been formulating this answer in his mind for weeks.

Petryk was getting into the swing of things. On Sunday, when Boss and Water went to a football match, Petryk stayed behind to guard the factory with Uncle Vasyl. It was scorching hot. They spent the entire day in the workshop under a fan. The old man dozed in his chair while Petryk read a book.

That was the kind of match worth telling future generations about. The team won with just one goal, but what magic Water pulled off! It was a one-man show—a goalkeeper's showcase! He saved two penalties and made a dozen other crucial saves. The opposing fans, who were quite numerous, sat silently like mice. Eventually, they started applauding Water. Even he did not know how he managed it.

The evangelist brothers were in some kind of trance. They had never seen anything like it, especially in amateur football. If anyone knew football, it was them—they had both played at the regional level, and Marko had almost gone pro, but he did not want to go without his brother. And there they were, standing by the sideline, watching in silence, not wanting to jinx the miracle. You could go on and on about that game. It was worthy of a newspaper article, complete with a picture of Water's smiling face, but by the next day, few people were talking about it. Only the brothers were still under its spell, hoping to experience such joy again.

In a simultaneous match, two teams were fighting desperately for the second-to-last and last places. It was there that an event occurred which overshadowed Water's performance. In the middle of the second half, a young student's tackle divided a thirty-year-old player's life into 'before' and 'after.' It happened by accident, not intentionally, but it happened nevertheless. He lay on the ground, screaming in agony, his hands reaching for his leg to try and set it back in place. His ankle was twisted at an unnatural angle. Blood was seeping out. From the sock he had put on over his shin guards, a white bone protruded. Everyone went silent. Only the poor guy's screams echoed across the stadium, cutting into everyone's soul. The student, pale as a sheet, stood off to the side, crying. Then he collapsed face-first onto the ground. No one said a word to him.

"We're just amateurs! I've got a small child. Who's going to feed her now? I'll lose my job . . . What have you done?!"

An ambulance drove onto the field and took the injured player to the hospital. The student was still lying in the center of the pitch, still crying. A cloud of uncertainty lingered over them both.

Outside the football field, life moved along at its quick summer pace. As if the world was ending tomorrow, Boss was determined to fix—or rather, to rebuild—the car of his dreams.

Some days, Water was dying to go to the city, and others, he yearned to grab a backpack and head along the riverbank. He wanted to properly prepare and conquer that river. Every now and then, he dreamed about it. He wanted to walk along the banks of the Stokhid, to see the swamps where so many people had found their final resting place during the First World War. To get lost in the river's branches and find himself again. To live for a while on its shores. But the river remained only in his dreams.

Water sat by the lake, watching the swimmers. He observed the strong young men swimming across to the other side and diving. He watched little children splashing around like clumsy puppies. He saw the young women gracefully entering the water, turning the simple act into a small ritual. He noticed parents teaching their children to swim. He saw the sun warming the bodies, making them glisten. Clouds dozed on the horizon.

Not far from the shore, a young father stood waist-deep in the water, talking to a friend. Just ten feet away, his seven-year-old son was drowning. Without any shouts or frantic splashing, he was quietly going under.

Water ran frantically along the shore, too afraid to go into the water. All he managed was to shout. His cry drew the attention of everyone swimming in the lake, even the boy's father. Boss, who had been talking on the phone nearby, came running. Everything happened quickly. Boss demonstrated the speed that had earned him a spot on the football team. He took a beautiful leap from the shore and swam with powerful strokes. Water stood on the shore, pointing at the boy. In no time, the kid was safely on the bank. He had swallowed a lot of water but was slowly coming to. People thanked Boss, while the boy's father, as white as a ghost, stood there unable to say a word.

"You should be a lifeguard," Boss said as he passed Water. Large drops of water rolled off his black hair.

"Very funny. A lifeguard who can't swim."

New changes were brewing in the workshop. A few days earlier, Hryhoriy had read an article about the divide between techies and humanists and insisted that it was all a matter of nature. He claimed that is how the brain works and, without naming names, assured them that nothing could change this.

Boss had completely forgotten that there was a world beyond his car. Petryk had somehow managed to get the keys to the Golf from him. Boss had already repaired it.

Water was irritated by the number of people at the factory after hours. He had grown accustomed to his solitude. What troubled him most was that his visits to Uncle Vasyl's neighbor could no longer remain a secret. Neither he nor she wanted that. The fear of gossip and speculation made them avoid meeting, despite being adults.

Water decided to ask Petryk to teach him how to drive.

"How long have you been driving?" Water asked.

"Since high school. We had an unusual school—all of us have graduated with driver's licenses. Back in our day, driving was as easy as swimming," Petryk replied.

Water said nothing.

"Sorry, I mean . . . it's like brushing your teeth. There's nothing to it."

As the sun sank toward the horizon, the factory's driving school began its sessions. The old German car struggled to start, often stalling until the novice driver learned to move smoothly. Eventually, the car drove confidently around the lake.

Yuriy's guests were arriving more frequently now. The familiar guard was no longer included. It became increasingly difficult to hide that they were interested not in the devices but in Yuriy himself.

Hryhoriy, who showed particular interest in the guests, always had his ears pricked up. His curiosity remained unsatisfied except for a single phrase: "In any regional center. If you want to be by the sea, just say so." After each visit, Yuriy would dissolve into contemplation. He was increasingly seen by the lakeside. Sometimes, in the morning, his entire family would gather there. Water watched them. Yuriy's son observed the fish jumping out of the water.

Hryhoriy tormented Dmytro, who would gladly converse with anyone but him.

"They won't change. They're just wired differently. We can grasp technology, but they'll never manage it. Poor souls. In this world, you need to create something with your own hands. Poor souls . . ."

Summer quickly dwindled away, indifferent to football victories or mostly empty conversations. Life moves on just as swiftly.

Dmytro spent more and more time in the city. Yuriy regretted letting Boss go, but things seemed to be moving along well. Dmytro continually pushed himself and made Herculean efforts whenever he had to interact with clients. These frequent meetings planted seeds of ambition in him.

Work became a mere routine. Even the radio, which had once been a reliable escape, no longer entertained. The songs on the air were repetitive and soon grew tiresome. The volume on the receiver was constantly turned down. Despite Water's efforts to listen, he could make out nothing.

Having exhausted conversations about humanists and techies, Hryhoriy found new topics—specifically, money. He spoke while sipping hot morning coffee by the lake:

"Besides the projected annual sum, I have saved up an extra ten thousand and don't know what to do with it. Water, where would you spend ten thousand?"

Water hesitated to respond, but when he grew tired of it, he said, "I'd donate it to the World Wildlife Fund."

Such conversations often repeated, though they had become tedious for everyone.

While conversations were ongoing in one place, work was in full swing in another. Boss's fortunes fluctuated. Some evenings, he would close the garage with a blissful face and drive his Golf to the village. At other times, it seemed he had not left the garage for days. When he argued with Oksana, which happened occasionally, his phone would go flying through the air like a comet. Once he had calmed down, he would search for it in the nettles and weeds that grew lush and stung his hands.

Amid daily troubles and football battles, the summer days grew shorter, even though the sun continued to blaze. No one was in a hurry, except for Boss, who worked tirelessly in his garage, sweating profusely. But when everyone finally learned why he was in such a rush, everything fell into place.

# 013

The wedding.

The first rumors about Boss and Oksana began circulating in early July. Everyone thought she was pregnant. It later turned out she was not, but by then, no one listened.

The women in the village gossiped, "Aha, he came here to play *football* . . ." The news of the wedding seemed to calm them down. The announcement should have reached the factory sooner—it seemed logical—but in reality, it was only when the last stray dog knew about the upcoming nuptials that Boss finally told Yuriy.

"We haven't chosen a date yet, but we're inviting you to the wedding. Do with this information what you will," Boss said.

Yuriy nearly fell out of his chair, but Boss calmly clarified the situation to his relief.

The idea to get married had not been his. Oksana had proposed it herself. "You know how Oksanas are; you have an Oksana yourself," Boss said. Yuriy silently agreed. They were not concerned that they had been seeing each other for just over a month. Boss was convinced that was enough.

The greatest wave of disapproval came from people whose opinions did not matter to them. The greatest support came from where it was needed. Since Boss was an orphan—at least, according to him—Oksana's parents became their main support. When the Head learned about the wedding, he called the Captain and asked when it would be possible to rent a hall at his restaurant. He then told the happy couple that he had already made arrangements and that they should choose a weekend in August. The Head became the driving force behind the ceremony. With his endorsement and parental blessing, preparations for the event began.

"Before I married my wife, I knew her for fifteen minutes. We've been living in harmony for thirty years. If you've decided, then it will be so. I will help in any way I can," said the Head.

His words matched his deeds. All that remained was to wait for August. Oksana's parents were very eager for the wedding. Boss took it calmly. His invitations were extended only to factory workers.

He rarely left the garage now. The buzzing of tools filled the surroundings day and night. While Water slept peacefully, music seeped through the concrete walls. In the morning, as Water drank coffee by the lakeside, the grinding noise shattered the silence.

Boss allowed no one into his space except Oksana. She started showing up more frequently—sometimes in the morning, holding her shoes in her hand, stepping through the cold dew with bare feet. The sun shone over the forest. Summer invisibly tethered everyone to itself.

Workdays blended into a tasteless mush. Happy people took out their spoons each morning, poked at dirty plates, and ate reluctantly. A certain tension had settled in the factory.

Petryk went away to take more exams. Everyone missed him. Yuriy's guests had probably gone away on a vacation because they no longer came by.

Water had grown so accustomed to the factory that he feared being alone. In the past, he had wandered through dozens of rivers, slept wherever he could, hundreds of times, but now he felt uncomfortable outside these walls. At night, he anxiously looked toward the forest. Sometimes, branches crackled on the ground from someone's invisible footsteps. The constant presence of unknown visitors made him turn on the radio. With it on, Water felt calmer. Troubling dreams gradually eroded his confidence. He wanted to pack his things in the middle of the night and run away.

The scorching heat arrived. The grueling football matches increasingly ended with victories. More people gathered by the lake. Cars crawled along the highway, leaving tire marks on the asphalt before vanishing into the hot air. Drivers' eyes ached from the glare. Only the dark forest promised relief with its coolness, but it could offer none. Meanwhile, Boss's garage hummed with activity and music.

Water and Boss often met by the lakeside.

"It's good that you're here," Water said.

"Are you alright?" Boss asked.

"Yes."

He did not dare admit that he was afraid, that every day he was overtaken by a multitude of small fears that had not existed before. It tormented him. Once, there had been only one, powerful fear. Now, it seemed as though everything was unraveling. Others were walking along his riverbanks now; others sleeping by his night fires. Women who had once welcomed him with open doors now opened them for someone else. Everything was changing, but people remained oblivious. Boundless madness governed the world, offering people hope of an impending end. But if that end did not come, the age-old complaints about the world would persist.

A week before the wedding, on Saturday, Water was practically forced into the city to buy a suit. He was to be a groomsman, and that came with obligations. The second groomsman was Petryk, as Hryhoriy and Dmytro had refused. Dmytro feared the added responsibility, while Hryhoriy found the role too trite.

So, Water went to the city. The bus driver, who for some reason did not turn on the radio but played three prison songs on a loop on an old tape player, ruined the morning for all the passengers.

The sun-heated streets of the city greeted Water warmly. After the markets, crowded with people who gulped their morning instant coffee, the sleepy streets seemed calm and contemplative. He liked everything he bought, although it meant spending part of his savings. Luckily, Yuriy had given him a bonus.

Water sat on a bench. Thoughts swarmed in his head. Scruffy city pigeons searched for food at his feet. Above him hung an equally scruffy sky. August was beginning. On streets he had grown unaccustomed to, people busily wasted their time. The city awaited rain, but the sky offered none.

Water did not wish to return to the factory. There were a few addresses he could visit, where he might be welcomed, but he did not want to go without warning, so he sat with his bag in the park. The beer warmed quickly. The air was unbearably hot, almost impossible to breathe. The heat drove Water from park to park. That was how the day ended. Water might have wanted to return to this city, but he always believed that only failures return.

By evening, the rain began, washing the dust from the streets, which now cooled in the twilight. The last bus left without him. He returned to the factory in the dark of the night. Boss was already asleep in the garage, having forgotten to turn off the light and the radio. Water had no choice but to listen to the music.

The next match hardly interested anyone—all were waiting for the wedding. Only the evangelical brothers, who after the third game focused solely on football, were fully immersed in it. The match was won with a minimal score. An extraordinarily amusing goal was scored by Kolya. The groom could not score, despite the presence of the bride. They had a lot of concerns of their own.

The entire following week was filled with those concerns. There were so many that it felt like they needed to be shared.

On Tuesday, Boss admitted he would not be able to finish his Phoenix before the wedding. He had known for a long time but had been reluctant to admit it even to himself. Perhaps it was just a futile attempt to manage the stress. Besides the car, Boss had a multitude of problems—and the closer it got to the wedding, the more unresolved issues there were. He needed to arrange for the cake, deliver the alcohol, bring in a makeup artist and hairdresser so Oksana would not have to travel far. He had to sort out transportation and find a photographer. And then there were the musicians and the emcee. But the worst part was that the Head was trying to interfere in every detail. It was understandable, given that Oksana was his only daughter.

The factory operated as usual, but the calm of daily routine was stirred by sweet anticipation. Everyone already knew their duties for Saturday, so they worked in peace. Yuriy was to transport the newlyweds—to the church, the registry office, the photo session, and then to the restaurant. Uncle Vasyl would entertain Yuriy's wife during this time, while his children would be picked up by their grandparents. Dmytro and Hryhoriy had only to eat, drink, and dance—nothing more was expected of them, and nothing more could be entrusted to them.

Water and Petryk were the groomsmen. Petryk was also scheduled to be the driver in the morning.

Uncle Vasyl's house became the groom's citadel—the place from which he would set out on his journey to becoming a husband.

The last night of bachelorhood was celebrated at the factory. A modest spread was set up on the broad hood of the Phoenix, which was covered with a tarp to conceal how far it was from being finished. Only a little alcohol was brought. Boss wanted to vent his feelings. The bachelor party felt more like a confessional.

"I can hardly believe this is real. That I'm getting married just a month after we met. It doesn't bother me at all. I want to jump and shout. I don't even know the words to explain how I feel. I really don't."

"Everything will be fine," Yuriy said.

"I know it will be fine. It's been so bad so many times that there's no other way. I've been thinking all week about how everything turned out this way. About childhood . . . You know, you're the only guests I have. And it's true, because I have no one left. My whole family died from carbon monoxide poisoning, and I wasn't with them. I got angry about something and ran away, and they all died—my father, my mother, and my two little sisters. My uncle, who raised me and taught me everything, passed away last year. There's no one left. If I hadn't ended up at the factory, I don't know where I would be. I don't know . . ."

"You need to rest," Dmytro said.

"Don't tell me I need to sleep too. You don't know what's going on in my head." Boss smiled and asked Water, "And why are you silent?"

"What should I say? I'm not getting married tomorrow, I'm just a groomsman," Water laughed. "There won't be any bodies of water there, so there's nothing to be afraid of."

"Weddings are expensive. Where are you getting the money for it?" Hryhoriy asked.

"Why does it matter to you? Maybe I've been stealing cars all my life, or took out a loan, or am waiting for you to give me money. What kind of question is that? Is there one fucking thing in this world that interests you more than money? Meet someone, get laid properly, maybe that will help." Boss threw on his jacket and went out into the night.

In the garage, everyone was silent. No one even tried to seize the moment to check out the car, where a bottle of cognac, barely touched, sat on the hood.

The first night of August . . . The sky was covered with heavy clouds. A few stars broke through the dark veil. The air already smelled of rain. This further irritated Boss because he did not want rain on the wedding day.

Yuriy's car headed toward the highway, illuminating the forest and the lake with its headlights. Water went upstairs. He knew well that Boss would manage everything himself, and it was better not to bother him now.

The man stood for a long time on the shore of the lake, signaling across with a cigarette. Then he pulled something from his jacket and threw it into the water. The heavy object flew about fifty feet before splashing into the lake. A breeze stirred. Boss returned to the garage, turned off the light, took the bottle of cognac, and locked the door. He lingered for a moment, signaling into the darkness from another spot, and then headed toward the village. Rain began to fall.

By morning, there was no trace of yesterday's rain. What had seemed well-planned and in order the day before now appeared unlikely to go smoothly. Countless things required immediate rethinking, and countless problems demanded urgent solutions. The two houses were filled with all of the world's chaos. So cozy they must have been there that the chaos had no intention of leaving and was making itself at home.

It all started with the hairdresser. Her car broke down. One of the Head's neighbors went out to help on the highway. Oksana was very nervous. The Head was even more so. This stern, experienced, and unshakeable man (as his subordinates would probably describe him, or as he would be portrayed in the wall newspaper, from which he sometimes seemed to have emerged) had turned into a bundle of nerves that day. He barely held back tears.

"I used to braid your hair for school, and I'll braid it for your wedding," the Head said firmly and seated his daughter on a chair in front of the mirror.

Oksana cried. She decided to trust her father—whatever happens, happens. Just as the Head had finished brushing his daughter's hair, the hairdresser arrived.

Then came the makeup, the voluminous white dress. The slender photographer darted around, capturing every moment through his lens. During the photo session, Oksana felt like the happiest bride.

"I hope it lasts for as long as it can," she told herself.

In the other camp, work was also in full swing. Boss had forgotten the champagne in the garage. Petryk took it to the restaurant early in the morning.

Yuriy and his wife arrived. They helped Water decorate the car with ribbons and balloons. Yuriy managed to calm Boss a bit.

"It's scarier than being drafted into the army. Don't worry, even if you forget something, it won't ruin the celebration. I forgot the fireworks at my wedding. We set them off on New Year's Eve, even though I got married in May," Yuriy said, attaching a decoration of two rings and two swans to the hood.

Soon, Boss was fully ready and watched his groomsmen in shorts and T-shirts dash around the car, decorating it with balloons, ribbons, and tulle.

Boss was short on people for all the traditional roles, but it went unnoticed. His small entourage, minus Hryhoriy and Dmytro who were running late, was ready to head to the bride's house.

Scattered clouds dimmed the August sun, but there was no threat of rain.

Everything proceeded according to tradition. The bride's family offered to give her to the groom for a symbolic payment of money or some vodka.

"You have the goods; we have the buyer."

"Let me see her first."

"Don't you remember who you're marrying?"

"For that kind of money, one could buy a brother out of prison."

"Why do you need so much vodka? You won't drink that much."

The evangelical brothers tried to barter Oksana for future football goals, but since they had already been drinking since the morning, no one paid them any attention.

Then the groom finally saw the bride . . .

After the parental blessing, which left everyone in tears, they headed to the village registry office. Dmytro and Hryhoriy arrived there. The ceremony went quickly and with excessive pomp. It could have ended like that—slightly dry and overly formal—but Water nearly doused the officiant while uncorking the champagne. Everyone laughed.

They walked to the church since it was close by. The priest spoke at length. Water tried hard to remember his duties—laying out the embroidered towel, handing over the rings. He completely forgot about the maid of honor, who was supposed to assist him.

Boss, though not very religious, was so moved by the wedding that he almost cried. He looked at Oksana and thought only one thing—he hoped it would last for as long as it could.

After the ceremony, the newlyweds headed to the photo session. First, they went to the lake, and later they were photographed in the forest near a sturdy oak tree Boss had saved from being cut down. During the session, Water got to know the maid of honor. She was Oksana's classmate, Svitlana—a beautiful woman with chestnut curls and brown eyes. Svitlana did not know anyone there, so Water felt it was his duty to keep her company.

Later, after the well-wishes and blessings, the bouquets and envelopes, the electric kettles, blankets, and bed linen, the Head gifted the groom a shotgun. The guests urged the groom to fire it, but Boss joked that the father-in-law had not given him any cartridges.

After the prayer and the first toast, a sudden sense of bitterness swept over everyone, and the newlyweds took it upon themselves to remedy the situation. The celebration finally kicked off in earnest— with drinking, games, and dancing.

Svitlana seemed to come alive, but she showed no interest in Water as a man or companion. She gave him a childish kiss on the cheek, though it carried a hint of mockery. As night fell, Svitlana disappeared with the right-side defender, who was already quite tipsy.

As twilight settled, the wedding grew more lively. Boss tried to be attentive to all the guests but struggled to keep up. The Head kept pulling him away, eager to introduce him to the entire extended family so everyone could see what a fine man was marrying their Oksana. Guests wanted to drink with the groom, ask him questions, and share stories, all while shouting over the music. Meanwhile, Uncle Vasyl sat alone, like a lost soul at a train station. Oksana's grandmother spent the entire evening reminiscing about her youth, recalling how she remembered Vasyl and his son when they were little.

"He was a good kid, very kind."

Uncle Vasyl grew sullen at these memories, as if he were sinking into the ground. He could not bring himself to drink, even though he wanted to. Then he apologized to the newlyweds and went home.

The Head kept asking for a fight.

"Someone has to fight. This is a tradition. Anyone but the two of us," he said before embracing Boss like a beloved son.

The district officer strutted around. Even when sober, he was not the most pleasant conversation partner, and with his bleary eyes, he struggled to find a kindred spirit. The officer took Uncle Vasyl's place and began to pour out his heart to Oksana's grandmother, while the old lady reminisced about how beautiful and young they once were.

"I'll have a drink, if you don't mind. Goodness, what a beauty Tanya is!" He drank, never taking his eyes off the saleswoman.

"And back in our youth . . ."

Weddings are magical occasions. So much happens there. It was here that little Ronaldo first got drunk—somehow it slipped past his parents. The boy experienced the unpredictable and thrilling effects of alcohol, which even Noah had once acknowledged. Then Ronaldo was sent to bed.

Yuriy and his Oksana left early to pick up their children. They were worried about their son but did not want to explain or make excuses. Dmytro and Hryhoriy celebrated as best they could. They sat with Oksana's uncle (the Head's brother), who talked about metals and how to work with them properly. The new acquaintance even wanted to go home for some welding to show off his brilliant seam, but his wife would not let him.

Petryk found his element. He danced with everyone, participated in all the contests, drank a bit but did not get drunk. He was everywhere—rocking the dance floor here, scribbling a rhymed toast on a napkin there, and then reading it aloud.

After the veil was removed and the headscarf tied on the bride, and after Svitlana caught the bouquet, the once-happy faces had grown weary. Many exhausted guests were still trying to dance, but only those who were well into their cups could manage it.

"Despite the newlyweds leaving us, our celebration continues. Let's dance until morning."

The Head's brother left. Dmytro and Hryhoriy placed a bottle between themselves and continued the banquet.

"We'll sleep at the factory," Hryhoriy commanded in a voice that was not his own.

"We'll walk there. I won't get behind the wheel," Dmytro said, as if justifying himself.

"We'll walk," Hryhoriy agreed. After a long pause, he continued, "It would be interesting to calculate how much all this cost. Serious money."

"Yeah, I'd pay off my loan."

"Come on, fill up my glass. And how much did we drink? If you convert it . . ."

His mind was churning with calculations.

"All you think about is money," Dmytro said, searching for something among the leftovers on the festive table.

"What else is there to think about? You all think I'm just greedy for money for no reason, don't you?"

"I don't think that . . ."

"Don't tell me stories. You all think that. But I'm saving for my retirement. I don't want to work all my life and die on this job. I'll work until I'm forty and then have some time to live. That's why I'm saving. Where it will go, to a business or real estate, I haven't decided yet. I still have money saved from my first college stipend," Hryhoriy said with a smile, signaling to Dmytro to top up his glass.

"You often visit different businessmen," he continued, "and haven't you ever wanted to live like they do?"

"I do want to!" Dmytro exclaimed.

"And what do you need for that? Right, money. And how did they get it? Earned it? No, they saved it, held onto it, didn't squander it. And what's wrong with that?"

"I'm not saying it's wrong . . ."

"There's no wrong except for the crimes that can land you in jail. Everything else you should do for yourself and not care what others think. The world is like a bag of lottery balls; it gets mixed up a million times, and no one knows how it will turn out. But you will always be your closest, most important person in life—only you. So, you need to take care of yourself. What is it that you want from life?"

"I want a good job without a glass ceiling," Dmytro said.

"And hasn't anyone ever offered you that?" Hryhoriy asked, but there was no answer.

Fewer and fewer happy faces were visible. The evangelical brothers were lighting up the dance floor.

"What a wedding!" they exclaimed.

The youth danced on the sidelines, careful not to interrupt the twins. Among the lively crowd stood rosy-cheeked Petryk, still radiant with happiness . . .

And at the end, after the newlyweds went off to count the

money, the fight that the Head had longed for broke out. Kolya landed a single punch that broke the district officer's nose after the officer had been too forward with Kolya's wife. Kolya then attended to the officer's bleeding. The officer left the scene in his blood-stained suit. This incident became the main topic of discussion for the following weeks. Surprisingly, the officer seemed to understand the situation. He did not press charges against Kolya and has refrained from visiting their store ever since.

Water found his jacket, took a bottle of whiskey, which had miraculously survived the night, from the buffet table, and left around four in the morning. He was not sure where to go. With so many drunken people wandering the village, the widow would not be pleased to see him. Lately, their conversations had dwindled to mere silence, lying in bed and staring at each other. He saw her appeal fading away, while she seemed to look right through him. And whenever he returned to the factory she so despised, she grew restless.

The dog did not bark at Water; it knew him well. It sat by the widow's house, wagging its tail. Both houses were dark, and the morning scent was already in the air. If such an hour finds you out of bed, life suddenly feels worth living.

The house was dark.

"Look what the cat dragged in."

"I came on my own."

The old man sat in the dark, puffing on his pipe. The chair creaked. Uncle Vasyl stood up and turned on the light. He then retrieved a pack of cigarettes from the cupboard and placed it on the table.

"Oh, and you're not empty-handed," he said and grabbed two glasses. "Want something to nibble on? I have some apples . . ."

"That'll do."

"What did you bring?"

"Whiskey . . ."

"Is it like moonshine?"

"Yeah, the kind a woman hid from her husband for ten years in an oak barrel and—"

"And you found it?"

"Yep." Water smiled.

They sat at the table. Smoke curled upward toward the ceiling, and the brown drink shimmered in the glass.

"I wanted to drink all that time at the wedding," said the old man.

"But didn't want to spoil the celebration?"

"Exactly . . . And where are those two shits?"

"They're still sitting there, but they're barely alive. They said they'd go sleep at the factory."

"Still have to get to the factory somehow . . . Now let me try some of that whiskey."

"More?"

"More . . ."

"Maybe not so quickly?"

"I said fill it up . . . I can't stand it anymore."

"What exactly?"

"I can't live like this, sitting here for years among the belongings of people who are long gone. I'm rotting alive. The alcohol doesn't work like it used to, so drinking is pointless. It's all pointless. That bitch won't even bring my grandson to visit, even though they live in my apartment."

"Have you tried going there?"

"No." The old man finished his glass. "Pour me more of that."

"I don't know what to say . . ."

"Say nothing. I just want to die, that's all. It would be better to burn down with all this stuff, but I want to leave the house to my grandson. The will is over there." He pointed at the cupboard.

Water was silent.

"It's been dragging on for so long. It's good you came, at least there's some company, but . . . What is there to say. Fill up my glass again and go."

"Alright."

There was still some whiskey at the bottom of the bottle. Water left it with the old man.

"Thank you," the old man said as Water opened the door and stepped into the morning.

"Don't mention it. It's all good."

When the door closed, Uncle Vasyl drank the rest straight from the bottle, spilling it down his beard. There was half an hour left until sunrise.

In the distance, the wedding music played on, wearily and without spirit. On his way to the factory, Water did not encounter a soul. He stepped off the highway, took off his shoes, and walked barefoot through the dew. When the bright sun peeked over the horizon, Water stood chest-deep in the lake, wrestling with his fear.

# 014

A few days later, about a dozen and a half cars were parked in the factory yard. First to arrive were the Head's relatives, who had requested various services while at the wedding. Some needed repairs, others inspections, and a few wanted routine maintenance. Friends, and acquaintances of acquaintances, soon followed. There was hardly any time left for his own car, but Boss did not mind.

Thanks to his hard work, the money kept flowing in. He and Oksana had already decided at the wedding that they would buy a home. The wedding gifts were not enough, so they needed to save a bit more to make the purchase. They hesitated to tell the Head, who was not ready to let them go from his tight parental embrace. But the newlyweds were determined to escape and build their own nest. There were plenty of vacant houses in the village, but all of them needed serious repairs. Oksana even considered finding a job in the city to earn a higher salary, but Boss persuaded her not to leave the school. In her limited free time, Oksana helped her husband in the garage, and in the evenings, tired and covered in grime, they would head back to the parental home.

The nights were growing colder. August still offered warmth, but it was clear that not much of it was left.

Things at the factory were not going well. Orders stopped coming in, likely because many people were on vacation. Yuriy waited and searched for new clients.

Everyone worked at a slow pace. There were also issues with

the supply of parts and components. Water and Petryk had more free time, and Uncle Vasyl had not shown up for work in a week. Water visited the old man every morning and evening. Uncle Vasyl barely spoke, staring vacantly somewhere beyond the village gardens. He always promised to return, and when he finally did come back to the factory, everyone could breathe easier.

Hryhoriy had been sulking since the night before the wedding, nursing a simmering grudge. He did not speak to Boss, rarely left the workshop, and kept his head down in his work. Dmytro spent less time in the city and more at his desk, pressing his heavy body against the radio, waiting for a surge of energy, a new challenge he might dare to face this time.

Yuriy spent more time with the children, who had taken a liking to the lake. They often sat by the shore, tossing stones they had collected near the factory into the calm water. More and more people were drawn to the forest. The sky overhead remained blue, but it was gradually losing its summer lightness.

"I'd like to live by the sea," Yuriy finally confessed.

"You haven't seen the winter sea yet—that's a whole different thing," Water countered.

"Oh, I've seen it. It's not that scary."

"Plenty of people have never seen the sea at all," Petryk added.

"Because they didn't want to," Uncle Vasyl said, spreading tobacco on the table.

"Because they couldn't," Petryk corrected him and continued, "Last year, my friends and I hitchhiked to the sea because we were underage and would have had problems with trains, but hitchhiking was a good option. And when our little group finally reached the shore, we wanted to cry. There were five of us, and none of our parents had ever seen the sea. They worked their whole lives for one reason or another, then in order to raise us, and never went anywhere. Some never even left the region, let alone saw the sea. Someday, I'd like to buy out all the train tickets and put all the parents who've never seen the sea on that train—let them go. That would be the happiest train to the sea."

"That's just how life was back then . . ." Uncle Vasyl said somberly, spilling some tobacco on the floor.

"And was that really a life?" Petryk asked, the fire in his eyes growing.

The question hung in the air, unanswered.

Hryhoriy tried to interject, "But everyone lived somehow . . ."

"You don't understand!" Petryk exclaimed, gesturing with intensity.

"I understand perfectly." Hryhoriy adjusted his glasses, got up from his chair, walked to the window, and stared into the distance.

"The happiest train to the sea," Petryk whispered.

They parted ways. They did not want to be together, did not want to talk. Each retreated into their own shell, lost in thought. Only two people remained upstairs; the others had gone down below.

"Have you ever been to the sea?" Dmytro, who had never seen the sea in his life, asked.

"I have," Hryhoriy replied.

The next morning, a man arrived at the factory. Yuriy was not there yet. Boss was working in the garage, no longer alone—he had already hired some assistants. Now there were three of them in the garage, not counting Oksana.

A white Land Cruiser smoothly pulled up right to the factory doors. Sleepy Water was sipping his morning coffee. He would not have minded some more sleep, but the noise of the newly established service station had disrupted his schedule.

Three people got out of the car.

"Good morning," greeted the man in a cream-colored suit. "I know Yuriy isn't here yet, so we'll wait for him, walk around, and see what you've got here."

"Go ahead," Water replied, clearly not in the mood for conversation.

Upstairs, the sounds of the national anthem drifted down from the radio. The visitors headed to the lakeshore. Mist hung over the water, and large fish swam near the shore, their sleek bodies visible beneath the surface.

When Yuriy arrived, the guests were still sitting by the lake.

"Good morning," the host greeted them rather curtly as he approached.

"Good morning. I've been waiting for you," said the man in the cream-colored suit.

He was quite tall. His disproportionate build made it impossible for him to move with any agility. He walked heavily and slowly. His long, thinning hair, with a noticeable bald spot showing through, was tied back in a ponytail. He smoked constantly. His two companions, dressed in denim outfits with sunglasses perched on their heads, resembled factory workers in uniform, ready for their shift. Both of them stood up and moved aside to give their leader space to talk.

"Lovely place. If you ever think about selling it, give me a call." The guest smiled.

"You'd have to get in line," Yuriy quipped.

"Oh, come on, I'm just joking," the guest laughed. "I don't have that kind of money."

His name was Illia Petrovych, but he quickly suggested they drop the formalities and use first names.

"My friends told me about your device. I have a small workshop with about twenty workers, and I'd like to make things better for them, to make them happier at work. You know what I mean," the guest smiled.

He made a positive impression on Yuriy.

"Are you interested in purchasing it?" he asked.

"Purchasing, yes. As I said, it's hard not to trust such glowing reviews."

"Then we should head up to my office."

"Great."

As soon as this tall and slightly awkward man stood up, the two in denim suits on the opposite side of the lake quickly headed toward the factory. Yuriy and Illia went upstairs, while the other two stayed by the car.

Illia came back down with two devices in hand. His companions immediately rushed over to relieve him of the burden. Then the white Land Cruiser suddenly took off and disappeared around the corner.

By evening, the weather had worsened. A light rain drove everyone indoors. Even Boss closed the garage and went home. He and his wife were getting used to each other, like people get used to dentures.

The night was restless. The rain stopped, but a powerful wind tested the strength of the trees along the forest's edge. Water was the only one who stayed at the factory. He tried to drown out the terrible howling with sounds from the radio, but it was futile. The wind was everywhere, sweeping through the first floor and whistling in the empty rooms. The old roof creaked under the strain of the fierce gusts, as if it might be torn off at any moment, leaving Water and his bed exposed to the black sky, where distant lightning flickered at the storm's edge.

Then, suddenly, everything fell silent, even the radio. The silence was deafening. A cold stillness crept in, searching for a new home. Silence . . .

And the front line of the forest could not withstand it. Trees fell, tall spruces snapped and groaned, breaking in half. They struck their neighbors, causing them to fall as well. Lightning illuminated the chaos. Wild animals trembled in their temporary or permanent shelters. The cracking of wood sent shivers down the spine. On the ground, a mix of timber, leaves, and needles had already accumulated. The lights went out, and the radio fell silent.

Water could not fall asleep until dawn. The storm had passed, and large cold drops fell from the black clouds.

In the morning, the rain was light and almost warm. Everyone came to the factory not to work, but to see what had happened. Yuriy had tried to call Water during the night, but without success. He was worried about him. Hryhoriy and Dmytro came as well, not knowing what else to do at home.

Water was making coffee downstairs over an open fire, while the others wandered around, staring at the gaping wound in the forest.

"Oh, so you're alive," Uncle Vasyl said.

"I thought the roof was going to blow off," Water replied, the fire crackling by his feet.

"The storm only hit the edge of the forest. Nothing terrible happened in the village," Petryk said. "Just a few fallen trees and some downed power lines."

"I see. I suppose everyone wants some coffee. Where's Boss? How did he miss this?" Water asked.

"Probably in his cozy nest, warm and snug with his wife," Yuriy replied.

"You can't build your own nest in someone else's," Uncle Vasyl said as he began his tobacco ritual.

"And what are we going to do? After we've had our coffee, of course," Water asked.

"There won't be power until evening," Petryk said, settling by the fire.

"We'll head home. I lent the generator to Oak," Yuriy said.

Dmytro and Hryhoriy had seen enough of the fallen trees and followed the scent of coffee.

The warmth of the fire was a welcome comfort.

"Now we can see just how important electricity is to us. They say it could completely disappear from the Earth," Petryk shifted the conversation to a new level.

"No way, don't say that," Hryhoriy jumped into the discussion.

"It's not me saying it; in this world, nothing can be dismissed like that," Petryk retorted, a hint of offense in his voice.

"But then people will invent something—we'll invent something. We'll find a way, plus there's green energy . . . "

"What you're saying is pointless. You tell people that in fifteen years they won't have any water, and they just shrug it off. You tell them not to drill wells to the center of the Earth, and they couldn't care less. This isn't some distant problem on the North Pole—this is right in front of you, it's happening tomorrow. Your river, in your own hometown, looks more like a stinking swamp than a river. And they keep polluting it, dumping copper, cadmium, zinc, mercury, phosphorus in it, and they don't believe that water could run out . . . "

Water went upstairs.

"That's nonsense. People will find a solution, invent something, figure out a way. There're so many bright minds in the world." Hryhoriy would not stop.

"Invent something? You invented a device for happiness at home, but has even one device made it into a warm, living home? No. The device that was supposed to help people live happily actually helps them work—often for the benefit of others. And this matter is no different. We'll have to pay, and pay dearly."

"We'll always have to pay, because money is—"

"When will you ever get enough of money?" Petryk snapped and went upstairs to join Water.

Yuriy spat on the ground and headed for his car. The others dispersed as well. Only Uncle Vasyl stayed behind, smoking by the wall.

"You all go. I'll walk."

By evening, the rain stopped. The power was restored, but it was not so easy to restore the atmosphere at work. Everyone remained gloomy for the next few days. It felt like something had broken in this machine. Boss returned with his team to the garage and could not understand what had happened to the people who had been so friendly and lively just the day before.

Around noon, Illia called and asked Yuriy to come by. His voice on the phone did not sound particularly friendly. Yuriy returned looking grim and silent, then asked everyone to gather in the workshop.

"This has never happened before. Our first negative review. I arrived, and that kind man started yelling. We managed to calm him down, but he had complaints. He said our device wasn't helping him. He said, 'I wanted the best for my people, but they're still unhappy, and productivity has dropped.' I told him our device doesn't brainwash people; it just amplifies their inner impulses. But he didn't care. He said I tricked him, that we're a suspicious operation. He's curious how many other people we've deceived."

"And the money? Did he ask for his money back?" Hryhoriy asked.

"No. He said we could choke on it . . . "

"Oh, then it's not so bad," Hryhoriy exhaled in relief.

"He's not planning to sue us since he's already tied up in court over the building for his own workshop, which he acquired through shady means. So, it's not critical. But one of his workers caught me by the car and shared something interesting. This guy runs a workshop where they make windows. Summer is their peak season—their earnings for the whole year. When there was too much work, their boss would lock his people in the workshop, and they had to work until it was all done. That's why he decided to buy the device. But on the first day he set it up in the workshop, the workers broke the windows, tore down the bars, and went home. That's the story."

"Interesting," Water could not help but say.

"You've just purchased happiness," Petryk said.

In the next game, the team secured a decisive victory. Boss

scored all three goals, and after each one, he ran to kiss his wife. The evangelist brothers were on cloud nine, their joy unaffected by any amount of alcohol.

"None of this would have happened without us," one of the brothers said.

For the next half-week, Petryk was absorbed in Ray Bradbury's *Dandelion Wine*.

"If you want to make the most of summer, you have to read it in these last few days," he advised.

But there were still a few days left before August ended. After the storm, which had left its marks on the edge of the forest, and several days of rain, the weather finally warmed up. Petryk had a plan.

He woke up early and walked to the factory before sunrise. He scolded himself for leaving so late. If Water was already awake and sitting by the lake with a cup of coffee, there would be no avoiding uncomfortable questions. At the lake, Petryk saw a few people heading into the forest to pick berries, so he slowed his pace and let them pass. At the factory door, his heart pounded like a blacksmith's hammer. From above, the radio played softly.

Petryk did not plan to steal anything; he just wanted to help. The tense atmosphere among the team demanded action. And so, the young man resolved to act.

He quietly climbed the metal stairs. On the second floor, he paused and listened to Water's snoring through the music. Petryk carried ten devices out of the metal room. He placed them around the factory and camouflaged them so they would not be immediately noticeable. He put them in the workshop, in the kitchen, and in the hallway. He even carried one into Boss's garage. Then Petryk took a bold step—he placed a device in Water's room.

After turning on the devices, Petryk grabbed a book from the workshop and headed to the shore.

No one noticed anything at the factory. No one remarked on

the sudden disappearance of the devices. The crew quietly took their places. Dmytro settled by the radio. Yuriy wandered about, looking gloomy.

Uncle Vasyl smoked even more, and Water appeared terribly exhausted, though not from physical labor.

Petryk sat and waited. The small tasks he had been assigned bored him to tears. The unnatural expressions of the so-called happy people from the device brochure irritated him.

Boss arrived alone. He came in to greet the rest.

Petryk watched the people and waited for some change. He was not sure what the device was supposed to awaken in the depths of their souls. How would it all unfold? The instructions said one device was enough for an entire house. But this was not a house, so there were about ten devices. Was that too many? Why had not the devices had any effect before? Could it be because of the metal room? Petryk's thoughts swirled, but an unexpected sense of optimism began to swell within him.

Yet it seemed nothing was changing. Uncle Vasyl clanged pots in the kitchen, trying to prepare lunch. Hryhoriy lifted his eyes from the microscope and gazed into the distance. Yuriy did not tear his gaze away from the computer. Water was stacking boxes in a column against the wall. The waiting gnawed at Petryk, and he wanted to go outside.

Petryk glanced at the gates and suddenly felt the urge to paint something on them. He returned to the workshop for paint. His faith in the device was slowly waning.

After someone's phone call, Yuriy began preparing a large batch of devices for shipping. Water brought them from the warehouse to the workshop and stacked them by Yuriy's desk. He planned to sort the orders and then focus on packaging after lunch.

Everyone went outside, except for Dmytro, who stayed in the workshop, saying he would finish soldering and catch up later.

"It's a nice day," Uncle Vasyl said, breathing steadily and calmly.

"Nice, nice," everyone agreed almost in unison.

The sky was clear, with not a cloud in sight. Storks flew in flocks, gathering near the main road. Summer was slipping away irretrievably. In the depths of the forest, silence dozed, occasionally broken by wild boars searching for food for themselves and their young. But they were so far in the thicket that their sounds barely reached human ears. Fish in the lake leapt from the water and lazily splashed back.

From the workshop window, thick black smoke began to pour out.

The garage doors opened. Boss, whom everyone had forgotten, removed the tarp from his car. The gorgeous gray Phoenix with a fiery-hot bird on its hood, drove out of the garage. The car roared to life, raising a cloud of dust, and sped down the road. Everyone stood with their mouths agape, watching.

"Fire!" Uncle Vasyl shouted and ran into the building.

Yuriy and Hryhoriy followed him. Water stood for a few more seconds, staring at the smoke, then, first slowly and then breaking into a run, headed towards the lake. At the shore, he stripped off his clothes, revealing a large tattoo on his back, and plunged into the water. The great Poseidon with his trident on Water's back shimmered in the sunlight. Then Water swam. His movements became precise and confident, his hands slicing through the surface, waves spreading outward. Water overcame his fear. He swam. He did not care that no one was watching.

Petryk stood by the metal gates, shaking a spray can. The idea for the painting had faded from his mind, leaving just the lines:

> *We'll all learn to live, as long as no one's teaching us how.*
> *Autumn will follow and erase the marks we leave.*
> *There once was a man who wished to quench the world's thirst,*
> *But he lacked half a spoon of water to achieve his dream.*

Three people were running towards the fire. The old man led the way. He stopped on the stairs, feeling faint. Yuriy, who was running behind, pushed the old man aside.

"Get out of the way, it's dangerous!"

Uncle Vasyl gasped for air. The production facility was already full of smoke. Hryhoriy ran past him. The old man slowly went outside to breathe. His legs wobbled. He sat down by the garage on a car seat that Boss had set up instead of a bench.

Yuriy went up to the second floor. Dmytro stood there smiling, satisfied with himself.

"All of it is burning," Dmytro said and coughed.

Covering his face with his hand, Dmytro went downstairs, got into his car, and drove off.

Yuriy ran into the workshop and saw his desk engulfed in flames, and a bottle of an unknown substance on the floor. Fire licked the walls and spread to everything in the workshop. Yuriy grabbed a fire extinguisher, broke a window, and threw it outside. The broken glass scattered down.

"Let it burn," he said and went downstairs. He saw Water swimming and went to watch him.

Water reached the opposite shore and, without pausing, swam back. Yuriy watched as the man, who just an hour ago had been terrified of water, glided smoothly and swiftly. Upon reaching the shore, Water collapsed onto the grass, exhausted. He lay silently, breathing heavily, while Yuriy sat nearby with a satisfied expression.

At that moment, Hryhoriy was the only one still able to act. He found a fire extinguisher, returned to the workshop, and managed to put out the flames. After ensuring the fire was out, he went down to the lake. Petryk trudged after him.

Water lay silently, breathing. His breath brought Poseidon on his back to life, and he threatened everyone with his trident.

"So, did you finish your drawing?" Yuriy asked Petryk gently.

"No," the boy hesitated. "I wrote a poem."

"Will you read it?" Yuriy asked.

"Maybe later. Actually, you'll be able to read it yourself."

"You did this?"

"Yes. I . . . I . . . thought it would be better, since we invented a device for happiness . . ."

"And are you happy?" Yuriy asked.

"Yes . . ."

"You turned on too many; we couldn't handle all that happiness."

"I don't know what's happening," Hryhoriy said, "but I managed to put out the fire."

He gestured towards the workshop's broken window—thin wisps of smoke were still seeping outside.

"Your work desk burned, and half of mine. Your computer, the parts rack. The window frame caught fire, several chairs, and some devices near your desk. Also, the display model and the microscope," Hryhoriy summarized.

"If my computer is gone, it's all over," Yuriy said.

"Don't say that . . ."

"And where's the old man?" Yuriy asked.

"He's sitting by the garage," Petryk replied. "I'll call him now."

Petryk ran there. Everyone remained silent, gazing at the lake. Water, with a dazed look on his face, still lay in the grass.

Petryk waved his arms, beckoning everyone to the garage.

"Let's go, something might have happened," Yuriy commanded. "Water, get dressed and come over too."

These words were enough to rouse Water from his stupor.

The old man sat in a chair, clutching his chest. A mask of bliss had frozen on his face. He was dead.

"He can't be found here like that," Yuriy said.

"What should we do?" Hryhoriy asked, his confidence unwavering.

"We need to call the police," Petryk said.

"No," Yuriy objected.

"But this is a crime . . . " Hryhoriy said.

"I don't want a police investigation at my factory, especially after a fire. I don't want unnecessary questions. We'll take him home. It's not unusual for an elderly person to die at home," Yuriy said and headed to pull the car up to the garage.

"We won't avoid questions; this is criminal responsibility," Hryhoriy repeated, but Yuriy ignored him.

By the time Water returned, the old man had already been placed in the car. There was nothing left of the living person; he had become an awkward burden to be disposed of—buried in the ground according to tradition. Water sat in the back, next to the body. Although the drive was short, it felt like an eternity. The old man's hand kept falling onto Water. All he felt at that moment was an overwhelming disgust and revulsion towards this situation and everyone alive in the car.

# 015

Everything unfolded very quickly from that point. The district officer arrived, examining the scene, sniffing around, and searching for evidence. The old man lay on the bed, but the officer was disturbed by the corpse's position. He ran outside, making urgent phone calls. Soon, other police officers arrived and took the old man to the morgue.

Yuriy bore the brunt of the situation—he kept repeating like a mantra that Vasyl had not been at the factory that day, even though he would often come there because he was bored at home. They decided to visit him, only to find this scene. The district officer sensed something was amiss; the old man's position seemed unnatural. He tried to probe every weak spot but found nothing. No one had heard or seen anything, not even the neighbor who should have seen something.

They spent the night in the old man's house, though few actually slept. Yuriy was constantly on the phone, trying to arrange the funeral and covering all the expenses himself. Hryhoriy went to sleep at the factory, saying, "I don't want everything else to go to waste." He promised to fix the window in the morning.

Water still could not shake off his revulsion. Petryk was sent home, even though he did not want to go.

In the morning, Water and Yuriy went to the morgue to collect the body. Yuriy already regretted his decision from the previous day. He replayed the situation in his mind a dozen times, analyzing every moment. Everything seemed to fit together like a puzzle, except for the decision to take the old man home. He did not understand what had compelled him to do that. Was it the eternal desire to maintain an unblemished reputation? But that did not seem right. What had the device amplified in him? Just yesterday he felt omnipotent, and today he was suffering as if he had a hangover. Yuriy was realizing his own insignificance, and it was a strange feeling. At least the district officer would not be able to dig up anything. Perhaps that would save him. But now Yuriy knew for sure that their production needed to be put on hold for a while.

Yuriy handled all the funeral arrangements over the phone. He found a van to transport the coffin and contacted a priest. Father Yosyp explained everything: if the authorities had no questions, they would hold the memorial service today and bury the faithful departed tomorrow due to the heat.

The district officer was waiting by the morgue.

"Good afternoon," he greeted.

"Well, it's not very good, considering the occasion," Water replied.

"For you, it's good. A heart attack . . . what a sudden and unexpected death," the officer said with a sardonic smile.

"We're all going to die someday. Why make a spectacle of it?" Yuriy asked.

"I don't like it. Corpses don't lie like this. I've seen dozens of them; they all curl up as if asleep. But Vasyl looks like someone broke him before he died. I won't leave this alone. Don't worry; if I find anything, you'll know immediately," the officer said and entered the morgue.

They closed the coffin. Water and Yuriy slowly carried it to the minibus.

"Don't scratch the floor! Lift it up, don't drag it," the driver said, but no one listened.

A wooden cross, with a plaque bearing the deceased's name written in silver marker, was also placed in the bus.

By lunchtime, the old man, cleaned up and dressed in a suit, was brought home in a brown coffin with gilded handles. People began to gather at the house almost immediately to pay their respects. Those who might not have even greeted him in life, now felt the need to confirm that he was truly dead. The house was so packed that the furniture had to be moved to the walls to clear a path for everyone who wanted to enter and see Uncle Vasyl in the coffin on the table.

The old man lay with his hands folded on his chest, his face turning yellow. The house was stuffy. The windows were covered with cloth so the sunlight would not disturb the dead. A few flies buzzed and landed on the body. Old women who remembered Vasyl as a child wept over him. Then they went outside, breathed the hot August air, wiped their tears, and dispersed. Distant relatives with their children, some of whom had never seen the old man and others who didn't even know who he was, arrived.

"Why are you crying, mama?" a little boy tugged Uncle Vasyl's niece at the skirt.

No one knew he had such a large family. He had never talked about it. People whispered that the old man had sent everyone away at his son's funeral.

In the evening, the priest arrived and filled the house with the aromas of juniper and incense. Breathing became even more difficult. After the memorial service, the relatives scattered around the village in search of a place to sleep. Some stayed at the house because it was not right to leave the dead alone overnight.

Women went to one room, and men to another. Women from the village came to replace the exhausted mourners. Their sparse tears smeared their makeup, dripping onto their hands and drying.

Water and Boss stood outside. In the light of the lantern, their jeans took on a purple hue. Neither of them could utter a word. It had grown dark. The cool August night settled heavily on the heads of the living.

The men sat in the kitchen, not in the mood for tears. The hunting season was about to open, they needed to wrap up the harvest, and recount yesterday's drunken adventures. The evangelist brothers arrived, even though they were not close to the old man.

"Would you like to hear a joke?" one of the brothers asked. They were still sober and wanted to remedy that.

"Go ahead, but don't expect a drink for it," said a tall man with a mustache, a cousin of the deceased, also named Vasyl.

"Oh, I know where to get a drink. Listen. Ivan goes to confession, and the priest says to him: 'Ivan, you're a good Christian; you go to church every Sunday.' Ivan replies: 'But I've sinned; there's Oksana in the neighboring village, and I went to see her while her husband was away.' The priest says: 'That's a human affair, go, I'll pray for you.' A week later, Ivan comes to confession again. 'And now what?' asks the priest. 'Well, I was in another village, there's Olya, and I sinned again.' 'I'll pray for you, go,' says the priest. A week later, Ivan comes again. 'And now who?' asks the priest. 'Tanya from the neighboring village,' replies Ivan. The priest is getting frustrated: 'I understand, young and unmarried, it's a human affair, but how do you manage all this?' Ivan replies: 'I have a bicycle.'"

"Vasyl was a tough man, but his little one, may the Kingdom of Heaven be with them both, how beautifully he played," said his brother.

"Vasyl was a good man too," Water replied, though he was realizing he might not have really known the man.

"He was . . . It seems like everyone was, and no one is," said Vasyl's cousin, who had last seen his brother alive at his son's funeral.

The women had calmed down a bit. Conversation had resumed in their room. The replacement mourners left, and the body was left alone. Outside, the wind had picked up, bringing with it storm clouds. The rain began to fall, driving the dust on the road, leaping from roof to roof, peeking into windows where people slept peacefully. It glanced into this house too but quickly moved on. The noise of the rain faded, darkness deepened, and the two conversations merged into one.

"He was a good man after all," said the elderly woman who had come to pay her respects.

"I never knew anyone better," said Boss, lighting a cigarette.

In the kitchen, the men could barely see each other through the cigarette smoke.

"I didn't know him well, but the fact that he tried to steer our whole family says a lot. Dad was terrified of him," said the niece very quietly, so as not to wake the child.

"Yeah. But we really didn't know much about him, and still don't," Water said, trying to find a comfortable spot on the bench.

"His wife died when she was quite young. He raised Kolya all by himself from a young age. Every summer we used to come here to visit Grandpa and Grandma. Kolya practically grew up here, playing with my Ira, and then he died so young. And Vasyl never remarried. He chased after Lesya, but she turned him down. Then she married Stepan, and he still beats her. She must have deserved it," said the old woman.

"He knew all about us. When I used to stay here overnight, we talked a lot. And there was a funny incident. I got drunk like a pig. The only thing I remember is that I couldn't open the door. I thought knocking was rude, so I just slept outside. Why not, the night was warm, only mosquitoes . . . But mosquitoes are no bother to the drunk. The old man found me in the morning, and I woke up already in bed. He joked that someone had left a child at the door overnight. He came out, and there I was, sleeping and drooling," Boss said with a warm smile.

"We used to visit them often when Kolya was still alive. Uncle Vasyl would take us for ice cream. We were so funny and covered in dirt, half the store's worth of kids—all with ice cream. I even went fishing with him. He taught me, and I actually caught something. But then I never went fishing again," the niece said quietly.

"We were still little. I asked him for a cigarette, and barely managed to escape. Dad used to say he was once a bandit, fought with the whole village over his wife, then his girlfriend, because they didn't want to let her be with him. He was a strong man. Even in his old age, he could hit hard enough to break bones," said one of the evangelist brothers.

"He loved all the children, and the neighbors' kids would often come by. He would show them how to weave baskets and make whistles from willow. Then they'd walk around whistling, and it drove us crazy," said the old woman.

"He was tough and healthy, never drank in his youth, and apparently didn't smoke either. He used to chase me for cigarettes. There weren't many like him in our family, and now there are none at all. It's a pity we wasted so many years over some grudges," said the cousin, a solitary tear rolling down his cheek, which he quickly wiped away.

"And that bitch never brought his grandson, even though she lives in his apartment that he gave to the boy . . . Did anyone call her?" the niece asked loudly.

"Is there no liquor in Uncle Vasyl's house?" asked one of the brothers.

"His neighbor called her. She said she might come. Maybe she thinks the house will be hers now," said the aunt, looking out the window. "What's it like outside?"

"No liquor . . . He was terribly afraid of this," Water answered and immediately remembered the joke about whiskey.

"Well, his neighbor is a good woman. She called us too." The niece was already quite sleepy and wanted to lie down beside the child.

"He was a good man," Water said.

In a moment, the rain outside had stopped, and it became quiet. Boss was the first to step outside to breathe in the post-rain air. There were no longer any obstacles to going home except for the mud underfoot. One of the women also went outside.

"It stopped . . . But how will I find my way home in the dark?" she asked Boss, but he didn't have a chance to answer.

"We'll see you home," the evangelist brothers replied almost in unison.

"Oh, how kind of you. If only you didn't drink, you'd be worth your weight in gold."

"Well, we're priceless already," said the brothers.

After they left, only Vasyl's brother remained in the kitchen, dozing over the table. In another room, the niece slept restlessly, wrapped around her son. Boss and Water stood by the door, watching the people disperse. The street smelled of rain, and the wind had calmed a little. There were no stars, no moon.

"Didn't we plan to meet here?" Water began.

"We did. Everything happened so quickly that I didn't even understand . . ."

"No one understood. And then Dmytro burned everything down."

"Would you have acted any differently? He probably got a good deal or a job, I don't know. He must have told everyone, including you, that he wanted to grow. He wanted a career, not to rot here. If burning down one room was the price to pay, who wouldn't do it?"

"And would you have thought long about it?" Water interrupted.

"I've done worse things, but now I have everything I wanted," Boss said, lighting another cigarette. "But everyone won in the end; no one's at a loss."

"Especially the old man . . ."

"What about the old man? He, like Dmytro, expressed clearly

what he wanted . . . And you? What did you want?" Boss started looking around for his car and then remembered he had come on foot.

"I don't know what I wanted, honestly. I grew to love fear. When it disappeared, I didn't feel relieved."

"Don't tell me that. I saw your pleased face when you came out of the water. Don't dwell on it too much. We're still alive, and we still have suffering to endure," Boss said, lighting the butt of the old cigarette and offering the pack to Water.

"And the device? What did it do?" Water asked.

"You know, I thought from the beginning that it was a scam. That Yuriy was just boldly raking in the money. Maybe that box did something to our bovine brains, but it didn't make us happy. All those reviews, to me, are lies. Maybe it does something, but happiness is in the mind of the beholder. Some people need money, some need a car, some want to be healthy, some want to be full. Does a plastic box packed with off-brand electronics really bring it all together?" Boss fell silent. Water was also quiet.

"Don't be silent . . . Tell me, did you ever believe you would swim again? That's what I want to hear. Because I don't want to think that among us there was even one person who didn't believe in themselves."

"But the device? They bought it, Yuriy cared so much about it, we heard so much positive . . ." Water could not calm down.

"Enough. If you know how to sell, you can peddle anything. A plastic box with a bright LED and a compelling story? Skilled salesmen will sell it in no time. The customers I crossed paths with were all suckers. If you spent so much time at the factory where so many devices were actually working, wouldn't at least something fall into the right place in your head?"

"I don't know. Maybe it didn't because of the metal room?"

"Want one?" Boss offered him the cigarette pack again. "I'm about to head home."

Water lit a cigarette. The empty street and the empty sky did not promise anything good. Maybe over the past six months something did fall into the right place in his mind after all.

Boss approached the old man's body and stared at him for a long time—watching as the skin yellowed, as if it had never held any life. He found Vasyl's pipe and tobacco pouch, tucked them into a pocket of his jacket, so the old man could smoke in the afterlife as well. He lingered a moment longer and then left, saying nothing to Water, and walked down the road, slippery after the rain. It was quiet, except for the dog from the neighbor's yard barking briefly before falling silent. The whole village was asleep. Only one house remained lit through the night. And then morning came.

Petryk arrived, followed by others. The house quickly filled up. The district officer moved around with a sorrowful expression on his face. The air was heavy with the scent of the corpse; the old man's mouth had opened. They had to tie it shut with a ribbon. The body was quickly turning yellow.

Closer to eleven o'clock, they brought the priest. He conducted the service in the house swiftly, then they carried the corpse outside. It was warm and windless. The water and mud underfoot were slowly drying up. The evangelist brothers had been digging the grave since morning.

About thirty people had gathered outside. The dog from the neighbor's yard whined. The neighbor, dressed in black, stood by the coffin, wiping her sparse tears and occasionally glancing at Water. Petryk stood, red-faced and wishing he could sink into the earth. The tension had stolen his voice. When asked something, he remained silent. Vasyl's brother arrived with his son. Everyone from the factory was there except Dmytro. He had vanished without a trace. Hryhoriy gazed silently towards the forest. Boss stood behind with his wife. Oksana was white as snow.

Yuriy stood by the coffin, once again reflecting on the events of the past few days. Although he had taken on organizing the funeral to distract himself, it had not helped. His gaze was vacant. He waited for it all to be over. In the crowd, a few women wept loudly, for the sake of appearances. The other women whispered among themselves, wondering if the daughter-in-law would come. She did not. The priest droned on with a nearly emotionless service. He did not know the deceased, as life had only recently brought him to this area. Uncle Vasyl rarely attended church.

"From the earth we came, and to the earth we shall return," the priest said. "What is life worth if it is just a fleeting moment before eternity? Before eternity, in which we will receive what we have earned in this life. Vasyl was a good man, and we can only believe that through his prayers and deeds, he earned the Kingdom of Heaven. We hope that his soul has finally found the peace it sought. We can only pray for his sinful soul, which the Lord will grant eternal remembrance . . ."

At these words, someone in the crowd sobbed.

"Once my grandfather told me that you stop being a boy when you're handed a child to hold, and you become a man when you are called to carry a coffin," Vasyl's brother said to Petryk.

Petryk clearly did not expect such a proposition. He was already feeling unwell. He kept thinking about what had happened at the factory, finding nothing in those thoughts but his own guilt.

When the old man was bid farewell from his home with three knocks on the threshold, Petryk's hands were trembling. And then, when they lifted the coffin outside, overturned the benches, and carried it to the car, Petryk broke down. He cried like a child and could not do anything about it, not even wipe his tears, as the wooden coffin rested on his shoulder. It was carried by four people: Petryk, Vasyl's brother, Water, and Hryhoriy. Yuriy was afraid to approach the coffin and kept his distance. They carried the coffin out of the yard and placed it in the car, draped in black ribbons and old carpets.

The procession slowly moved toward the church. Along the way, people detached from the procession one by one and returned to their homes. The church service was conducted quickly, and they carried the old man to the cemetery.

The evangelist brothers had long finished digging the grave and were sitting in the shade of a monument covered in green moss.

"So many of them this year," one of the brothers pointed to a new row of graves, the crosses of which were hidden among mounds of sun-bleached wreaths.

"It seems like they're calling each other. This year, Petro Yakymiv was the first. And then it took off—he called a neighbor, and that one called a classmate, and so on, half a row of graves. They and Uncle Vasyl were also in the same class," said his brother.

"And how many were born? Two or three . . ."

"You'd better start pouring, because soon they'll come, and we'll have to bury him."

"We dug so long, and there's still water at the bottom. We're like devils in the mud."

"Come on, or they'll say we're useless again."

"And we haven't even done anything useless in a while."

"Well, eternal memory to the old man . . . "

"May the earth rest lightly upon him . . ."

The procession moved slowly. Strong men bent like trees in a storm under the weight of the coffin. It seemed as if the old man had gained weight. The mud under the men's feet had formed a crust. Because of this, the procession moved slowly and unsteadily. The coffin was tightly sealed, the sun's rays reflecting off the lid. High in the cloudless sky, storks circled, gathering under the forest and ignoring the sinful people below.

The priest impatiently watched the slow procession but did not dare to urge them on. From the depths of his cassock, he retrieved his phone and checked the time. He was dissatisfied. Funerals always took a lot of time, and walking was required—this was not some christening. Once, Uncle Vasyl had said he wanted to lie next to his wife, but his son was already buried there. He would have to lie where they placed him.

The evangelist brothers hastily hid their modest meal behind the monument covered in green moss and began to create the appearance of work. But everything was already prepared; they were seasoned at this, as they say. They placed the heavy coffin on wooden stretchers above the grave, which had a mix of earth and water at the bottom. The brothers took pride in this work:

"Vasyl, we picked the perfect spot, just like for our own."

A woman with a wreath approached the procession. A gentle breeze rustled the black ribbons with the inscription "From a Beloved Grandson." Tall and dressed in black, she stood to the side and looked at the coffin.

"Shall we open the coffin so you can say your goodbyes?" the priest asked.

"No need, I'll say goodbye this way," the woman replied quietly.

The service ended quickly. No one spoke a farewell. The priest frequently and nervously glanced at his phone. The coffin was lifted with ropes. The twins removed the wooden stretchers from beneath it. The rope scraped against the coffin with a dull sound. The old man was gently lowered into the grave. Everyone took a handful of earth and tossed it into the grave. The muted thud echoed in everyone's mind. When the brothers began shoveling earth into the grave, it seemed that the lid might not hold. The child clung to his mother, hiding his face in her skirt.

The priest and the deacon left the cemetery. The evangelist brothers filled the grave. Several wreaths and a wooden cross lay to the side.

"If you need anything from the house, you can take it. Just leave the key with the neighbor. I'll be selling the house anyway; it was left to the grandson," said the daughter-in-law, already preparing to leave.

"There's no need to take anything. I'll buy the house from you," Water said, agitated.

"My phone number is with Nadya. Call me tomorrow afternoon," the daughter-in-law said before turning and leaving. Her long hair fell out from beneath her black scarf and cascaded onto her shoulders. A car was waiting for her by the church.

"Please join us for the memorial lunch at the restaurant," Yuriy announced to everybody.

"I'll go see to my people and come," the neighbor replied, slowly making her way between the rows of graves to the other side of the cemetery, where her son and husband were buried.

"We'll definitely come, just let us finish covering the grave and put up the cross," one of the brothers said.

"And change our clothes," added the second brother.

"Just try to be quick," Yuriy requested.

"The vodka won't even have time to chill . . ."

People finally exhaled. A sense of comfort settled over everyone. A warm breeze caressed their somber faces. The green grass by the well-tended graves boasted a few scattered flowers. The neglected graves stood as reminders, symbols of lost love. The world changes, people come and go, but the graves remain in place.

The sun began to blaze. The brothers quickly erected the cross and arranged the wreaths on the grave. They gathered their tools and headed to the wake.

"Aren't you coming?" they called out as they left, but no one responded.

Petryk and Water remained by the grave. Above them stretched the August blue sky, its serenity interrupted by circling storks.

"I think they're checking how the young ones have learned to fly," Water said, shifting his gaze from the sky to his feet. "I'm not an ornithologist; I'm just saying what I see, and it seems perfectly logical to me. Observing nature, I've realized that everything in it is logical. Everything has a clear explanation that anyone can understand, provided they don't have utterly bovine stubbornness. They have a long journey ahead. They need to assess how ready the young, the old, and the sick are, and who needs to be left behind. And they leave them. It might annoy us humans, but we act in a similar way. They need to experience the flight, and they do everything for it. The hardest part is for the first one, who faces all the air resistance; after that, it's easier. And somewhere in the middle of the flock, flying is as comfortable as riding behind a truck on the highway. I've always been curious about who becomes the first and how he is chosen. Now I think he volunteers, taking on the responsibility and the mission of cutting through the air. He's a reluctant leader, and until the flock finds him, no one will fly anywhere."

Water lifted his head to the sky and pointed with his finger.

"That big one, like the one we saved with the old man. It would be symbolic if he volunteers to lead the flock. They're just like us, only it's hard to see. They're emotional, jealous, uncompromising, and outrageously brave. They cling not to the nest but to each other. Sometimes, taking care of oneself is the best way to help others. That big one is definitely one of us. For some reason, they didn't settle well at the factory . . ."

The air smelled of autumn and farewells.

"I—I—I have to live with it," Petryk said.

"We all have to live with it . . ."

# 016

The exhausted crowd was forced to confront the high mountain that blocked their path. About a dozen men struggled up to the summit, leaving behind women with crying children, the elderly, and those who were afraid. It was hard to understand what they hoped for, but this was the path they had chosen and had to follow. At the very least, the mountain could offer them the chance to look around and decide their next move.

Somewhere midway up the mountain, they rested on a large plateau, from which forests stretched out in all directions. The plateau was covered in grass and moss, from which large stone boulders emerged. It seemed like a place where they might settle. At the foot of the mountain, there was a forest where they could hunt and gather food. They had encountered many animals along the way—enough for sustenance and hides. Wood for construction was abundant, and the place was safe. What was lacking was the most crucial element—water. The small streams they had seen in the forest could not quench the thirst of the entire tribe, so any hope of staying here was as slim as a child's pupil. After resting, they continued their ascent. The grass underfoot gave way to bare rock and twisted roots covered in moss. It was damp. Scattered bushes, struggling to reach the sky, pricked at the bare bodies of the men with sharp thorns. Nearer to the summit, the sound of gurgling water reached their ears, and they realized they would remain here. This sound gave them strength. They rushed towards it, their feet bleeding from the stones jutting out from the green carpet. Before their weary eyes lay a ravine, where water bubbled up from the depths and spread across the slope. The chief approached the spring, scooped up a handful of water, and drank. It was cold and pure; he drank and drank. Smiling broadly, showing his decayed teeth, he invited everyone to quench their thirst. The youngest wanted to climb higher to see what lay beyond. Beyond were even higher mountains, their peaks cutting through the clouds. Only gods could live at the peaks, and humans were forbidden there. But on this smaller mountain, they would make their home. The main thing was to befriend the deities, not anger them, then everything would be fine. They filled containers with water to take down and let the thirsty people taste their new home. The tribe, which had not yet known chains, extended like a chain up the plateau.

Life, however difficult, took on a new rhythm. People lived under the sun and reached for it. They built their primitive homes. They made utensils and carried water from the summit. They died up there on the mountain. Their bodies were carried into the forest, where everyone found peace. Game was carried up, and water was brought down. Of those who had first come here, none remained. Even the infants who had cried in their mothers' arms were long resting in the forest, where their frail, old bodies were decomposing in the earth. And someone made a decision. Someone alone.

"We will no longer fetch water; let it come to us."

And so, they gathered stones, chipping pieces from large boulders and carving troughs into them. The work lasted for years. During this time, they transitioned from foraging to primitive agriculture—the first seeds planted yielded generations of crops. Then the life-giving water flowed in a thin stream through the troughs from the spring to their large settlement. The forest receded from the mountain, and expansive, cultivated fields pressed close to it. People were born and died, hunted and grew their food, and the water flowed through the troughs. They prayed to the gods living in the clouds on the neighboring mountain but did not go there to avoid disturbing and angering them.

However, comfortable life spoiled them. They increasingly complained about their fate. They lamented those who hid in the clouds. They regretted that they could not be near them. The gods had given them only water; what other blessings and treasures did they refuse to share? Some called for ascending into the clouds and settling there, as there was no more room on the plateau and new homes were creeping downward. The forest had fewer wild animals. And what vast herds roamed the boundless, cloud-hidden expanses, concealed from human eyes by the elusive gods?

The bravest, armed with spears, went to the mountain of the gods. When they returned, they reported that the gods would not let them come and that the cliffs were so steep that only a bird could reach them. They too wished to fly.

Years passed, and people continued to think about how to detach from the earth and fly. They did not care about what would happen if game disappeared or if the crops did not grow. People had no enemies except wild beasts.

One sunny day, instead of a rushing stream, only a thin trickle flowed through the troughs, and by evening, it had completely dried up. The tribe rushed to the spring, stumbling over stones and searching for paths long unused. Everyone who could run did so. But there was no water. The bottom was visible, the stones polished by years of water. People peered into the pit with animal fear. Someone threw a stone in, and it landed with a dull thud.

"This must be a joke from the gods," said a man. "The water will return; where else can it go? Its only way out is up the mountain, to us. Until then, we will fetch water from the forest streams and survive somehow. We've survived worse."

Everyone dispersed to their homes, slightly calmed. The next morning, they spread out into the forest with empty containers to search for water. The streams were shallow, but it was enough for now. Every day, people carried containers of water to the plateau, falling and spilling it down the slope. Driven by thirst, they descended to refill their containers and repeated their journey. Formerly cheerful conversations were replaced by irritable silence and crying. The women sang rain songs, but the sun scorched all hope. Gradually, the water also disappeared from the forest. Animals left in search of water. The leaves underfoot crumbled to dust, and the trees dried up.

One day, a small spark fell from the sky.

People gathered on the plateau and watched in horror as the forest burned, their crops went up in flames, and the fire-driven game fled out of sight. They fell asleep to the crackle of flames—dreamless. At night, flames were visible from the mountain, licking everything around. Terrified, people fell into a trap, like beasts. Water supplies were scarce. The earth blackened with ashes. There was no escape from the smell of burning.

They decided to plead with the gods. To apologize. To beg. They found someone who had never spoken ill of the gods and decided to lower him into the well, hoping that prayers and pleas would appease the deities. The rope to lower the volunteer was to be made from women's hair—so the unfortunate one would feel the support of his fellow tribespeople. A volunteer was quickly found. He was the son of the man who had once suggested moving to the mountain of the gods.

For several weeks, the settlement shaved the heads of all the women, braiding the hair into a rope. From all kinds of hair—young and black as tar, thin and gray. Although many women lived in the tribe, there was not enough hair. Then they cut the hair of children—little girls and boys. Their soft, youthful hair was woven into the braids of the adult women. The rope grew longer and longer. The fires had died down, but the shallow forest streams, clogged with burnt trees, were dirty and dead.

When the village ran out of water, the people climbed to the top of the mountain to the well, in a last desperate hope. The men carried the rope over their shoulders. Shorn girls led the young volunteer. He was naked and completely unarmed. The boy was wrapped in the rope, and the strong men lowered him into the cave. At first, he saw nothing in the thick darkness. His bare feet touched the cold, damp stone. He ventured further into the gloom, feeling the smooth, cold stone beneath him, but there was no water. The boy screamed, prayed, and pleaded, but received no sign. When they pulled him up, he was exhausted and terrified; he collapsed onto the bare rock and wept.

By evening, the sky opened up and rained. Tiny, sparse drops fell to the ground, and people collected them in whatever they could find. The rain fell on their tired faces, on the buildings, and on the mountains, extinguishing the few remaining fires. People realized that the gods had heard them, but were not satisfied with just that one prayer.

In the morning, the men set out hunting. They went further and further, but found no suitable game—only ashes. Tired predators devoured bones, finishing off the grim carcasses of burned animals. The catch the hunters brought back to the village was meager and had required a great deal of strength. It could not save them; it could only prolong their suffering.

Then the people decided to offer the gods their most precious sacrifice—children. Ten little girls and ten boys who were already standing on their own were chosen. Stone axes crushed their heads. Blood flowed onto the parents' hands and onto the grass. The children were then carried to the well, hoping that the sacrifice would be sufficient, for they had nothing else to give.

The miracle did not happen, though people continued to wait for it. At night, wolves howled beneath the mountain, drawn by the scent of the sacrifice. Their howling seeped under the skin, driving away sleep. People stared into the darkness, terrified of what might emerge from it. They set a watch by the bodies to keep wild beasts from dragging away the sacrifice meant for the gods.

The gods did not accept the sacrifice. The small bodies lay by the well. When they were no longer guarded, wild animals scattered the corpses across the mountain.

Then the young man who had descended into the cave said they needed to leave and find a new home. Not everyone agreed, but most followed him. It was a heavy burden for him, but he was made to carry it. The young man ordered the destruction of all the empty houses so that no one would ever settle there again. And they left because they had somewhere to go.

All who remained on the mountain stayed there forever . . .

◆

This was the first dream I had outside the factory walls. I didn't understand its meaning for a long time. I left the factory three days after Uncle Vasyl's funeral and spent another week at Boss's place. We played another match and managed to win. We ended the season ranking fourth. But that's not the point—this isn't even about me.

Yuriy left a week later. In seven days, he settled all his affairs. He moved his family to live by the sea. Now his little son breathes salty air every morning and watches the weightless sea. Meanwhile, Hryhoriy is running the factory. He brought in some woman. Under her watchful eye, he is starting a new life. They make children's toys, though I don't know which ones. Hryhoriy told the district officer in the store that things are not as wonderful as they seem, but he is holding his own. He pays a symbolic amount for rent. Hryhoriy kept a few tools—begged them from Yuriy. He has taken on the obligation to pay Bereza a certain amount every month—as compensation for the lost finger, which Yuriy had dutifully paid. I thought about staying, but Hryhoriy was not ready to pay me the same amount I used to get. It's fine; it's like a weight off my shoulders. I'm free again. Nothing came of it with the widow, and it couldn't have worked out anyway.

Yuriy left without saying goodbye or explaining anything. Deep down, I know he is happy. Dmytro disappeared, though I think he's doing well. I can only wish them all success. Yuriy calls occasionally; we talk about nothing. Or rather, we talk about everything but the past. Sometimes his son lets me listen to the sea and invites me to visit, saying that the fish don't jump out of the water there.

I bought a house. To make a long story short, I couldn't buy Uncle Vasyl's house because the daughter-in-law set an exorbitant price. It's still for sale, but I doubt anyone will pay that much. My new home is much cheaper. A village, on the verge of dying out, guards a river and forests, and has taken me in. About a hundred people live here, and there is a shop. A bus stop is eight miles away, which suits me just fine. And I'm already making some provisions for winter. The main draw is the river. It's good to be by the water.

Step outside the house, and you'll see the river. The current is quite fast, but here the river widens and slows down. The water carries white foam and willow leaves. It's cold now, but sometimes I dare to go in at midday. I walk a few dozen steps into the depth and then swim, surrendering to the current, which carries me to the next shallow spot. Here, fish are caught, and there are almost no people. While it was warm, the occasional rafts and canoes with cheerful travelers floated by, but now there's no one. I gather the trash carried by the current and try to help the river. There's a lot of trash. No one else will clean it up.

A neighbor is teaching me how to fish. We spend whole evenings talking and drinking his mead. He's as old as the hills, and he still manages forty hives. His sons come by from time to time to help, take the honey, and sell it in the city. The old man sees me as an assistant.

I've been stung by bees a few times already. I think it will be fun. I still have some savings, so I can get through the winter here. Fall, winter—here. Spring, summer—away.

But that's not the point. Today is a rainy day, early November. We all gathered together again. Everyone except Dmytro, of course. Today we buried Boss. He was killed in a car accident. He crashed into the oak he had once refused to have cut down. The car was instantly turned into scrap metal. Nothing useful could be salvaged from it. There was no one else in the car. Boss always drove recklessly when he was alone. But no one expected this. Poor Oksana . . . Today at the cemetery, she stood like a living monument. The tragedy was that, despite the baggy clothes she put on to hide her round belly, everyone could see it. And Boss knew, I think. That fool . . .

There were many people at the funeral. The Head was black with grief and tried to keep people away from his daughter. It rained. The entire football team carried the coffin—and it was no short distance. A long human river with wreaths and flowers trailed behind them. People wept bitterly, especially those who had lent him money for the wedding. The evangelical brothers walked by the coffin, wiping bitter tears from their wrinkled faces. Everyone was there . . .

Yuriy stood aside, crying. At Uncle Vasyl's funeral, he hadn't shed a single tear, but now he couldn't stop. Oak, who brought good news, for someone always has to bring good news, couldn't hold back his tears. Petryk arrived. He was no longer the Petryk who had been Boss's groomsman at the wedding. A student, withdrawn and distant. I hope everything goes well for him. Hryhoriy was with the same woman who had taken over the factory. He greeted me and went on his way. Later, I was told her name was Oksana. You could tell right away—she'll make a man out of him.

I exchanged a few words with Yuriy. Everything is fine with him. He invited me to visit. I'll see—maybe I'll go sometime.

I'm struggling to come to terms with Boss's death. I spent a lot of time with that fool; he taught me much. I'm infinitely angry with him. I didn't go to the wake; there were plenty of people without me. The rain doesn't stop. It's cold, the kind only November brings. I walk along the highway, with bare trees lining the sides, leaves scattered on the grass, where they will rot. A weasel in its white winter coat hurries to braid the horses' manes. In the fields, young wheat is turning green, and the village slowly disappears behind me. I'll have to come back here, at least to visit the cemetery. Cars speed by, large droplets of water spraying out from under the wheels. No one is likely to pick up such a drenched traveler. I walk on, while autumn burns out like a match before my eyes. They say this winter will be special. A winter that could finally change us.

# Ihor Mysiak

Ihor Mysiak, born June 16, 1993 in Lviv, was a contemporary Ukrainian poet and prose writer. He studied history at Drohobych Pedagogical University and actively participated in the Revolution of Dignity. From late 2014 to mid-2015, he served as a military paramedic in the Azov Brigade.

Mysiak won several literary awards in Ukraine, including Khortytsia Bells (2018), Irpin Parnassus (2018), Zhytomyr TEM (2019), and An T-R-Act (2020). His work has been featured in *Literary Chernihiv*, *Dzvin*, and various anthologies.

In March 2022, a month after Russia invaded Ukraine, he joined the Territorial Defense Forces, fighting in the liberation of Kherson and later in the intense battles near Bakhmut.

His debut novel, *The Factory*, was published in Ukrainian soon after, a sign of hope during the early weeks of the full-scale invasion that Ukraine would stand. Ihor's life was cut short at the front line when he was killed by Russia in the spring of 2023.

## Hanna Leliv

Hanna Leliv is a freelance literary translator working between Ukrainian and English. She was a Fulbright fellow at the University of Iowa's Literary Translation MFA program and mentee at the Emerging Translators Mentorship Program run by the UK National Center for Writing. Hanna has been collaborating with a range of Ukrainian and international publishers, and in 2023-24, she was a translator-in-residence at Princeton University.

## Yevheniia Dubrova

Yevheniia Dubrova is a writer and literary translator from the Donetsk region of Ukraine. She holds a BA in English and Creative Writing from Dartmouth College and is an MFA candidate in Creative Writing at Vanderbilt University. Winner of the 2024 Lando Grant for refugee writing from the de Groot Foundation, she writes about displacement, loss, memory, and what endures, and translates fiction, poetry, and plays from Ukrainian.